A CURSED DRAGON

[Deanna Cooner, PhD]

Stones in Clay
PUBLISHING

A Gathering of Dragons
Copyright © 2019 by Deanna Cooner, All rights reserved

Stones in Clay Publishing
P.O. Box 1302
Newcastle, Ok 73065

Living stones, being built up as a spiritual house for a holy priesthood, to offer up spiritual sacrifices acceptable to God through Jesus Christ. 1 Peter 2:5,
But we have this treasure in jars of clay, to show that the surpassing power belongs to God and not to us. 2 Corinthians 4:7

Cover Design and Graphics by Mindi Stucks
Book Design by Gary Cooner
Edited by Jeanne Marie Leach
Published in United States of America
ISBN: 978-0-9989522-6-0
Young Adult Fiction / Religious / Christian / General
2019.6.26

Stones in Clay
PUBLISHING

One who has truth,
cannot be enslaved by lies

He said to them, You are those who justify yourselves in the sight of men, but God knows our hearts; for that which is highly esteemed among men is detestable in the sight of God. Luke 16:15

OTHER NOVELS BY DEANNA COONER

The Dragon and the Mask

A Gathering of Dragons

Contents

1

What is it?

Assemble yourselves and let us go into the fortified cities. Let us perish there, Because the Lord our God has doomed us and given us poisoned water to drink, for we have sinned against the LORD.

---Jeremiah 8:14

DR. ZAY TROYE stood beside his mentor and supervisor, staring into the steel cage four floors beneath the science lab. His eyes focused on a most bizarre creature.

"What is it?" he muttered.

"The subject of your research to fulfill your fellowship requirements?"

Zay shook his head and put his hands on top. "No way!"

"Then the fellowship will be offered to another student, and you will sign a legally binding silence contract."

Zay studied the creature by closely observing it from the hind quarters with hooved feet to the long serpentine body holding the head of a cross-eyed, three-horned dragon twenty feet in the air.

"How?"

"President Reagan signed a line item for genome research, and financing has been distributed to fourteen universities of which we are one."

"No, I mean how did this thing come into existence?"

"That is the question you will answer during your two-year fellowship with the university."

"Why me?"

"Didn't you apply for a post-graduate fellowship?"

"Well, yes, but—"

"You thought you would be working with chimps?" Dr. Winegren smiled.

"I don't know what I thought, but I never imagined this." Zay couldn't take his eyes off the creature stirring in the cage.

"Do you remember me?" Dr. Winegren asked Zay.

"No, should I?"

"I came out to your dad's farm when you were a young boy. I took some soil samples with a questionable and flammable substance on them."

"Oh yeah."

"You know what I discovered about those samples?"

Zay ducked his head, remembering the dragon drool on his family's farm.

"No."

"I discovered a reptilian creature usually found only in fantasy novels."

Zay didn't speak. He knew the creature. The family called him Nisroch, the god of agriculture. He didn't want to think about it. "Is there a connection?"

"I don't know."

"Where did you find this thing?" Zay asked.

"Couple of students ran into it on campus and brought it to me."

"Oh." Again, Zay didn't ask any questions; he knew his brother-in-law and cousin were the students. He also knew that occurred at least six or seven years ago.

"Identifying strange creatures is not my career choice." He took hold of the bars and stared up at the creature.

Dr. Winegren ignored his statement. "You will have a work-study undergrad working with you. I will be your supervisor. You will conduct labs for my classes in addition to your study of this creature."

"What am I supposed to study?"

"It's DNA."

A mixture of revulsion and excitement surged through Zay's body. He would certainly have original research.

"Do I have a choice?" Zay asked.

"You can reject the fellowship."

The creature roared and quickly moved its head toward Zay. He jumped and stepped back until he hit the wall. "I don't like snakes," he yelled.

The creature turned his head sideways and peered into his eyes. Zay stared back with his mouth agape.

"Be careful. It may hear and understand both what you say and what you think."

"It looks like pure hate and smells like a slaughterhouse."

"That's a good description. Not only does it smell like death, it looks like it hates everything, including itself. The thing is an abomination."

"What does that mean?"

"It's goal is to kill you. It's dangerous."

Zay wrapped his arms around his stomach and inched toward the elevator door. "I gotta get out of here."

Dr. Winegren didn't budge. He looked down at his fingernails. Then he pointed up at the ceiling in the cage.

"You see it?"

"I see a grotesque monster staring at me."

"Look above and behind."

Zay shuttered at the suggestion. He raised his head and focused on the small area between the creature's head and the ceiling.

"Whel," he let out the strange sound and covered his mouth with his hand.

"The creature provides you with physical matter, but your quest includes that faint image behind this poor misshapen dragon."

Once the two men were on the top floor, Zay fell down on the couch under the window. Dr. Winegren handed him a glass of water.

"I know it's a lot, but with DNA research coming into vogue now, you have a whale of an opportunity with that creature."

Zay gulped the water. Dr. Winegren sat down behind the desk.

"It makes you thirsty to be down there, like the moisture is sucked out of the air."

Zay nodded as he drank the water. He couldn't get enough. Dr. Winegren was right.

"Your duties will be overseeing the work-study student. If you choose to reveal our secret pet to him, you will have some help feeding Phobus."

"Feeding? Who?"

"I named him Phobus."

"Why?" Zay wrinkled his forehead. "Why give a monster a name?"

"It helps to know the difference between the fearful and that which is behind it, causing the fear."

"Still not getting it." Zay said between gulps.

"A phobia is a fear of something, so I call the monster Phobus because he stirs fear in all who see him, but he's the image, not the real danger."

Zay wrinkled his brow.

Dr. Winegren raised his hand palm up pointing toward the steel door leading into the basement. "It's okay, you'll understand in time."

2

A Troubled Soul

> I have set My face against this city for
> harm and not for good, declares the Lord, "it
> will be given into the hand of the king of
> Babylon and he will burn it with fire."
>
> ---Jeremiah 21:10

ZAY SETTLED INTO the university research lab
assigned to him. Today, his work-study student would
meet with him in the student union building. Then Zay
would determine if he would be a lab assistant or a fetch-
it.

While waiting for the appointed time, he enrolled in his
required class, molecular biology. With his head down
reading the class schedule both for himself and his lab time,
he tripped over a large object. He stood and brushed his
clothing then searched for the object which caused his
embarrassment. He dropped his hands to his side, and his
jaw dropped at the sight of the body of a horned bull.

Remembering his embarrassment, he inspected the grounds for observers and breathed a sigh of relief when he didn't spot anyone pointing and laughing at him. The early morning hour provided isolation and covered both his blunder and horror.

Then he heard a voice from above. Zay swiveled his head in the direction of the speaker. He saw a young man, tall and lanky staring at him from the upper level of the garden area.

"Did you see this?" Zay stammered.

The young man nodded and descended the steps to Zay's level. "Do you know why it's here?" The young man asked.

Zay didn't answer the question but posed a new one, "What's your name."

"Ronnie." The young man answered with a tremble in his voice.

Zay squinted his eyes and waited for the young man to give voice to the words choking in his throat.

"Dr. Troye?" Ronnie squeaked out in a strained voice while kicking at the grass.

Zay watched the young man kicking the bull that lay bleeding all over the grass. "Why is it there?"

"The bull?" Zay pointed to the animal.

The young man nodded.

"Don't be frightened; I think the delivery man made a mistake." Zay cleared his voice as he spoke. He gave the young man a quick and slight smile.

"I hope it wasn't meant for the cafeteria." Ronnie raised his head, smiled, and released a chuckle.

"Well, it's food for something." Zay smiled hoping to relax the young man. "I'll call maintenance and ask them to take it to the proper place." He put his briefcase under his arm and thumbed through a stack of envelopes. Ronnie watched him.

"Is there something I can do for you?" Zay asked the young man.

After an uncomfortable minute, Ronnie answered, "I have an interview appointment with you as your work-study assistant,"

Zay nodded and smiled. "I see. Is your last name Walton?"

"Yes."

"Then your first task is to help me relocate a two-thousand-pound bull before it gathers a crowd."

"And flies," Ronnie added.

Zay laughed and repeated, "And flies."

Suddenly, both Ronnie and Dr. Troye slammed into a wall—an invisible wall. They rubbed their noses and reached out with caution. Neither of them felt anything or saw anything.

"Did you feel that?" Ronnie asked.

Zay nodded. His hands shook, and he dropped the files and papers. Ronnie helped pick them up. His hands were shaking too.

"Did you hear anything?"

"I heard a loud clap of thunder and ran into something hard," Ronnie answered but didn't look up at Zay.

"Do you know what it was?"

Ronnie shook his head and kept his eyes down. He put his hand out to see if the invisible wall still stood in front of them.

"Follow me," Zay instructed Ronnie. They make a wide loop around the invisible barrier.

Once the two reached the science building, Ronnie spoke, "Did you see something?"

"No, I heard the same thing you did and felt it." Zay unlocked the microbiology room door. He forgot about their meeting in the student union. "I have a difficult chore to do. Can you help me?"

He picked up the phone and dialed the number for the *Used Cow Factory* "Yes, I received my order but it was dumped on the front lawn of the campus, can you come move it to the proper place."

Zay listened as the man on the other side spoke.

"It's okay just let the new driver know my orders always go to the east side of the science building. There is large steel trap door on that side. Dump the animal into the door.

Zay hung up and headed toward a metal door at the back of the lab. He unlocked it and motioned for Ronnie to follow him. They entered a small room with an elevator on one side and a set of stairs on the other. Zay pushed the down button on the elevator.

"I thought we were on the ground floor." Ronnie mused as he entered the open elevator.

"We are; this elevator is for the basement levels."

"How many?" Ronnie stared at the button panel on the elevator holding six buttons.

"Four."

"Why six buttons if there are only four floors?"

"I guess to add to the confusion. I really don't know."

"Is there anything on those floors?"

"That's a quest we will have to undertake someday." Zay smiled as the elevator door closed. He wondered why it never occurred to him to check the other two floors. Dr. Winegren didn't mention them, and Zay hadn't noticed until now.

Once the elevator stopped, Zay looked at the boy directly. The two men stood eye to eye, one the post-graduate professor and the other a third-year student.

"What you are about to see is real, awful, and bewildering."

Zay headed out of the open elevator doors without giving Ronnie any explanation. But once Ronnie turned the corner he realized there was no need for explanation.

They stared into the largest yellow eye with a distinct vertical reptilian iris.

Ronnie gasped and placed his hand over his mouth. With great difficulty he managed to mutter, "What is it?"

Zay didn't answer him instead he stared into the eye of the creature and muttered, "So it's dead, it's still food." Zay spoke to the creature in a thirty-foot-tall steel cage. The creature roared and slammed his body into the bars. He opened his maw and let his sulfur-scented breath fill the room with odious repugnance boosting the visible horror.

"What are you studying?" Zay opened a conversation with Ronnie while he furiously worked with some buttons on a panel in the wall.

"Microbiology. Are you talking to that thing?" Ronnie answered and asked while holding his nose and staring at the beast with wide eyes.

"Great, you're in the right place. And yes, it can place its thoughts in your mind."

Ronnie laughed out loud, "I said microbiology, not strange animal husbandry."

Zay joined him in laughter. "Believe it or not, that's what goes on in my lab."

"So, what are you going to do with the bull?" Ronnie asked as he stared at a huge metal door above the monster's head.

"I feed it to my microbes." Zay peered at Ronnie from the side of his face and smirked.

"You must have some gigantic microbes." Ronnie smacked him back with a jab. "Is this thing what you call a microbe?"

Zay smiled. "No. We keep them in the freezer upstairs. This bunker is for the incubator."

"Incubator?"

"Yea, I ordered the bull for that monster's dinner. We take tissue samples from the monster and study its DNA"

"Sweet." Ronnie bobbed his head up and down.

"Ah, I got it." Zay exclaimed.

"Got what?"

"The code to open the door to the bin." Zay pushed the last button and a loud crash from outside permeated the room; the sound of metal and hydraulics. A trap door near the head of Phobus opened, and the bull came sliding down. The ogre snapped it up before it hit the ground and closed his huge mouth around it. A knot appeared in the freaks' throat about the size of the bull.

"That will calm him for a while."

Both men kept their eyes on the creature with the serpentine head and neck and the grotesque horns bent around its face as it settled down on the floor.

"That's clever?" Ronnie whispered.

"I had this hydraulic bin installed after I hauled my first load of meat down here. I decided there had to be an easier way. Besides, the *Used Cow Factory* doesn't care why I want the animal, they are glad to make the sale."

Ronnie nodded his head at the complicated method of feeding a huge monster.

"Are you afraid they will find out what you have down here?"

"No, the bin doesn't open down here until I put the code in. They never see it and if they hear it, they think it's mechanical."

"How often do you feed it? Ronnie asked.

"As little as possible." He said to Ronnie, "Come on over slowly."

Ronnie obeyed and stood next to Zay.

"Is it safe?" Ronnie asked.

"Down here is never safe and don't ever forget that."

Ronnie's whole body started shaking, and he froze.

Dr. Troye touched his hand. It was cold. "Don't make any sudden moves and you'll be okay. I don't think the creature can see detail, only movement. The cage is made of titanium steel, and it has held this creature for nearly ten years."

"Yet, there's always that weak moment in the movies . . ." Ronnie muttered.

"What?"

"You know, in the movies when something goes wrong that isn't supposed to go wrong."

Zay laughed his reference. "I can tell you are going to keep me entertained."

"That's not my objective, but if it gets me a better grade, I'll sing for ya."

"Only if you can sing."

"Oh, I can sing, the question is whether I sing well?"

"Point made." Zay slapped him on the back. Phobus raised his head and made a squawking noise.

"No sudden moves, remember?" Ronnie reprimanded Zay.

The door closed inside the beast's cage. the Doppler sound of the truck leaving could be heard, and the creature settled down on the floor.

"His rear!" Ronnie pointed and exclaimed.

"Don't!" Zay grabbed Ronnie's pointing hand.

"But . . . His backside looks like a goat," Ronnie stammered.

"It is."

"I'm confused."

With Ronnie's statement, the creature raised its head and looked into Ronnie's eyes.

Ronnie gasped. This time he saw both eyes and one of them didn't look serpentine; it looked. . . human! The creature opened its mouth and put it against the bars of the cage in front of Ronnie.

"Human teeth too." Zay pointed out to Ronnie. "On the second row in the back."

"What? . . . Is . . . I . . ."

"This is the big question; what is it and how did it come to be. But the bigger question is what do we do with it? Phobus is our project."

"A deformed dragon?" Ronnie screamed out at the creature.

The dragon closed his jowl and stared at him.

In a surprise action, both Ronnie and Zay heard the gravelly voice speaking directly to their minds, *the planting of seed is singular, but the harvest comes in multiples.*

Then the dragon turned its head away, circled inside his cramped cage, and settled into a corner.

Ronnie's face turned pale and his body went stiff. "What does that mean?"

Zay shrugged his shoulders. "Come on, let's get out of here. With a full belly, he'll settle down for a few days."

Ronnie followed Zay to the elevator in silence. Once they arrived at the ground floor, Ronnie slumped onto the couch beneath the only window in the room. Zay handed him a glass of water and took one for himself. They both gulped as if they'd escaped a desert.

"I can't explain it, but every time I go down there I come up thirsty."

Ronnie refilled his glass and gulped it down. He nodded but didn't stop drinking.

Zay joined him with a second glass. "Now that you've met our house guest and his appetite, I'm putting you in charge of ordering his dinner. Check with the zoo.

Sometimes they have animals they need to discard. Animal shelters can provide small snacks for him, but the Local *Used Cow Factory* is usually our best bet. The fresher the meat, the longer it keeps him calm." Zay patted the water stand. "Be sure you keep plenty extra bottles on hand for our water cooler."

Ronnie nodded and said, "If feel like I could drink one of those five-gallon bottles."

"Some days you will. Being in the presence of that thing sucks the moisture out of you."

Ronnie stared at Dr. Troye and shook his head. "Who knows about that thing?"

"Not many, a few of the microbiology professors, the necessary administration, and one student—you."

Is that all?" Ronnie asked.

"No, a few graduates know. Remember, it's been here nearly ten years. It's rather remarkable the whole campus and community doesn't know," Zay explained.

"Where did you find it?" Ronnie asked.

"Actually, it was my brother-in-law and cousin who found this thing."

"How?"

"They found it half-wrapped in a burlap sack, and the dragon head was biting its goat rear. It was a lot smaller then."

"What did you call it?"

"Phobus."

"The name fits; he's scary." Ronnie shuddered as he made the statement.

"It's our jewel in the rough right now for our research."

"What's the research?"

"This school is one of only fourteen research labs which received grants from the National Institutes of Health to be an active part of the human genome project."

"Wow." Ronnie's eyes grew big. "That's a biggie?"

"Yes, it is. I credit this little critter with our success in obtaining the grants."

"Grants?"

"Yes, we received a private grant from the Celera Corporation."

"So, this is our test subject?"

"No, I didn't mention this critter in the application, but he is a well spring of genetic information. As far as I can tell, we have human, reptilian, and mammal DNA in that one creature. We don't have to waste time finding test subjects."

"You think that thing was hatched?" Ronnie mused.

Zay nodded.

"I think it was created in a laboratory, so this is all it knows. Speaking of laboratory, do you know how to extract DNA from a molecule?"

Ronnie shook his head.

"Then your first assignment, learn the process, because that is what we do here." Dr. Troye handed Ronnie a textbook.

Returning to his task, Zay recoiled when he felt the cold prickly presence of something unseen touch him. At the same moment, he caught a glimpse of Ronnie's blond head and felt a surge of compassion for the boy only five years his junior. He shook his head to bring himself out of the strange daze. He glanced around the room and saw a quick glimmer of red. Something either winked or revealed itself for a second. A new surge of fear crept up his spine. The same fear he had felt on the farm as a thirteen-year-old boy facing a dragon.

Zay's flesh buckled up into small bumps as his nervous system reacted. He shuddered. Then he stepped back away from the apparition. He kept watching for more visible signs of the dragon. Instead, he heard the victorious roar of a pride of lions.

3

Vampires

> I will first doubly repay their iniquity and their sin, because they have polluted My land: they have filled My inheritance with the carcasses of their detestable idols and with their abominations.
>
> --- Jeremiah 16:18

CHRISTINE SANDERS DRIED her hands on the dishtowel after finishing the dishes. She'd let them pile up so high it took her nearly two hours to wash, dry, and put them away. The worst were the pans she had left. *Why do I do this to myself?*

Boom! Some of the clean dishes scattered on the floor. "What the heck was that?" she shouted out loud. She picked them up. *Thank goodness for Melmac non-breakable.*

Marcy Odom, her roommate and a clean freak, should be grateful. Christine filled the role of slob in their community household. Even with the differences in personality, they seldom disagreed. Marcy paid the most rent, and Christine washed the most dishes and did the most cooking. The shared apartment located on campus gave them quick access to campus classrooms and a quick trip back between classes for guilty pleasures like taking the time for their favorite daytime television drama—an old rerun called *Dark Shadows*.

Christine filled two glasses with their favorite soda. She glanced at the clock and knew Marcy would be coming in soon. She took the sodas to the living room and turned on the television set. The old television took a while to warm up and get a decent picture, although, it was almost always a little snowy.

Marcy always finished class early on test days. She studied and knew the answers, so Christine hurried getting everything ready before she arrived. The rasp of the front door caught Christine's attention, and she turned to see Marcy with hands full and short of breath.

"Has it started yet?" Marcy said as she came into the kitchen and plopped her purse and books on the table Christine had just cleaned. She took her seat on the couch. The place with the most pillows, one for her back and one for her feet. Being short had few advantages, but Marcy quickly learned to compensate for her five-foot-two-inch frame.

Christine picked up Marcy's things and transferred them to her bedroom. When she came back, Marcy was gazing out the back window.

"Guilty conscience or expecting a guest?" Christine asked.

"I don't know, just looking."

"You're just paranoid." Christine joked as she sat down.

"Me?" Marcy exclaimed, "You're the one—"

"I know, I'm the one who's always looking over my shoulder."

"It's time for the show to start. Shh."

The hand-me-down black and white television set stared back at the girls with its snowy eye. Christi worked with the dials and managed to get a clear picture. "Now, if it will hold for the next thirty minutes, we can be happy."

"I applied for a Sears credit card today, if it comes through, we can get a new television—in color," Marcy added.

"That would be nice," Christine muttered, not paying attention as she pulled on her costume.

"Ready for some soda, fudge, and witchcraft?" Marcy asked.

Christine cracked her red lips in a curve and revealed her white teeth as she rubbed her hands together and said in a playful growl, "Let's open the book of shadows and see what comes out."

Marcy laughed at the antics of her friend with her plastic vampire teeth over her own. "You even dress the part."

"Of course, the better to enjoy the trip with *Barnabas Collins*. This show may be old, but it still sends chills up my spine," Christine intoned.

This daily ritual of watching a soap opera about vampires, witches, and sorcerers and sometimes dressing as the characters was the girls hidden secret. Marcy threw back a big gulp of soda.

"Did you make the fudge?"

Without acknowledging her question, Christine asked, "Do you think the Bible says anything about vampires?"

"Let's ask Mrs. Holloway tomorrow. That should be a fun way to get her off her lecture," Marcy suggested.

"Did you make the fudge?" Marcy repeated.

"Of course," Christine said. "What good is a little evil without a lot of sweet. Does the Bible really say to kill witches?"

"Yep," Marcy answered as she went to the closet-sized kitchen and picked up the fresh pan of fudge.

"That seems harsh." Christine pondered the thought. "Marcy, you're quite the Bible expert, why kill witches?"

"Because they bring evil demons into our lives."

"Then what the heck are we doing?" Christine grinned and turned up the volume. The conversation stopped. Their attention turned toward the television where the vampire filled the screen and spoke in tones befitting their anxiousness of safe fear.

"It's entertainment," Marcy answered before the commercial ended and the show started. Neither would be talking now.

The camera moved up the stairs, slowly stopping at the top where a figure stood dressed in white with a thick veil covering the face.

"Who's that?" Marcy whispered?

"Either Kathryn or Angeline?" Christine muttered.

"Could be."

The white figure started walking down the stairs slowly. The camera cut away and turned on the face of Barnabas. Christine pulled a throw up over her legs and shivered.

"Is it cold in here to you?" she asked Marcy.

"I'm fine," Marcy answered. "But I have a blanket over me."

Christine shuddered with a violent motion.

"You're really shivering. Are you sick?"

"No, just cold."

Marcy moved in closer to Christine, and they turned their attention back to the show. As the white clan figure crept down the stairs, Barnabas walked toward it. He stepped in front of the form and reached out to raise the veil . . .

Suddenly, Christine let out a blood-curdling scream.

Marcy jumped up and looked at Christine who was now kicking and batting the air. Her scream changed from one of surprise to a high-pitch of absolute terror.

"Hey, it's only a show," Marcy said as she grabbed Christine's arms and tried to calm her.

"Stop! Leave." Christine screamed, and a small trickle of blood formed in the well at the base of her neck.

Marcy stepped back and let go of Christine. "What the heck is that?"

Christine didn't answer, she kicked and batted the air as her face twisted in a horrific look of fear.

By this time, their neighbor, a hulking football player, broke the latch on the door.

"What's going on?" he shouted as he took a stance, ready to defend their honor.

"She started screaming like she's being attacked, and look, she's bleeding. I don't know why," Marcy tried to explain as she shook her head and tears flowed from her eyes.

Christine continued screaming, kicking, and batting the air as if she were fighting with someone.

"What's attacking her?" the neighbor yelled. "I don't see anything or anybody."

"I don't know," Marcy answered.

As Marcy and the neighbor watched in horror blood trickled down Christine's arm.

Marcy gasped.

The neighbor stood and watched the flow of blood as Marcy swabbed it with tissue and Christine groaned.

"What do we do?" The neighbor asked her.

Another unearthly screech joined Christine's, and Marcy turned toward it. It was coming from the television, and the horrendous face of a huge dragon atop the white figure filled the screen. Marcy reached over and turned it off.

Christine went flaccid and draped across the couch, her eyes stared unseeing at the ceiling. The neighbor turned toward the door.

"Don't leave us," Marcy called.

"I'm going to call an ambulance; we've got to get her to the hospital."

Marcy threw cold water on Christine's face. "Wake up, please wake up."

Christine turned toward Marcy and blinked, "Do you see it?" she said in a groggy voice.

"What?" Marcy asked as she dried Christine off. Her skin was ice-cold, but at least she was breathing.

Marcy heard the wail of the ambulance and breathed a sigh of relief. She forced herself to look at the puncture wounds on Christine's forearm. She muttered, "Did Barnabas bite you?"

Christine tried to smile as she shook her head, "Not Barnabas."

"Then what?" Marcy attempted to keep her voice calm.

"It ... hurt." Christine mumbled with a thick tongue.

"What?"

"The planting of seed is singular, but the harvest comes in multiples," Christine muttered. Then with clarity of expression she looked deep into Marcy's eyes and added, "It's harvest time."

Marcy stepped back from her roommate. It may be her body, but it wasn't her voice. The voice was strong and . . . deep like a man.

Christine dropped back into the demeanor of confusion and pain. Her face twisted into a look of agony and she moaned, "Ugly dragon."

4

Blood Identification

> O LORD do not Your eyes look for truth? You have smitten them, but they did not weaken; You have consumed them, but they refuse to take correction. They have made their faces harder than rock; they have refused to repent.
>
> ---Jeremiah 5:3

ZAY SLIPPED INTO the lab early. Working with organized memory, he sat up the lab. His meticulous habits of control and storage made the task a mindless one. His mind focused on the day's assignment or the questions he brought to the lab for answers.

His brother-in-law, Daniel Holloway, called in the wee hours of the morning and asked him to come to the hospital. Upon his arrival Daniel led them into an empty patient room. He pulled out several vials of blood and handed them to Zay.

"I don't know if this is against hospital policy or not, but I don't want to take a chance on having to cut through a process of red tape and explain my concern."

Zay looked at him with a furrowed brow. "So why are you giving this to me?"

"The patient claims she was bitten by a dragon." Daniel whispered.

Zay nodded and slipped the vials of blood into his pocket. "Anything specific that you're looking for in the blood?"

"Answers."

Zay patted Daniel on the back, "me too, brother. I'll call you if I discover anything important."

"Thanks," Daniel said and he quietly opened the door and peered out into the hall. "It's empty." He said and the two men stepped out into the dimly lit aisle.

Zay placed the freshly drawn blood sample he had taken from Daniel's patient, known only as Christine S. next to the rack of other samples Ronnie had drawn from Phobus. With the samples clearly labeled, he pondered which tests to do on the limited amount of blood. He decided to set one vial aside in the refrigerator in case one became contaminated.

Today, Zay's train of random thoughts started with the details of a wild story his cousin told him about the time the creature was found eight years ago. His smile grew wider with the memory of his reaction; he hadn't believed them.

Then Dr. Winegren introduced him to the same creature eight years later. He became a believer in the wild story pretty quickly when he came to face to face with the beast. He went downstairs to make sure the organism still resided in the cage. He was there coiled up in the corner in its usual position. Zay almost felt sorry for a goat trying to carry the awkward length and bulk of a dragon neck and head.

This monster reminded Zay of a poorly cut puzzle. One of those 5000-piece puzzles with the cover image on the box faded or lost. Zay hoped the genome project would reveal this monster's origin and composition.

This morning his brother-in-law, Dr. Daniel Holloway, had presented another puzzle piece to the dragon's origin. The blood samples from Christine Sanders led Zay to probe for a connection between Phobus and Christine.

It was Christine's description of the attack she suffered which offered the implication. Zay understood Daniel's analysis. Christine's roommate, Marcy, kept chattering about the attack in strange phrases such as *red*, *big*, and *snake*. She answered every question with the same words, followed by a loud groan. As the adrenalin seeped from her body, exhaustion replaced the hysteria.

Daniel wrapped Marcy in a blanket from the warming oven.

She sighed and relaxed a bit, but her body shivered involuntarily even though the Texas fall temperature still held the leg of the summer heat. Marcy rocked, muttered, and sang until exhaustion took her into a deep sleep on the pull-out couch in Christine's room.

The bizarre incident and fantastical description of the attack presented Zay with the questions of the day. "The simple step is the best first step—set a baseline."

That morning Zay called his twin brother Rance, a financial broker. After relating the details he knew about this student, Christine, he asked the question that only his brother and father could understand. "What does the phrase mean? And why the added words, *the harvest is now?*"

Rance groaned. "Not again. Have you asked Barbara?"

"No, I don't want to bother her. She has her hands full with three kids and the pregnancy crisis center."

"Yeah, I guess so, but she may understand better than any of us. We haven't had any dragon sightings in ten years."

Zay laughed at the analysis. "I guess you're right, but the phrase finds its way to us frequently. Why do we keep hearing it?"

"To me, the phrase is pretty simple, not necessarily a puzzle," Rance responded. "On the other hand, the fact that it keeps appearing is a puzzle."

"I hadn't thought about that," Zay said.

"It sounds like something God would say, not a dragon."

Then Rance changed the subject. "How's your project coming along?"

"We received our lab equipment yesterday. We can start our genetic study on the creature. It appears we may have a victim of a dragon attack to study. And she isn't a Troye." Zay added with emphasis.

"What are you looking for in that critter?"

"It's origin and a means to destroy it."

"Don't we already know the answer to its origin?" Rance raised his voice a bit.

"It's not a fallen angel. It doesn't have the power of the dragon we saw. But—" Zay stopped.

"But what?" Rance prodded.

"There's a dragon behind it; a magnificent dragon."

Rance laughed, "That's an oxymoron. I can't imagine any dragon being anything but awful, not magnificent."

Zay joined him in laughter. "You're right, but this one has the scales of beauty. I only saw a small glimpse of him, but it was breathtaking."

"Maybe in more ways than you can imagine," Rance warned. "I still don't understand what your purpose is with this critter you can see and the one you barely see."

"I'm pretty sure, based on the details surrounding the capture of that thing along with objective observations, the ugly critter is the result of a manufactured mistake in a lab."

"So?" Rance asked.

"If there is a lab that can create life and in such a deformed manner, what else is that lab creating?"

"Oh, now I see your dilemma, you are both scientist and detective."

"I guess so," Zay answered.

"Sorry, brother, I can't help you with your mystery or your puzzle. I have put that time out of my mind, and I don't ever want to relive it."

"I understand, but I have to face the problem, and I know I can find the answer. I have the education, the intelligence, and now I have the proper equipment and financing," Zay boasted.

Rance chuckled and rubbed his hand over his chin, "It's all about money, brother. Money runs and rules the world."

"I know, but that's your world, not mine, I just want all my equipment to arrive."

At the moment Zay voiced his wish, he heard Ronnie come in the door making a lot of noise. Before he saw Zay on the phone, he pronounced their good fortune.

"Hey boss, it must be Christmas, we have multiple packages and they are all from Celera. We've got new toys." Ronnie said with a joyful lilt.

"I gotta go, brother, my golden ticket just arrived."

Zay stepped over to help Ronnie unload the boxes. He opened one of the smaller packages and pulled out a fluorescence-activated cell sorter. He yelped and held it up for Ronnie to see.

"You ready to isolate some cells?" Zay said in a sultry invitational voice.

"I guess this means we got the grant from Celera?" Ronnie asked Zay.

"Yes, and it also means we are officially a part of the national genome research project."

The two men grinned. "If we can't get our answers now, we are poor microbiologists," Zay said in a soft voice while tearing into another box of equipment. Ronnie joined him as they spent the afternoon unpacking their treasures.

"We'll get everything set up and start working on the project tomorrow morning." Zay announced as the equipment piled up on their floor and work tables.

The next day, the two men arrived at their workplace early with excitement in their steps. They pulled on their lab coats. "Get three tissue samples," Zay instructed Ronnie.

"Which three?"

"One from the student Christine Sanders, one from the mammal part of the monster, and another from the reptilian part of the monster."

Ronnie stood there as if frozen in thought. "You want me to draw blood from a monster?"

Zay couldn't help but laugh at the terrified expression on Ronnie's face. He went to the supply closet and gathered a gun and syringe. "Fill this with the tranquilizer and shoot him with it. It takes a few minutes for him to collapse. It works faster if you get it in the neck, but the rump is easier to hit."

Ronnie relaxed and sighed.

Once Ronnie came back to the ground floor with his two test tubes of blood he asked Zay, "Do you think we can get a homogenous group of cells from each?"

"We better, it's the only way to see the individual cells in their purity," Zay answered.

"Yeah, I thought that too," Ronnie said with a slight grin and a wink. "Purity is overrated."

"Hey, we're talking about cells, not behavior," Zay gently scolded.

"I know, but you said your dad told you God gives us pictures of the things He wants us to know. Maybe this is a picture that homos really are pure."

Zay shrugged his shoulders. "Let's see what the day reveals from under the microscope before we start relying on empty preaching. Shall we?"

Christine begged Dr. Holloway for details, or rather more details.

"There's nothing more to tell," Daniel groaned.

"So, I was bitten by a snake. That's all you can say? What about that—"

"That what?" Daniel encouraged her.

"I don't know, if I was bitten by a snake, how come nobody saw it?"

"They are known for sneakiness, you know."

"It came out of the television," Christine yelled at him. "Why won't anyone look in that blasted television set?"

"They did, and there was nothing there," Daniel explained. "Did you see it before it bit you?"

"Yes, it came right out of the screen, the horrible, open mouth of a snake, a huge snake, it looked like a . . . a . . . dragon."

Daniel didn't say anything, but he made a note in his own private notebook. "Can you describe it?"

"Yes. Horrid."

"Did you see the whole animal?" Daniel continued.

Christine dropped her gaze to her hands which were fidgeting with the edge of the sheet. "No, I was trying to get away from it. It was dreadful," Christine cried as she described her ordeal. "That wasn't the worse part."

"What was the worse?"

"His eyes . . ."

"What about them?" Dr. Holloway prodded.

"They looked like buckets of hate."

"What does hate look like?" Daniel spoke softly but could feel his rapid heartbeat.

"Piercing, as if the thing wanted to rip me to shreds."

"Did you feel it had the power to hurt you?" Dr. Holloway asked.

"I'm in a hospital, it *did* hurt me." She held up her arm and pointed to her neck.

A slight blush rose to Daniels' face.

Dr. Zay Troye entered the hospital room of Christine Sanders. Zay was familiar with her blood chemistry since Dr. Holloway gave him blood samples, but this was the first time he met the actual person. Dr. Holloway introduced Zay to Christine, "He's a biomedical engineer. I've asked him to help us find your monster."

Zay sat down in the chair beside her bed. He took her hand in his and smiled. In a soft voice he said, "Now, I need to know exactly what happened from your point of view." He gave his full attention to Christine as he listened to her tale.

She didn't stay on topic but wandered back to her childhood. She had become a ward of the state at the age of ten and spent most of her life in foster homes. At age fifteen she entered her last foster home where she would live until she attended college. She stayed in touch with the family, but they lived a thousand miles away.

Zay understood why she had to give her background with the last sentence. She was apologizing for not having any family with her. He felt an emptiness in his spirit with her confession. He made a mental note to talk to Barbara, his sister, to find some family support for her.

Zay couldn't help but notice Christine's unusual beauty. Her face would cause a man to freeze in fear and gasp with lust. She was beautiful, desirable, and fearful.

He rose from his seat and said, "I'll be visiting you from time to time."

"I'll be the researcher on your case, and I'll keep you informed if we find anything to explain what happened to you."

"Dr. Holloway wants me to see a physiatrist, Dr. Greenstein. What do you think?"

"I'm not a medical doctor, but I know Dr. Greenstein. She's fair and thorough. It might be a good idea; after all, you've had a unique experience."

"Not too many people get bit by a television screen." Christine gave him a weak smile in spite of the swelling in her neck and chin. He smiled and patted her hand. With that motion, he took a closer look at the bite on her arm. Her skin stretched beyond its limit at the site. He then looked at her neck. It had the double puncture wound of a snake bite but looked different than her arm. It wasn't as swollen, but it pulsated as if it had a heartbeat.

"What do you think?" Zay asked Daniel.

"It looks and acts like a snake bite."

"It had huge fangs," Christine interrupted.

"Are we are ever going to be rid of those things?" Zay moaned in a light voice.

"What do you mean?" Christine asked with wide open eyes that were gathering a mist of fear in them.

Zay regretted his statement and her acknowledgement of it.

"Christine, you're not the first to see a dragon," Daniel interjected.

"Really, who else has seen one?"

"Both Dr. Holloway and I," he answered, keeping his voice low and calm.

Christine relaxed and lay her head back on her pillow. She focused her eyes on the ceiling and said, "Were you bitten?"

"My wife, his sister was attacked." Dr. Holloway answered.

"I've wondered why it attacked me and not Marcy."

"It may have been random, with no reason," Zay answered. "But know your case is top priority to me."

"So, I'm your guinea pig?" She smiled at him.

"No . . . well, yes, I guess you are." he returned the smile.

When everyone left her room, tired overtook Christine and she fell into a restless sleep. She tossed on her bed as a nightmare embraced her.

She tried to scream, but only garbled moans were heard by the staff. She opened her eyes and saw a dark shadow coming toward her, and it was coming out of the wall. She sat up, and now fully awake she gasped and let out a shriek of terror.

The shadow swallowed the shout, and no one responded to her. She searched the nurses' station through the glass for help. There are two nurses there, each busy with their paper work. They are oblivious to her dilemma. She screamed again and tried to get out of bed. She fell and scrambled toward the door.

Finally, one of the nurses saw her in the hallway.

"Oh, my dear," the nurse yelled.

"Help me," Christine muttered and looked behind her. The shadow is no longer dark. Color fills the outline form of blackness—a deep red.

The nurse came and helped her back into bed. The shadow stood behind the nurse. Puffs of smoke floated over the nurse's head as she spoke softly to Christine and kept talking in a gentle voice. This calmed Christine because the shadow kept its distance behind the nurse. She pulled a sheet up to Christine's neck and a blanket afterward.

Christine attempted to take the nurse's hand and realized she is trapped in restraints the nurse applied while calming her.

"You. . . you. . . tied me down!"

"It's for your safety, dear."

"Can't you see it's coming after me? You've got to get me out of here!" Christine thrashed around and cursed.

The nurse smiled and left the room, closing the door behind her.

Christine shouted as loud as she could. "It's the terror of the night called Leyla."

The nurse stopped and observes Christine for a moment, cocking her head to one side. "What did you say?"

"I said, please don't leave me alone with this terror."

"You're not alone. We're close by; your call button is within your reach." The nurse closed the door and left.

As the door clicked shut, Christine stared wide-eye at the vile creature standing before her. .

"You are mine," he responded with a hiss.

"Who are you?" Christine yells out at him.

The nurse stops her paper work and walks to the door of Christine's room where she hears Christine talking. She stands there a minute and listens, then she returns to the nurse's station and tells her co-worker, "Christine must be hallucinating, she said the terror of the nightimaged named Leyla was with her. Do you understand that?"

"It's from the Bible."

"Really?"

"Yea, in Psalm 91."

The nurse grabbed up a Gideon Bible from under the counter and looked it up.

"Your right, in verse five it says, 'you will not be afraid of the terror of the night,' but what is Leyla?"

"I think that was the name of the terror of night."

"That would make it a person, a thing, something besides a feeling."

"Now you know, she's seeing monsters."

"How'd you know this?" The first nurse asked her.

"I just heard a sermon on it on the way into work today. Interesting, don't you think?"

The nurse checked on Christine again and noticed she appeared to be talking to someone. She fought against the restraints and her hair was wet with perspiration. She returned again to the desk and asked her co-worker, "She really is afraid, do you think I should remove the restraints?"

"I think we can, we can watch her close." The co-worker said. The two nurses rose to go to Christine's room. When they approached her room they stopped at the door and listened for a few minutes. They both gasped at what they heard and saw.

"Who are you?" the shadow spoke.

"I'm a nobody."

He sighed. "You're an important person in my kingdom."

"What do you mean?"

"Quiet," he hissed, making contact with her leg.

Christine pulled her leg away, but she felt a cold, silky touch wrapping around her legs and her body.

"Be still."

Christine opens her mouth to speak but discovered her voice had no sound.

He laughed as he wrapped his serpent head around Christine's entire body.

She saw a smoky haze and a loose shadow. "Help!" She turned toward the two nurses standing in the door way watching.

"Nobody can hear you."

"What are you doing?" she demanded as she wriggled and tried to escape the clutches of his muscles tightening around her.

The thing sneered and answered, "Planting a harvest."

5

A Desert Place

Woe, is me, because of my injury! My wound is incurable. But I said, Truly this is a sickness, And I must bear it." My tent is destroyed, and all my ropes are broken; My sons have gone from me and are no more. There is no one to stretch out my tent again or to set up my curtains.

---Jeremiah 10: 19-20

THE THIRST SO deep, the creature's inside skin felt as though it roasted in the beam of a summer sun like a salted filet. The wind removed whatever moisture its body may contain. The dragon could feel the gnawing of dryness chewing up its body from the inside out. The physical torment gave way to mental desperation. Madness descended upon its mind.

A strange world of white consumed the windy landscape. The blasts of wind so cold they burned. The ice below it as hard as steel, the wind around it as hot as fire and the sky above . . . gloomy.

The white night sun surrounded it like a friend who protected from the stimulation of colors, hope, and loneliness. The strangeness of the dark mixed with continuous light muddled a chaotic mind. All hope shattered in the swirling wind of icy blasts. No guideposts or landmarks exist. A howl from the bowels of fear made its way to the brute's throat, but before it could be heard, it was stolen by the wind. It's in a land so unforgiving and cruel even a dragon cried for mercy.

Its scales frozen to hardened cold skin. Not even the cold heart of the beast could beat. It's eyes normally burning hate on lesser creatures upon which it used sharpened claws to lacerate and feed on the hardiest of animals. Alas, it mattered not what weapons it held in its control, for there exists none other than itself. With a flick of its split tongue, the beast searched for the scent of fear, which betrays hidden prey. Sadly, the only fear it found lived within itself.

The creature squinted its eyes and saw a rise on the horizon. With punishing steps, the beast approached an opening that was level with the ground. It trudged toward it with head bent against the wind. Perhaps it may find peace from the wind where hunger and thirst will leave it in death.

When it reached the edge of the precipice, stairs winding down into the hole appeared. It didn't think about it before it wound its long neck over the rail of the steps.

Its scaly frozen body passed the head in a freefall down into a dark abyss. Rising from the coiled heap of hurt, it waited for the eyes to adjust to the blackness. It heard the whoosh of wind through a tunnel but felt no movement, yet still keenly aware it senses there are others present. Again, the flicking tongue test the air for a possible meal and liquid. It raised the head slightly when it sensed no heat from the other creatures hovering around with unseeing eyes.

"What is this place?" it muttered to the nearest imposing figure.

"Who are you?" the large figure jumped back and followed the voice to the ground.

"I don't know," it replied.

"Do you have memories?"

"What's that?"

The large creature leaned over and stared at the unknown misshaped creature. With bright golden eyes fixed on it he asked, "Are you the cursed one?"

"Again, I don't know if I'm 'the one,' but I'm cursed with thirst."

The large dragon breathed heat on the smaller creature. "That should help for the moment," it said and then turned its huge body around, knocking the smaller creature onto a tail as long as a Lebanon cedar was tall.

The little one shouted in anger, "How does that help my thirst?"

The tall one stopped and roared. "Do not yell!"

"Where are we?"

"It's called the Abyss by the Holy One. We call it Tartarus."

The smaller creature moaned. He had no memories, but he instinctively knew Tartarus was not a good place. "How did you get here?" it asked the large dragon.

"I was cast in here."

"Can you get out?"

"No."

The small one whimpered then shivered. "Can I?"

The large creature stopped and turned his mammoth body to look at the small dragon. The red dragon knocked the little one off his tail. "Don't get back up there," came a demanding roar from the large beast.

"I can't keep up."

"Then leave."

Each step the large dragon took pulled the two dragons deeper into darkness. The little dragon goat sat on his haunches, hissing at the darkness. A deep guttural laugh from the large beast mocked him in return.

"Please tell me. . ."

"Tell you what?"

"If I can get out of here and how."

"Look, those of us condemned to this place failed in our quest. If you will take it up, then maybe we can get you out."

The little dragon held on to every word. "I will. I will" it said. The funny looking monster would promise anything to get out of this place.

The large dragon sat down on the hard ice and studied the mismatched eyes of the little dragon and laughed.

"What's so funny?" Little dragon asked.

"You may be part of our mission. Where have you been? How'd you get here?"

"I don't know. What is the quest?"

The large dragon said. "You are proof it can work."

"What do you mean?"

Without acknowledging the little dragon's question, the red dragon spoke to little dragon about things it didn't understand.

"Our boss, Annika, took the power of the earth from those slimy humans. But then the Holy One—" The red beast stopped and spat on the ground with a grotesque face. "Provided a way for them to get it back with a child."

"Our leader Samzaya found a way for us to intermingle with the humans by taking wives from them and having children with them."

Little dragon watched the big dragon pace. The smoke coming from the side of its mouth revealed a growing anger. "Why?" Little dragon asked. Big dragon looked down on it and roared, "We pollute the blood line, then the Holy One's plan would fail."

The little dragon flicked his tongue out to taste the air. It sensed no danger in spite of big dragon's anger. It turned the head back to the big dragon and asked the obvious question, "What happened?"

"We ended up here and He destroyed the human race."

"Can't see how that helped," the little dragon drawled.

"He kept one family back. One man, Noah, was not yet infected with the dragon blood. The Holy One started over."

"How did you end up here?" Little dragon asked.

"He does not tolerate disobedience. When we chose to leave our spiritual realm as watchers and become part of the human realm, we angered the Almighty. He creates, He sets the boundaries. When we cross them, we face His wrath and His judgment." Big dragon spoke with a roar and told the little beast how the dragons ended up in the abyss, with a booming voice growing in harshness. Little dragon kept quiet and lowered his head. The reverberations of the dragon's tirade bounced off the walls of the cavernous place they occupied. The other dragons plodded along in their routine. Big dragon sat down on his haunches and snatched little dragon with a strong claw. Little dragon stared at a face that struck fear in the gut.

"You are not like us." Big dragon observed. "Do you have powers?"

Little dragon whimpered, "Don't know."

"You could be the key to our latest plan." The big dragon roared.

"What do you mean?" Little dragon gawked at big dragon.

"We hide the Holy One from the eyes of the humans." The big dragon laughed, and the sound bounced throughout the underground chambers.

"How could we know our quest to stop His plan would fail? But I have a sure-fire plan to destroy His happy little home. We distort the image by destroying the attraction. After all, it was the Holy One that gave them their free choice." Big dragon raised his head and howled with glee. Little dragon raised the awkward head attached to the small goat. The ideas the big dragon spoke didn't make sense, but the words made the big dragon happy.

"Teach me, wise one." the small dragon said and bowed the deformed head, even though the weight of it toppled his back end when the dragon head lost its center of balance. The big dragon appreciated the sign of submission, but chuckled at the poor creature's clumsiness.

"Your ugly enough to be the key to making our plan work."

"What do I do?" the little dragon asked as he bounded to leap on the big dragon's tail. The big dragon moved his massive tail, and the little one hit the hard ice, skewing his horns a little more and causing his face to puff up a little.

"I told you not to do that. Remember, you must obey every command we give. I am Belial, one of the fathers of rebellion against the Holy One."

Little dragon roared a small humble roar of admiration.

Big dragon stood and turned toward the blackness of the abyss. "Go back" was all he said.

"How?" Little dragon asked.

"Through a portal."

"I don't know what a portal is." The little dragon whimpered.

"Try the airwaves," the voice said before it disappeared.

The airwaves? What is that? Little dragon stood and looked around. White, hard ice surrounded everything in this place. Little dragon walked back toward the mouth of the cave. Once outside, he looked around. When he looked up he saw the air moving in waves. "Is that the airwaves?" the wimpy creature roared. No answer came.

Walking around in curiosity to find a way to mount the airwaves the clumsy slow dragon coiled the long neck around itself and ran in circles. Pictures flew toward him in rapid succession like a slow framed movie. With great effort the deformed beast ran to catch one. The pictures would disappear before the dragon goat could gather enough control to jump at them. It had both the sure foot of a goat, with the awkwardness of a stumbling ostrich.

Soon, it tired and stopped. The pictures kept coming. It watched as the pictures surrounded him in a constant movement of images, much like a carousel ride. The pictures included children watching television commercials, adults watching movies, teens reading magazines, men watching football, and the stream continued with no break.

Then it appeared before the creature's eyes. This was the airwave. The importance of the picture started the creature without reason. Two young women, one dressed in costume, watching the dragon with rapt attention. The brute didn't know what would happen when he uncoiled his neck and reached toward the woman staring into his eyes. It only knew this was the wave to catch. With a stretched neck the dragon felt the pull from an icy wilderness into the comfort of warmth.

It escaped Tartarus. With mouth agape, the body of the deformed dragon whipped through the air until it landed next to one of the women. She screamed. The dragon sunk his spear like teeth into her arm and held on while pulling the rest of the awkward body out of Tartarus. The woman kept screaming. The other people ran around him. The task accomplished, the dragon suddenly felt terror. The other humans moved and prodded the woman and the dragon.

The woman kept screaming and hitting and kicking him. The others held her. They did not appear to see him. Suddenly, little dragon saw Belial race into the room and grab the woman by the neck. The woman stopped thrashing and fell into a stupor.

The dragon determined it best to lay dormant beside her. The dragon felt warmth. It still clamped its death onto her arm. It needed more information about this world. It heard a roaring sound. Big dragon winked at him.

"Good job, little one."

6

DNA Extraction

The word which came to Jeremiah from the LORD, saying, Hear the words of this covenant, . . . 'Thus says the LORD, the God of Israel. 'Cursed is the man who does not heed the words of this covenant. . . Listen to My voice, and do according to all which I command you; so you shall be My people, and I will be your God in order to confirm the oath which I swore to give a land flowing with milk and honey."

---Jeremiah 11: 1-4

ZAY CLOSED THE lid on the centrifuge and turned on the timer. Learning to extract DNA and map the genome excited him as a scientist. On the other hand, the results he discovered with his primary test subject in the basement, disturbed him. On impulse, Zay decided to go back to the dungeon and see if the beast still slept from the tranquilizer given him earlier. If so, he would draw a new sample.

The dragon lay curled in the corner of the cage in the same position Zay had left him earlier this morning. He quietly put the key into the lock box to open the door to the cage. The beast didn't move. Zay proceeded on. He could feel his hand shaking as he approached the dragon.

One swipe of the beast's claw could eviscerate him so quickly he would be watching his guts fall out of his body before he saw the strike. Each visit could be his last. With that pleasant thought skipping around his mind, he could feel his body reacting to the physical fear. The hormones in his system exaggerated his body movements. He could control the mind skips, but the body jerks were a bit harder. He pulled the syringe from his lab coat pocket and visually selected a vein.

At least dragons possessed large veins which made it easier to draw blood. The skin beneath the scales remained tender so the needle plunged easy. The vial filled with the dark-red liquid and Zay turned his gaze to the monster's eyes. They were flitting. Either the dragon slumbered in REM sleep or he was about to wake up, and Zay prayed to a God he didn't believe existed to keep the thing asleep.

Once the vial filled, he quickly exited and slammed the cage door shut. The noise woke the dragon. It was not in a pleasant mood. He roared and released a plum of fire. Fortunately for Zay, this deformed dragon had a deformed flame thrower and could only pulse a flame a few inches from its mouth. Zay escaped before the flame touched him.

It often felt as though the dragon crawled around his mind. He remembered his dad told him how Nisroch, the dragon on the farm, communicated through mental images. One look at the horrific mistake made in a lab told Zay it probably didn't have the ability to reason, think, and communicate. However, he was certain this dragon was more than the eye could behold. The spirit of scheming coming from the dragon sent cold chills of fear running through Zay's body.

He remembered his father's teaching when they faced the dragon on the farm, "Let your fear take you by the hand and lead you to the core of your faith. There you can stand and never fall, for greater is the God of your faith than the god of this world."

That sounded good, but Zay knew the biology of the human brain. It worked in ways contrary to his dad's teaching. There existed two parts to the super computer in a person's head. The logical thinking sat atop the most primitive reptilian survival brain with no processor logic at all. The stupid part of the brain would steal all the mainframe power of the intelligence when it got scared. That made a person go from awesome to stupid in the span of a heartbeat. Right now, Zay felt his stupid mind in full operation.

His smart reasoning reminded him hourly of the awesome opportunity to learn from the DNA structure of a most bizarre creature. His stupid brain saw the spirit behind the creature and wets its pants. Zay begged his logical brain to overcome the scared mind because when stupid is in control, well . . . it wore wet pants.

According to his dad, the only cure for the stupid was to cut out the stuff that caused the fear. Zay laughed at the absurdity. Phobus sat in the ground below him, and that terror possessed a physical body with a tangible horror.

Zay took a deep breath and let it out slowly. He sat down on the couch and waited for the shaking to pass. In time, stupid brain would get distracted and smart brain could resume control of the body. Each time he faced the vile creature, it took longer for stupid brain to go away. Zay gulped his water, refilled it, and gulped again. He knew the fear had passed when he didn't lose any of the water due to his shaking hands.

While gulping his last glass of water, he heard his dad's voice in his smart brain. "Replace the fear of what you see with the reflection of the Holy One, seen in Jesus Christ."

Buster Troye, Zay's dad lived with a dragon on his farm and confronted him. Buster spoke from experience not exaggeration. Still Zay didn't know how to carry out his dad's advice. All he could see was a distorted creature wanting to devour him.

He put a drop of dragon blood in three test tubes and a drop of human blood in another three. He dropped them into the buckets of the centrifuge and closed the lid. While it ran to separate the white blood cells from the red, his mind returned to the persistent question that consumed his every thought. How did a human become a dragon goat?

He shook his head in bewilderment. Again, he imagined what his Dad would say, "Have faith in the wisdom of the Holy God." I no longer have any faith. It floated away from me like a leaf being pulled away on a rapid stream and fading into the white caps.

The centrifuge ding startled him, and Zay's reasoning processes returned to full operation. He rose from his stool still thinking about the question. As he pulled the test tubes from the machine, he stopped and stared at them, furrowing his brow.

There in front of him was a profound fact. The bands of color appeared on all the tubes: dark red on the bottom, a small band of white blood cells, and the yellow tinted plasma on top. He focused his attention on the bands which represented part of the answer, an elementary principle found in the physical not an elusive faith.

The rapid spinning of the centrifuge separated the heavier white blood cells from the red blood cells leaving separate bands of serum, white blood cells and red blood cells.

Zay pulled the tubes out and held them in front of his face. Three layers in our blood, each distinct but separate in their purpose, yet all are needed for the blood to nourish the body. "Amazing." He said as he put the tubes in a rack.

He needed the white blood cells to isolate the DNA. The white cells served as the commander giving the red bloods cells their instructions. The red blood cells delivered oxygen and nutrition to every part of the body based on the white blood cell directions. Red blood cells operated as the freight train of life.

No matter what one's religious status, the human body served as one of the biggest mysteries of all the cosmos and one of the best road maps to understanding the origin of man. Still, the process of separating the genes from the DNA presented a mystery.

He took notes on every step of the process, even recording his own random and sometime silly thoughts about a process. He left a blank page after each process in order to make later notes as the gene code revealed itself to him through experimentation.

His personal notes flowed from his pen, 'The human experience of life separates truthful instructions from perceived but unproven thinking. Thus, allowing the individual to find a purpose for life, whether it was true or not.' The notes may be personal but Zay reasoned like a scientist. To be truthful, it had to be reproducible under like circumstances. He titled his personal opinions: Observation of Opinion. This way he didn't have to reproduce an unimportant detail which simply fascinated him.

Observation of Opinion: By the principle of separation, DNA can be observed in its purity rather than its purpose.

The written statement caused a random thought to come to Zay. By separating a person's life from proper direction, a person can believe whatever is given them; therefore, a person does not need faith. They need proper and truthful instruction.

Zay sat down and pondered the notation. People don't need a god, they need science. With a bit of sarcasm, he addressed his dad's teachings in his notebook and said out loud, "According to my dad, this would be a picture illustrating how separation from the Word of God leaves a person vulnerable to lies."

"I thought this was a science lab, not a theology class," Ronnie said as he walked in on Zay's progressive thinking.

Zay jumped at the sound of his voice. "Sorry."

"You mean you think lies caused the thing in the basement to change from human to thing?" Ronnie mocked his boss but carefully. He needed Zay's grade and recommendation.

"No, I'm not anywhere near an answer to that question."

Ronnie picked up Zay's notes and read. "Interesting, I wouldn't have pondered the basic cell structure, but I think it provides a foundation, in the very essence of life."

"Exactly," Zay answered while focusing on his test tubes.

"You were talking about the instruction from the Word of God. I don't get how a book of fairy tales and stupid rules have anything to do with that creature."

Zay chuckled. "I know what you mean."

"Yeah, I don't care much for that book. But you don't strike me as the Bible thumper type, so how did you get to be such an expert?" Ronnie stopped and looked at Zay when he asked the pointed question.

"My dad."

"That's an advantage you had that I didn't."

"What happened to your dad?" Zay turned back to his work.

"He died in Vietnam when I was five years old."

Zay turned and looked at him, "I'm sorry."

Ronnie shrugged his shoulders

"Did your mom remarry?"

"No, she said there wasn't another man in the world like him."

Zay smiled. "That's the way I feel about my dad. He fought in WWII, but his biggest battle was against a dragon."

Ronnie gasped and looked at Zay. "Whad'ya say? A dragon?"

"Yeah, but he looked like a dragon, not like that abomination in our basement."

Ronnie groaned and grabbed his stomach.

"What's wrong," Zay asked as he put his work down and grabbed Ronnie before he hit the floor.

7

The Psychiatric Wing

> I know, O LORD, that a man's way is
> not in himself, Nor is it in a man who walks
> to direct his steps, Correct me, O LORD, but
> with justice.
>
> ---Jeremiah 10:23-24

MARCY ODOM BEGGED Professor Barbara Holloway to go with her to visit Christine Sanders in the psychiatric wing.

"I don't know how to approach her," Marcy pleaded.

"Okay, I'll go with you."

When they arrived, the nurse told them Christine showed violent behavior with bizarre voices and words. She entered the room first and informed Christine she had visitors.

Marcy's heart still beat in the rhythm of a salsa dance. Because she knew the possible source of the behavior. Mrs. Holloway taught psychiatric nursing at the university and she was the wife of Christine's physician, Dr. Holloway.

Marcy felt comfort in her presence when she entered the strange world of Christine's room.

Christine stood facing a small window with bars over it. Stagnant air filled the square pen-like room with a disinfectant smell. The place was clean but void of color or life. Marcy wished she had brought a plant, a flower, or even a piece of colored paper—anything to break the dull insipid green of the room. Other than one institutional looking chair, there was no place to sit except on the broken-down bed with a rust-colored frame.

Mrs. Holloway remained calm as they waited for Christine to acknowledge them. The nightmare slowly unfolded before Marcy and Mrs. Holloway as Christine turned to face them, Marcy's mouth fell open and she gasped. Without saying a word, she ran from the room to the lobby. She buried her head in her hands and wept. Her body shook, not from the weeping but from fear that gripped her to her bones. The same dragon she witnessed explode from the television set smiled at her from Christine's body.

Mrs. Holloway stayed a few minutes with Christine before she approached Marcy in the lobby. She leaned back and sighed. "I'm sorry."

"What happened to her?" Marcy asked between sobs.

"Can you tell me what you just saw?"

"I can, but I don't want to tell you."

"It wasn't Christine was it?"

Marcy held her head down, looking at her hands, twisting her fingers around each other. She shook her head and sniffled. "Is she sick?"

"Marcy, did you see something besides Christine?"

Marcy nodded.

"What was it?"

"The same thing that attacked her," Marcy whispered. Mrs. Holloway put her arm around her. She leaned into her shoulder and wept.

Barbara Holloway raised her head and whispered a prayer, "Help us, Lord. Only you can free her."

Marcy squeezed Mrs. Holloway's hand when she heard her say the short prayer. "Amen," she said.

"She's so pale and drawn, like something is sucking the life out of her."

"That's probably a good description."

"I should have turned off the television," Marcy said, whimpering. "Did you see . . ."

"The dragon?" Barbara calmly finished Marcy's question.

"Uh huh." Marcy stared at Mrs. Holloway, waiting for her answer.

"Not like you did, but it made itself known to me," Barbara answered.

"Why are you not shaking like me?"

Barbara sat up straighter in her chair and took one of Marcy's hands. "I've fought a dragon before . . . and . . . I won."

"Really? How do you win against a monster?" Marcy said between gasps.

Barbara shook her head, "Prayer and Bible knowledge. We don't know what goes on in a person's life that brings a dragon to them. But Jesus knows."

"Where. . . I mean how. . . what is a dragon?"

"A dragon is the physical image of an evil spirit. I think it can be a demon, or a fallen angel."

"What's the difference?" Marcy wiped the tears off her face as the conversation brought her to a somber state.

"It is believed the fallen angels are the ones that rebelled against God and fought with Michael and his angels like it says in Revelation 12:7-9. It clearly states the dragon is the devil."

"Are you saying the devil is in Christine?"

"I'm saying what the Bible says. We have to consider the whole Bible to have understanding."

"What do you think that thing is that attacked her? A demon?"

"Demons are different than fallen angels."

"How so?"

"People that study that kind of thing think the demons are the children of the fallen angels."

"Now you have me really confused. I didn't think angels could have children."

"They took on human form and came to earth to take human women for their wives. In Genesis six, it clearly says they had children with human women."

"Wow."

"Yeah, I know, they are making themselves known more and more."

"Why?"

"By reading the book of Jeremiah, there is a progression of rebellion against God."

"What was that progression?"

"First, they brought in idols. That actually happened during Solomon's time about 400 years before Jeremiah. But during Jeremiah's time, the people were mixing the worship of the idols with worship of God. They would spend their nights in sexual parties, sacrifice their children, and worship those wooden idols. The next morning, they would go to the temple and make sacrifices to God, or Yahweh."

"You said they progressed. How?"

"The first step was distorting God's message by the prophets. The prophets served as the Bible for God's people then."

Marcy sighed. "We're doing the same things, aren't we?"

"I think so. We want to have our fun without guilt, so we change the meaning of God's Word."

"Do you think Christine is rebellious, and this is why the dragon is taking her over?"

"I don't know Christine, but I do know she needs our prayers."

"How do you know prayers will help?"

"I had a demon try to take me over. My family and friends prayed for me. That was the only thing that saved me from being possessed."

Marcy's mouth dropped open. "Wow! So, you know, you really know?"

Mrs. Holloway smiled and nodded at Marcy. "Tell me about Christine."

"I know Christine had to practically raise herself."

"What do you mean?"

"She was in and out of the foster care system. When her dad died, her mother became a drunk."

"What happened to her dad?"

"Her mother killed him."

Barbara sighed heavily. "Dare I ask why?"

"I only know what Christine told me, and she was just a baby when it happened. She said her mother told her he was about to kill her, so she grabbed a butcher knife and killed him first."

"I guess that's when the state stepped in?"

"Yeah, she spent as much time as she could with her mother, but since she's rarely sober that wasn't much."

"How did you two become friends?"

"We met at college. I think Christine was looking for a sober friend. I was the only other one sober the night we went to an after finals party."

"Does Christine drink?" Barbara asked.

"Not a drop. she said she would never touch the stuff. Christine's vice is men."

"Does she have a boyfriend?"

"Always, sometimes two or three."

"She's so pretty," Barbara observed. "I'm sure she has no trouble getting boyfriends."

"One would think, but in reality, she draws the lewd weirdos."

Barbara nodded and put her arm around Marcy. "It's not easy growing up without a father."

"Did you?"

"Did I what?"

"Grow up without a father?"

"No, I had a wonderful daddy." Barbara smiled at the mention of her father.

"How do you know what it's like to grow up without a father?"

"Through my best friend and now cousin by marriage. Her father went to prison when she was a teen. I shared her pain even as you share Christine's," Barbara answered as the two women rose to leave the psychiatric wing.

At that moment, they both heard a gut-wrenching scream coming from Christine's room. Marcy gasped, and a tear flowed down her cheek. Barbara took her hand and squeezed it. Neither spoke, for the terror in the scream took their voices.

With shaky steps, Marcy walked to her car with Mrs. Holloway supporting her.

"What can I do?" Marcy asked her.

"Pray for her," Mrs. Holloway answered. "Get others to pray for her and trust our sovereign God."

Marcy waved goodbye to Mrs. Holloway and got into her car. She sat there for a few minutes and cried. Five minutes later, she wiped the tears from her face, turned off the car, and started back into the pavilion.

"I can't leave her like this; I need to see her," Marcy said to herself before she headed back to Christine's room without following Mrs. Holloway's instruction. Marcy didn't pray first.

8

The Exchange

> This evil people, which refuse to hear my words, which walk in the imagination of their heart, and walk after other gods, to serve them, and to worship them, shall even be as this girdle, which is good for nothing.
>
> ---Jeremiah 13:10

AN EERIE QUIET surrounded the hallway to Christine's room. There were no buzzers, clatter of carts, conversations of staff, and no moaning or screaming. An aide walked out of a room and locked it behind her. Marcy couldn't help herself, she took a peek into the little window of the room. She saw a man sitting on the edge of the bed, eating.

She looked at her watch and smiled; lunchtime. With an explanation for the quiet, she continued down to the end of the hall. The light faded as she approached the room. She hadn't noticed that with Mrs. Holloway. She felt herself thinking about movies she had seen like, *Nightmare on Elm Street*, and *Fire starter*. A silly thought entered her thinking, I wonder if Freddie and Drew Barrymore are here? She chuckled to herself. But it was a nervous twitter.

Once she reached Christine's door, she peered in the window first and gasped. A huge reddish-purple reptilian creature was in the room with her. Marcy slid against the wall and wrapped her arms around herself. It was the same creature from the television. Taking a deep breath, she stood with a deep breath and resolve and turned to the window. She saw only Christine this time.

Her body slumped in a pitiful pose on the edge of the bed, picking at a tray of food. She picked up a morsel with her fingers and put it in her mouth and chewed a few times before she swallowed. She pushed the food around on the plate, picked up the cookies, and put them in her nightstand. She acted as if she were listening to something. Suddenly her head spun toward the door.

Marcy locked eyes with Christine.

She snarled.

Marcy moved away from the door. While her addled mind searched for her next move, the door opened, and a smiling Christine invited her inside. Marcy took a hesitant step inside the room. She heard the door close and latch behind her. She turned toward the door and reached for the knob to open it. It was locked. How did Christine get it open? Before she had time to think about the problem, Christine put her arm around Marcy.

Marcy responded, grateful to see her friend and not a monster. They held each other in a loving embrace. Marcy released the embrace to move away but found she couldn't.

Christine held her tight. Marcy felt something odd poking her in the back. It hurt. She pushed hard away from Christine. She still didn't escape the embrace; Christine held her tight. Marcy pushed harder, but the leverage Christine had over Marcy in height gave her a distinct advantage in this tug of war.

Marcy felt finger nails digging into her back. They felt like claws. Christine didn't like long fingernails. This felt strange. Then the horror of the dragon entered her mind, and she looked at Christine, or rather the image of Christine. The eyes were those of a serpentine dragon and not the eyes of a human.

Marcy screamed at the top of her lungs.

With the screaming came a tighter grip pushing the air from her lungs, silencing her screams. Christine tossed Marcy onto the bed. She held her with one hand. Marcy couldn't break the strong grip Christine exercised over her body. With Christine's other hand, she removed Marcy's clothes.

Panic consumed Marcy. She tried to scream again, but her voice didn't come out. She kicked, and Christine slapped her legs with a burning and painful contact. Marcy saw blood coming from her thigh. She managed to keep one hand free and threw a punch at Christine's face. Her fist slapped across a leathery surface. Then the dragon revealed his face and bared his teeth.

Marcy passed out.

She awoke with the horror of the face still before her. She screeched, and this time she could hear her voice. It reverberated in an empty room. She ran to the door and turned the knob. It didn't open. She banged on the door screaming. Soon, she saw the aide and an orderly standing in front of an open door.

"Oh, thank you, there was—" Before she could finish her statement, she felt the pierce of a needle being inserted into her arm. She glared at the nurse. It was the last thing she saw before the room disappeared in a dark haze, and her legs crumbled beneath her.

Christine walked out of the psych wing. She smiled as she moved past her caretakers. They didn't notice because they were all running toward the screaming woman locked in Christine's room, Marcy Odom.

"Get her still!" shouted the nurse to the attendant.

"No, I'm not supposed to be here," Marcy screamed. At that moment, the nurse found her deltoid muscle and injected a strong tranquilizer. Marcy searched the face of the nurse with fading light in her eyes and muttered, "You don't understand . . . she esca—"

"What'd she say?" the attendant asked.

"Not sure, but sounded like she said escape," the nurse declared. "We better put restraints on her and keep a close watch. We can't let this one escape. She's dangerous."

The attendant nodded and carried out his supervisor's instructions. When he left, he turned the key in both locks on the door.

Marcy stared at the door as everything faded from her view. How did this happen?

Christine walked into the parking lot and looked around then rambled through Marcy's purse for car keys.

After she found them, she scanned the parking lot for the car.

Once in the car, she slipped off the shoes. Marcy stood at five foot two while Christine topped off at five foot six. She couldn't wait to get the tight, pinching shoes off her feet. However, she liked the short skirt.

Once Christine arrived at the apartment she shared with Marcy, she looked around for any signs of the ... what would one call it ... the monster in the television?

The dragon spoke to Christine. his voice felt warm and familiar now. She no longer feared him. Instead, she liked having him close. He whispered about a woman named Patti Pan. He told Christine to find her.

She searched her memory for someone named Patti. Where do I start? The dragon didn't answer her. I wonder if he knows where she is?

She knew this gig only worked as long as the hospital staff believed Marcy to be Christine. How had the dragon accomplished that? It didn't matter. She needed to fulfil a quest, and for that she needed answers or an address. She examined the chair where the monster overtook her and ran her fingers over the blood spots on the arm of the couch—her blood. Then she looked around her bedroom.

Gosh, you're a slob. She noticed the scattered magazines on the unmade bed, with titles like "Cosmopolitan," and "Marie au Claire." She scanned the closet contents. This was her world, where she lived, yet she couldn't remember any of it. Why not?

She cleared the clutter from the one chair in the room and sat. The walls were filled with pink flowered wall paper and matched the chair she occupied. The crumpled spread on the floor revealed a similar pattern as well as pillows, also thrown on the floor.

Well, I guess you like flowers. This décor did not please Christine at all, yet it was her room where she lived. She shook her head and wrinkled her eyebrows and spoke out loud. "If we stay here, this is changing."

With no clues to be found in the messy room, Christine opened the closet. At least these clothes would fit her body. She pulled out some clothes and changed, leaving Marcy's clothes lying on the floor with the others. She then walked across the hall to Marcy's room.

There she found an immaculately clean room decorated in a tasteful blue one-piece coverlet on a French Provincial bed and matching dresser. The nightstand held a radio and a stack of books. On top of the stack lay an open newspaper, turned to an article about an attack in student housing.

She wondered into the living room and stood in the middle. "What do I do now?" She asked the empty room, but a deep gruff voice answered her question.

"Find Patti and find your baby!"

9

The Next Generation

> Thus says the LORD, "Cursed is the man who trusts in mankind and makes flesh his strength, and whose heart turns away from the LORD.
>
> ---Jeremiah 17:5

SHARON SET THE table for their guests while Michael prepared a fire and did the last-minute cleaning. She joined him after she finished.

"How's dinner?" Michael asked when he saw her coming in.

"It's ready. How many do you think are coming?"

"It's hard to say. This is a new group, and frankly, I'm a bit apprehensive."

"How so? Sharon ventured.

"This is the first group I've led with children of those killed and missing in action."

"I never thought about them." Sharon said.

"Me neither. I know how to relate to fellow soldiers, but how do I relate to that kid whose dad died before he was born?" Michael moaned as he set a side table with ice, soft drinks, and tea, and then started a pot of coffee.

The doorbell rang. Sharon answered it and saw a group of young adults—both boys and girls. This was a new wrinkle; many of the children of MIA and KIA soldiers were female. Would Michael be able to relate to a girl whose father died fighting in a war no one understood.

"We'll be having dinner tonight." Sharon pointed the group toward the dining area. As soon as the timid group of youths were seated, Michael gave an introductory speech.

"Tonight, we get to know each other and discover what each one expects from this group."

The shy group of young adults chatted among themselves. Michael watched Sharon take the casserole out of the oven. He approached her. "Let me take that."

"Thank you. Is anyone else coming?"

"Yes, Zay."

"Why is he coming?"

"He wanted to introduce his lab assistant to our group. Is that too many for you?" Michael sat the casserole dish on the table. He gave her a squeeze and a wink.

"No. I'm okay, just thinking about Zay. Working in that lab has changed him."

"We're trying to encourage Zay," Michael explained.

"I know, what would you do if it were you taking care of that horrible creature?'" she asked him.

"Remember, it was me and Daniel who found the vile thing and sent it to the lab."

Sharon shook her head and moaned. "I remember that night, still gives me chills." She shuttered. "I can't think about it. It scared me too bad."

"We thought we killed the thing. We blasted it with a shotgun. Yet it was alive when Dr. Winegren put it in the cage at the lab. Surprised us all."

"Did you recognize the people dragging it?"

"Not at the time, but now I think the woman might have been Patti. The man, I never saw him before or since."

The doorbell rang, interrupting the conversation. It was Zay. Michael leaned over and whispered in Sharon's ear, "Let's not discuss any of this with Zay."

Sharon nodded, and they sat down to dinner. Michael led in prayer.

Sharon looked around the table at each of the guests Their furrowed brows and shallow, polite conversation revealed their deep concern. Sharon rose and brought back dessert and coffee. The table came to life, a little. When all had finished eating, Michael invited them into the living room. Zay sat on the edge of the couch next to Ronnie.

"Do you want me to stay or go?"

"It's okay either way."

Michael handed a paper to each guest.

"I'm glad to see each of you here. I want you to introduce yourself, again. Now that we have eaten together, we know each other a little better, but we need to introduce ourselves with our whole name and the name of our lost parent."

"Seriously?" Ronnie asked looking at Michael.

"Vietnam survivors gather as brothers, we know. You are survivors too, but you don't know. That's why you sit loosely next to each other, each in your own world of pain." Michael explained the reason for the exercise.

The group became slightly more animated with the explanation. One of the young women spoke up, "I don't know any of that information."

"Just tell us what you know," Michael responded. "And if you don't know anything about your lost parent, tell us about yourself."

The first one to speak up knew all the info about his dad, and once he shared it with the rest of the group, he couldn't stop talking. He faced each member directly and spoke about his dad.

Ronnie listened to the veterans tell the agony of leaving a wife and child behind. The children were always pre-born or very young. Ronnie fit into that group. He listened for their unit, hoping he would meet someone who knew his dad.

One girl spoke up and said, "I was twelve when my dad left. I have memories of him, but I miss him still. I loved him, and more than that, I needed him." The girl wiped the tears from her cheeks. Sharon handed her a tissue as her tears flowed freely.

Ronnie put his arm around her, and she smiled a thin-lipped smile at him. He realized in that moment they may not know each other, but they were kinfolks through the tragedy of a war fought before their time.

"I don't know that I ever grieved for my dad because I didn't know him."

Another young man said, "I grieve for the memories and life activities I never had with him."

The pensive group nodded. Ronnie caught a tear trekking down his cheek before anyone noticed. He wiped it away and said, "Me too."

"Can you share some of the trials you've had growing up fatherless?" Michael asked when the conversation came to a lull.

Feeling empowered by the group and his identification with it, Ronnie took up the conversation.

"I'm not sure who I am. My mother talks about him a lot, but she paints a picture of a perfect man. When I was growing up, the people at church would say to me, 'Take care of your mother. You're the man of the house.' I didn't want to be the man of the house. I could never be as good as my dad."

The girl next to him nodded and patted his hand. The next one to speak up was a young man. "My mother remarried before my dad was cold in the grave. It didn't last. She married one more time, and when it failed, she only associated with other women, until finally she brought a woman home to live with us. From that point on, I wasn't abused or put down like my step-dad did, but I was ignored. I've been in a lot of trouble, and I'm hoping this group can give me some understanding of what I'm supposed to do with my life."

Michael nodded but inside he groaned. "This group will introduce you to the One who said He would be a father to the fatherless and a mate to the widows."

The group focused on Michael's face as he said, "Jesus Christ."

10

Psychiatric Medicine

> Righteous are You, O LORD, that I would plead my case with You; Indeed I would discuss matters of justice with You; Why has the way of the wicked prospered? Why are all those who deal in treachery at ease? You have planted them, they have also taken root; they grow, they have even produced fruit You are near to their lips but far from their mind. But You know me, O LORD; You see me; and You examine my heart's attitude toward You.
>
> ---Jeremiah 12 1-3

DR. ABBY GREENSTEIN stood face to face with Christine Sanders. "Look at me," she demanded.

Marcy looked up at the doctor. "Plea loo me," she pleaded, hoping the doctor could tell the difference between herself and Christine.

Dr. Greenstein looked at the chart and realized the woman was excessively drugged. "Do you hear him talking?"

"With?" Marcy asked with thick tongue.

Dr. Greenstein made a note in regard to Christine's loss of weight and muscle tissue. Christine was shrinking all over. She drew herself into the fetal position which made her appear smaller, but it did concern her.

"Are you eating?" she asked.

"Ifff can. . . har swallow." Marcy answered.

Dr. Greenstein cut back on her medications. They would get nowhere like this. Marcy slid to the floor, and catching herself, she ambled to the closet. She opened the door and held on. Dr. Greenstein kept writing. "Loo, loo," she groaned.

Dr. Greenstein walked toward the closet, closed the door, and helped Marcy back to bed. She took her hand and stroked it. "When you are not so drugged, we'll talk, OK?"

Marcy nodded. Hope brought a small smile to her face.

After Dr. Greenstein left, Marcy stumbled toward the closet again. She opened the door and counted the chalk marks. The first ones straight and in line, but starting with the third mark, the lines wiggled and slopped, but still they were there marking the time Marcy had been locked up in Christine's psychiatric room. Twenty-one days! *Doesn't anyone miss me?*

Dr. Troye called the roll for his class. He didn't really pay attention because he needed the time to get his thoughts together. "Marcy Odom." No answer. He marked her absent and noticed she had been gone all month. She must have dropped the class. *That's a shame. She is one of the exceptional minds at the university.* He sighed at the loss of her in class. Not only did he want to discuss her ideas, he wanted to get to know her better. After reading her paper, he saw potential for her as a lab helper. Ronnie did a good job, but Zay needed another set of hands and another point of view. He made a mental note to check with the registrar to see if she was still enrolled. He really needed her help with his current project—a transhuman/chimera/dragon or all of the above.

The dean of students, Dr. Allen, answered her phone, "Hello."

The voice on the other end sounded strained as she introduced herself. "I'm Elena Odom, I'm calling about my daughter Marcy."

"What can I help you with?"

"I haven't heard from her in nearly a month. She doesn't answer her phone. She usually calls me two or three times a week. I'm worried."

"I understand. Give me your number, and I'll check on her and get back to you."

"Thank you so much."

Dr. Allen wrote the number on her desk calendar, but she didn't write a name or message beside it. After hanging up the telephone, she continued her previous task. A shadow crossed the room, and the number and the caller were forgotten.

Marcy felt a tear trickle down her face. In spite of the medications injected into her, she knew she had to get herself out of this jam. She no longer jumped when her 'roommate' revealed himself, even though she felt insane fear when he became visible.

"Having a good time?" he mocked her after Dr. Greenstein left.

Marcy squirmed and tried to escape the reptilian face only inches from her head. She hated snakes, didn't care much for frogs and avoided alligators, yet this face in front of her held more repulsive features than all of those mixed together. If it weren't for the drugs harnessing her central nervous system, she would be screaming and running for the door.

"Only if you die," she mumbled.

"I get stronger. You get weaker. Guess who will die first." He extended his forked tongue and touched her face. She groaned and turned away from him.

"How did you get into our apartment?"

"You opened the door for me."

"No, I didn't," Marcy argued in her mind, but in truth she wasn't sure if that was correct or not. She didn't say anything more. She thought about the last Bible study she remembered. Her focus changed from the red horror to the Scripture. She struggled to remember and, in the process, forgot about the dragon. It pulled away from her and vanished.

Marcy relaxed and continued to trace the memory of Scripture. The study came from Jeremiah 23:25-26. "I have heard what the prophets have said who prophesy falsely in My name, saying 'I had a dream.' How long? Is there anything in the hearts of the prophets who prophesy falsehood, even these prophets of the deception of their own heart."

Marcy lay back on her bed and took deep breaths. The anxiety of facing the creature passed as her breathing settled into a regular rhythm. She still wouldn't be able to speak clearly, but at least her thought processes functioned with clarity.

She pondered the Scripture and smiled as she remembered her mother telling her that the Holy Spirit would give one the right words at the right time. Maybe this was a case of the right words. If so, then what did they mean, and how were they going to help get her out of this dreadful predicament?

Marcy reasoned within her mind, who are the prophets? Her understanding of a prophet included an ancient man dressed in a white robe, standing in the middle of a town, and shouting at the people passing by. Her current image didn't stray too far from that image. If this Scripture had any meaning to her situation, there had to be a person who was a prophet.

Who could it be? She moaned out loud. "I don't know." In a bolt from the blue, she shouted, "Preachers?" With the word she sat up. A thought was coming to her, but it was struggling. It was a battle. "Jesus, help me," she shouted.

An orderly rushed into her room. She gazed at him, clear-eyed, and with clear voice asked him, "What is a prophet?"

The orderly stepped back, evidently surprised by the clarity of her voice.

"I guess one who tells the future."

Marcy shook her head. "I don't think that's completely correct."

"Okay." The stunned orderly took Marcy by the elbow and led her to the chair. "What do you think?"

"I think it's a person who speaks truth about what the future can be." Her speech was becoming slurred again.

"Yes," the orderly agreed.

Marcy knew he was humoring her because she had repeated his answer, but she didn't say it all. She muttered, "A prophet speaks the truth from God and reveals God's plan. . . unless he speaks from his own thinking, then—" Marcy stopped, sat down, and eyed the orderly, "I'm hungry," she said.

He smiled and answered, "That's the best thing I've heard from you in three weeks."

He left and locked the door behind him.

Marcy really was hungry. She leaned her head back against the chair and sighed. She whispered a prayer, "Show me how to get out of this joint. The people here make empty promises. They truly think I'm Christine."

The orderly returned with a dish of ice cream and a side of chocolate syrup. He sat it on the bedside tray and pulled it in front of Marcy. He handed her a wooden spoon and said, "Enjoy."

Marcy gulped the ice cream, it tasted wonderful. She hadn't eaten in three weeks because of the drugs. Her nourishment came from a tube they put in her nose.

The charge nurse came into her room a few minutes later and picked up the empty ice cream dish. "If you eat like this for the next few days, we can disconnect you from that thing." The nurse pointed to the tube taped to her nose.

At that promise, a great peace overcame her which begged for physical rest. She lay down on her bed and fell into a deep sleep. Soon she was snoring.

The sound of the lock didn't awaken the patient. The nurse stepped in with a syringe filled with Nembutal, a strong tranquilizer. She heard Christine snore and smiled, leaving the room with the syringe still filled.

Marcy's body rested in her normal biological rhythm without the drug interference. During the rest, she was given a dream or a vision. She didn't know which, even though she knew it was a message to her in answer to prayer.

He stepped into Marcy's line of vision. Marcy smiled. She knew him. He reached out and took her hand. "My child you are not forgotten; you are assigned here. All you must do is study and rest. Soon your task will be evident, and you must be armed and ready." He kissed the back of her hand and backed away into the light from which he had come.

Marcy slept soundly the rest of the night. She awoke knowing she had regained her non-drugged alertness. The memory of the dream gave her a peace which surrounded her with warmth in the middle of a storm. An umbrella of light rested above her head.

11

Waiting

> If you have run with footmen and they have tired you out, then how can you compete with horses? If you fall down in a land of peace, how will you do in the thicket of the Jordan? For even your brothers and the household of your father have dealt treacherously wi9th you, they have cried aloud after you. Do not believe them, although they may say nice things to you.
>
> ---Jeremiah 12:5-6

MARCY DIDN'T JUMP when she heard the lock turn. The sound no longer struck terror in her soul since the dreaded hypodermic needle no longer followed the sound. A medication nurse entered with a little white paper cup filled with colorful baby button pills.

Marcy prepared for the charade of swallowing the disgusting mixture of poisons. She put her tongue in the small space between her gums and cheek, where she would hide the toxins until the nurse left. She sighed, wanting it to stop but knowing any objection to the pills might bring back the needle. Any escape would be fruitless if her mind surrendered to the zombie-like status the staff desired.

She had to act as though she were Christine in order for the mixture of mind-numbing and soul-killing treatments to end. No escape would be possible until she got her head back on. The door opened, and Marcy squealed. She couldn't help herself. She saw the strained face of her mother.

"Momma!" She cried. Then she saw the big burly orderly behind her mother.

"I'm sorry, I thought you were my mother." She added. She winked at her mother, whose jaw dropped. She had to think fast, a difficult thing coming off that stew of drugs she had been given over the past month. "You're Marcy's mom, aren't you?"

She nodded. "Yes, Christine I am." She winked back at Marcy who breathed a sigh of relief at the secret code.

The orderly stepped in behind Mrs. Odom. "You have half an hour for visitation. If you feel threatened in any way just press this button. I'll be here."

Mrs. Odom nodded at the instructions he gave. As soon as the door closed she turned toward Marcy. A huge grin expressed her relief and happiness. She spread her arms and took Marcy into them.

Marcy whispered in her ear. "Don't speak, they listen to everything."

Mrs. Odom sighed, backed away, and took off her coat. "How are you feeling, Christine?" She opened her purse and took out a pencil and paper. "Do you mind if I set on the edge of the bed with you?"

"No, not at all. How's Marcy?"

"I haven't seen her in a while or heard from her, until today. She's not handling your situation well, but I think she's okay," Mrs. Odom related to her daughter that she had been looking for her. She wrote down on the pad: *What's going on?*

Marcy responded properly to the conversation but wrote another note. *She escaped and left me here. No one looks at my face. They think I'm Christine. How did you find me?*

"I pray for you every day."

Marcy nodded and smiled at her mother's comment.

Mrs. Odom put her arm around her, pulled her close to her side, and whispered in her ear, "I look for Christine, and I find you. Do you know where Christine is?" Marcy shrugged her shoulders.

The two kept the facade up for the next half hour, and Mrs. Odom gathered as much information from Marcy as possible.

After she left the room, the orderly shut the door behind her. Mrs. Odom turned to him and said, "What's wrong with her?"

He shrugged, "It's my job to keep them clean, fed, and medicated. Beyond that, you have to talk to her doctor." He didn't wait for a response but left Mrs. Odom standing in the hallway, confused and scared. *How will I get her out of here?*

Ronnie scanned the hospital room. "How did I get here?" he asked and was surprised when a voice answered him. A figure stepped out from behind a door. Ronnie pushed the sheet away from him and slung his feet over the edge of the bed, only to be met with a crippling pain.

"Not so fast, young man." A stern voice from the nurse reverberated through him.

"How did I get here?"

"You had an appendicitis attack." She calmly said as she looked at the bottles hanging next to his bed that were connected to his arms.

"Oh." He nodded and watched her. "How long will I be here?"

"That's up to your doctor, but he won't let you go until you're stable."

"Who is my doc?"

"Holloway."

Ronnie laid back on his bed. The nurse finished her routine then asked him a few questions about his pain and bodily functions. She patted him on the arm and smiled.

"You have a visitor; do you feel up to it?" she asked him.

"Yeah, who is it?"

Before the nurse could answer, Zay walked into the room. "Your boss and the one who rescued you."

Ronnie smiled at him. "Thanks."

"Anytime. I can't let my best lab assistant leave me."

"Any progress on the DNA strand?" He asked.

"It's time to start mapping the sequence. That's why I need you to get better quick. This is new territory we're entering."

"What happened that I ended up here?"

"You fainted, Phobus roared, and I panicked. I did manage to call for an ambulance to get you."

Ronnie laughed and then grabbed his side. "Oh, that hurts." He moaned with a slight chuckle.

Zay shook his head and raised his hands in the air shaking them. "What are you laughing at?"

"Imagining you panicked. You're the calmest person I have met."

"Not really, it's more like I'm oblivious."

"I can see that, especially when it comes to girls."

"What do you mean?" Zay wrinkled his brow.

"Girls all over campus try to get your attention, and you don't see any of them." Ronnie mocked his friend.

Dr. Troye blushed. "I don't have time for relationships," he said in his defense.

Ronnie smiled. "We all need someone at one time or another."

"It would be nice to have someone close enough to discuss my concern. Trouble is what girl wants to listen to my woes and discoveries?" Zay smiled at him.

Ronnie turned his gaze away from Zay's face and asked, "Does it have to be a girl?"

12

A Mystery

> Why then has this people, Jerusalem, turned away in continual apostasy? They hold fast to deceit, they refuse to return. . . everyone turned to his course, like a horse charging into battle.
>
> ---Jeremiah 8: 5-6

ZAY DIDN'T ARGUE with Ronnie when he insisted he could recuperate from surgery and still help on the project because he needed him, even if the only skill he had to offer was note taking. With Ronnie disabled, this meant the care and feeding of the monster fell on his shoulders again. It took a lot of time, energy, and courage.

That could be a good thing because Ronnie's question about his choice of a mate followed him like a cloud on a rainy day. A cloud which hung over his head endlessly. The question continued at a slow pace. It needled Zay with its implications. Until this question arose, Zay assumed he would marry a woman someday when he found the right one. But the question brought up another question; why wasn't he looking for a wife? Many of his college classmates had a wife and one or two children.

Every slide Zay observed spoke a new concept to him. Unfortunately, it wasn't about DNA but about his own thinking. He was twenty-six years old, never had a date, and didn't think about girls. Of course, as a scientist, he had to add the other factors; the last eight years were filled with classes, studies, labs, and applications for postdoctoral positions. He had no social life because he couldn't work it into his schedule. With that thought, he was able to turn his attention back to his work. He did have a deadline to meet. Which meant he still didn't have time for dating.

Zay searched for the sonic sound wave included in his materials. Maybe it would give him some intact proteins which could be used for lysis of the cell membrane. After placing the tissue sample in the sonication machine, he pulled other samples from the freezer. He used every method of separation he knew and hoped to get a good, solid cell sample so he could reach undamaged DNA in the cell. Once he isolated a cell, he would add enzymes to one sample and detergents to another, hoping to open the cell membrane. "Why is this so hard?" He sighed. "Because you don't know what you're doing," he answered himself.

Ronnie quit writing and sat up. "Dr. Troye, that's the very definition of a new science; we don't know what we are doing, and that's why we do an experiment, record the results, and start over with a new one. We'll get to something that will consistently isolate the cells intact and allow us to look inside them."

"Consistency. That's the problem." Zay said, not in response to Ronnie but rather in response to his thought processes. The separation of the white from the red blood cells came easily, but from that point on, Zay was trending for new discoveries using old scientific theories to prove new ones.

The Mendal Inheritance Theory started in 1863, since then the search for DNA and the method of inheritance plagued origin scientists for decades. He was the new scientist who needed to learn the old history of the discipline of origin and inheritance in order to continue forward. He chuckled at one of his dad's favorite sayings, "Son, don't pull the fence down until you know why it was put up in the first place. The mean bull may still be in there."

His attempts to break away from his family's religion proved to be as hard as opening this cell membrane to gain access to the contents of the cell. The old religion of simple-minded people no longer answered questions. It took the sophistication of science to know the origin of man, not an ancient fairytale. Still, that old fairy tale and all its sayings hung on like a desperate man clinging to a cliff.

So it was with a family membrane also. Zay depended on his brother-in-law; he loved his sister; he needed his brother's advice; he couldn't imagine not having his mother's love; but he wanted to be cut free from his dad's constant preaching and his Bible.

Ronnie's question about girls popped up again like a single kernel of popcorn in a hot skillet but with added information as the other kernels slowly popped around the first. The toughness of the cell membrane must be for the protection of the genes. The cell either held delicate tissue or fantastic information, or both. The family cell membrane protected its members and their secrets.

13

Manipulation

> We waited for peace, but no good came:
> For a time of healing, but behold, terror!
> ---Jeremiah 8:16

DRESSED IN BLUE jeans and a chambray shirt, Zay jumped into the pickup with his dad. The gentle wind blew through his hair, and a big smile covered his face when he said, "I forgot how much I enjoy coming to the farm."

"Maybe you should consider moving back here. You know your sister and your cousin are both returning in a few months."

Zay nodded and turned his head away from his dad. His stomach churned both directions. "You know I have another eighteen months on my fellowship."

"That's nothing in the whole scheme of life."

"I know dad, it's just that—"

"You don't want to come back?"

"I can't come back until the puzzle of the monster in my lab dungeon is solved."

"Don't look for that to happen." Buster pointed to the field. "Remember that?"

Zay nodded. The two men sat there staring at the soil as if it were going to speak.

"Does he still show up?" Zay asked as he kicked the dirt.

"Not as often. But the ugly thing shows its vile face in a heartbeat when I take my eyes off God's image and start putting my focus on the things in this world, like corrupt politics that injure people." Buster sighed.

"Why?"

"To test me." Buster took a deep breath. I fail the Lord a lot these days."

"I don't believe that." Zay sneered.

"It's hard, son," Buster touched Zay on the shoulder. "It's hard when your kids are hurtin."

Zay turned his head away from his dad. "How'd you know?"

"About age sixteen, you asked me why all the other boys talked about the girls."

"I remember that." Zay smiled. "I also remember your answer."

"What was it?" Buster prodded.

"You said, in time I would understand." Zay threw a dirt clod across the field.

"Do you?"

"Not really, is something wrong with me?"

"Son, there's something wrong with all of us. Right now, you're focused on your scientific studies."

"Do you think I could be gay?" Zay stared down at the ground, and he hoped his dad wouldn't turn him off. As much as he wanted to be free of his dad's religion, he couldn't stand the thought of not having his dad's relationship.

"Son, if you're gay, then you're not a happy man. I don't know of any homosexual that is happy."

The answer took Zay by surprise. "What do you mean?"

"There's not much goodness in homosexuality. In fact, I can't think of any."

"Dad, would you still love me if I am a homosexual?" Zay whispered.

Buster grabbed his son by the arm and pulled him close to his side, "Son, there ain't nothin' in this world that could stop me from loving you."

"Dad, do you know homosexual people?" Zay asked when he realized his father's statement about not knowing any happy homosexuals.

"Yes, son, I do. And don't ask me who. If they want people to know, they'll tell. It's not my place to share a friend's secrets."

"Friends?" Zay gazed at his dad with his mouth open.

"Yes, son, I have friends of all kinds."

"But I thought the Bible taught that Christians were supposed to hate gays . . . I mean homosexuals."

Buster laughed. "That's a common misconception. Truth is, Christians don't care whether a person is homo or not."

"Then why—"

"Why do Christians speak out against it?"

"Yeah." Zay slowed down his long stride to keep in step with his dad.

"Because God told us to warn people about the dangerous things in this world which hurt them and separate them from God's love. That's all we are supposed to do. It's not a Christian's job to rescue a person in danger, it is our job to point them to the One who can rescue them."

"Does God love homosexuals?"

"The same as He loves me because the things I've done are just as bad."

Zay cleared his throat. "I can't imagine you doing anything to make God mad at you?"

"Son, God doesn't get mad at us; He becomes sad when we turn away from him. He tries to bring us to faith and trust in Him then He can keep us from the dragons in this world."

Zay understood the statement. He often thought Phobus could escape the dungeon and destroy them all. "I understand that."

"How are things at the lab?" his dad asked.

"My lab assistant is a third-year microbiology student. He and Dr. Winegren can handle the lab right now. Their number one job is feeding the beast."

Buster nodded. "The beast will never be satisfied; its appetite is insatiable. A dragon will devour until it's destroyed everything, even itself."

Zay knew he had to return as soon as possible, but at that moment, he didn't ever want to return. He wanted to stay there. He wanted to have more discussion with his dad. He wanted to work the soil and study it for better crop production. In spite of their differences regarding religion, he liked working beside his dad.

They moved long tubes of aluminum irrigation pipes from one field to the other by sliding them into the hooks on the side of the pickup and moving them to the next field then opening the water valve for the water to flow through them.

Zay's job was to open the smaller valves at the beginning of each row of vegetation and let the water flow gently down the rows to nourish the plants. Zay found the irrigation process relaxing, simple, and amazing. It reminded him of the cell production he observed under the microscope.

"Dad, why did you become a farmer?" Zay asked as they walked over the turn row to the next field. The sun shone brightly, and the clouds floating lazily in the light-blue sky cast intermittent shadows on the fields.

"It's who I am; it's what I know." Buster answered his adult son.

"Did you ever want to be something else?"

Buster cocked his head to one side and bit his lips in a pose of deep thought. "Nope, just a farmer."

Zay smiled at him and shook his head. "What if you had the opportunity to go to college?"

"I would've gone, so I could be a better farmer."

Zay laughed at his response.

"You see, son, I like to be outside. I like to plant the seed and watch it sprout and grow. But mostly, I like being able to talk to God all day long. He teaches me a new lesson every day, and most of them are here in the fields, not in a fancy church." Buster smiled at Zay and sat the last water tube on the ditch mound.

"What's on your mind, son?" Buster ventured to break into Zay's thoughts.

"I can't hide anything from you." Zay chuckled.

The two men climbed into the pickup and poured themselves a drink of water.

"Dad, I've got a deformed dragon in my lab, and I don't know what to do with him."

"What do you mean deformed?"

"He's half dragon and half goat and has crooked, twisted horns. The shaggy torso of a goat holds the neck and head of a dragon. His eyes are off-kilter, they're still yellow, but one's clear and looks like a human eye, the other one is . . . well the vertical iris is at an angle."

"Sounds ugly." Buster said in a flat voice.

"He is."

"Sounds like a distorted image of a cursed dragon."

"Exactly, not that I want a dragon in my lab, but . . . I almost feel sorry for him, and I think there may be some human in him."

"You mean, he ate a human?" Buster turned and gazed at Zay.

Zay laughed. "I don't think so. Although. he could. I think he was created from a human."

Buster shuddered. "That's an insult to God's image."

The necessity of returning to the university lab brought Zay back in three days instead of the five days he planned. He rubbed the back of his neck. The muscles screamed for relief from his bent position. He stood up and stretched. Maybe he should seriously consider moving back to the farm.

Ronnie hadn't arrived yet. Zay's request for another assistant, specifically naming Marcy Odom fell on deaf ears. He hadn't heard from the Dean of Students office in two weeks, an unusual length of time since a waiting list for jobs usually produced someone within days and sometimes hours.

Ronnie was a great assistant, but his body needed time to heal. He helped as much as he could, but feeding the monster amounted to a phone call to find a meal. The lab wasn't the priority in his life.

Marcy might be the same, if she was still a student.

He would take the two part-time since they would provide Zay with two of the most brilliant minds in the microbiology department.

Besides, Marcy was about to graduate, and as soon as she did, Zay planned on asking her out. After his conversation with his dad and watching his mom and dad together, he realized he truly wanted a mate, and he wanted that mate to be female. He also discovered part of his delay came because there were few girls who shared his passion for the scientific. Turned out Marcy was more than a brilliant mind. His happy thoughts led him to chuckle as he pictured her short frame against his lanky six feet. He decided the reason she was still unattached was because the boys looked over her. In Zay's world, she stood out as the only girl on campus that garnered his attention. Most people assumed Zay was a little bit on the sweet side of a relationship with Ronnie, based on their long hours hunched over microscopes.

He didn't care about the reputation he earned from working with Ronnie. He respected Ronnie and his work, and he needed Ronnie's mind now more than ever. Besides, he was the only student who had seen the beast downstairs. Zay sighed as he thought about the beast and their work. Ronnie needed some guidance—more than he could give him. Zay didn't really care about Ronnie's personal decisions as long as it didn't affect his work. A smile appeared on Zay's face as he recalled his dad's comment and the truth of it. Most people whether they were Christian or not didn't care about another person's sex life.

Zay knew the results of their research would most likely be horrific or unbelievable. Either way, he wanted to keep the circle of those who knew to a minimum.

A strange sound much like water falling into hot grease grabbed Zay's attention. The pop and sizzle startled and confused him. He didn't see anything, but the sound continued.

"Looking for me?" The words sizzled but were clear.

Zay stood and backed toward the door. Sweat formed on his upper lip. He opened the door and scooted out. At that moment, he realized he hadn't fed Phobus yet. The popping sound came again.

"Keep looking; you'll find me."

Zay stood in the stairwell landing, his feet frozen in place and his heart threatening to jump out of his chest.

"Dr. Troye?" Ronnie said as he took the last stair on the landing near where Zay stood.

"It's talking to me," Zay said, his voice quiet.

"Who?"

"That thing."

"Phobus?"

"No, something else."

Ronnie shuddered and noticed the quiver in Zay's hands as he held his coat up to his face like a napkin. Ronnie took Zay's elbow and led him back to the lab door. He opened it and took Zay to the couch.

Ronnie's inquisitive mind provided Zay the ability to discuss out loud and find solutions, almost as if they were one mind. In some ways they were since they were both focused on finding the origin of their resident monster. Other than that, they actually knew very little of each other's lives and thoughts.

For Zay, the creature was his life. It felt as if Ronnie suffered from the same malady but in a different way. Zay noticed how Ronnie often compared himself to the little monster. Ronnie would say they both have screwed up chromosomes. Then he would look at Zay as though he wanted to say something but couldn't.

Ronnie hovered over Zay. "I've kind of known there's something else in the lab with us, but you said you heard it?" He looked closely at Zay. "Your eyes are dilated. What do you see?"

"Glimpses of a reddish and purple sunset. It's a disturbingly beautiful scene. It's . . . a beautiful dragon, but its beauty is disgusting. I want to admire it, but at the same time I'm repulsed by it."

Ronnie sat next to Zay and followed his gaze. He gasped. "I see it."

Zay shook his head, the two stared up at the ceiling.

A roar came from the basement and the vision disappeared.

"I haven't fed him today."

"Me neither."

Both of them moved with lighting speed since they entered into crisis mode knowing it would bang on the walls and roar, arousing the entire campus with curiosity.

The creature made quick work of any meal. Large meat-eating creatures often grow two or more rows of teeth. Sharks, for instance have rows of teeth. Phobus's teeth didn't fit that pattern. The second row of teeth bothered Zay. They appeared to be disconnected from the body, as if they were an image rather than reality. They were small like deciduous or baby teeth in a human. What possible use would a dragon or chimera have of human baby teeth?

Zay couldn't even articulate the question. He grabbed the school van keys. "I forgot I went shopping this morning." He said to Ronnie.

Ronnie went downstairs to open the feeding chute. Zay pulled the van around to the secluded backside of the science building where he would drop his load—five large dogs, several cats, a raccoon, and some turtles. A good size snack for the beast. They would have to go 'shopping' again tonight. The next bull wouldn't arrive for another week. Keeping the monster fed tried their emotions with constant death. Zay often wondered why they didn't let it starve to death.

Sharon sighed as she turned the light off in the twins' bedroom. It had been a busy day, and she had forgotten to eat dinner. She went to the kitchen and poured herself a glass of milk, grateful her work day was completed.

Michael had taken Zay and Rance camping. He said Zay needed to get away from the lab, and he and Rance needed to make plans. The two of them were seriously thinking of moving back to Church Creek Falls. With the next generation reaching adulthood, the community slowly increased in population. Michael and Rance decided they needed to help rebuild their hometown. Their plans included a bank and a law office. No matter how small an area, the reality of taxes, disputes, and money matters loomed over the community.

Sharon liked the idea of moving to Church Creek Falls. Even though it wasn't her hometown, it was a place of family. Much wreckage still littered the area, even after fifteen years, but the hope of a new beginning permeated the small, growing population.

Zay mentioned moving back and opening his own agricultural biology lab. It sounded like a great family reunion. If only the chimera would disappear, it could become reality and not wishful thinking. Michael and Daniel would never leave Zay alone with that beast.

Michael settled in a lawn chair and held his stick with a marshmallow on the end over the campfire. The glow of the fire lit up the faces of his two cousins and cousin-in-law, Daniel, who decided to join them at the last minute.

Daniel laid his perfectly cooked marshmallow on a graham cracker covered with a piece of chocolate. He smashed another cracker on top and crammed the sweet treat into his mouth. Rance pulled his stick holding a cooked marshmallow out of the fire and ate it. He put another marshmallow on the stick. Zay let his marshmallow fall into the fire. He held his empty stick over the fire letting it slowly burn.

"Better keep your mind on it this time if you want to enjoy the taste," Rance teased as he put another marshmallow on Zay's stick. Zay fist-bumped him on the shoulder.

"I'm glad you were able to join us, Daniel," Michael said.

"Barbara pushed me, said I'm a dull person."

The group laughed.

"She's right," Rance confirmed.

"Zay, how's the research going?" Daniel asked him.

"I'm looking at the DNA of a monster. What do you think?"

"Creepy from the monster, exciting on the exploration side."

"The monster has a dragon head and a goat body. I've found both serpent and mammal DNA. I also found . . ." Zay paused.

"Found what?" Daniel encouraged.

"I've had some trouble getting the cell membrane open, so I pulled from the mitochondria."

"Did you find anything?" Daniel asked, reaching for another marshmallow.

"I did, but I don't know if it's good info or not."

"What's wrong with it?"

"It's human."

Daniel sat back, and his jaw dropped. "That means a human mother?" Daniel shuddered.

"Yeah, the DNA in the mitochondria is from the maternal side only."

"Does anyone else know?"

"Not yet."

"What are you going to do with the information?"

"I don't know; it raises more questions than anything." Zay's voice raised in pitch with the comment.

Michael reached over and put his arm around Zay's shoulder and patted him. "There's more to this than you can handle. You need help."

"I know, but where am I to get this kind of help? I've applied for a lab assistant. I even asked for Marcy Odom. She saw the thing attack Christine, so she knows."

"We understand," Daniel said. "When we found the thing, we felt the same way, there was more to it than we could explain."

"Where did it come from?" Zay asked Daniel and Michael.

"We're not sure. There were two creatures dragging it. One was Patti Pan and the other . . . we thought was the demon that was terrorizing Barbara."

"What were they doing?"

"I heard Patti ask him what they did with their mistakes. The man said, they usually burned them.

"So, whatever they were doing, this one was a mistake?" Zay asked.

"The real question is what happened to the ones that were not mistakes," Daniel mused. Rance nodded and added an addendum to the questions, "And what are the non-mistakes?"

"Oh!" Zay put his hands on his head as if he had a sudden ice cream headache. "Are you trying to say, there's something out there like this that isn't a mistake."

14

Confusion

> Let everyone be on guard against his
> neighbor; and do not trust any brother;
> because every brother deals craftily, and
> every neighbor goes about as a slanderer.
> Everyone deceives his neighbor and does
> not speak the truth, they have taught their
> tongue to speak lies; they weary themselves
> committing iniquity. Your dwelling is in the
> midst of deceit; through deceit they refuse to
> know Me," declares the Lord.
>
> ---Jeremiah 9: 4-6

CHRISTINE WOKE UP with a fuzzy head and blurry vision. Looking around, she recognized her apartment but didn't know how she'd arrived here. Only chaos filled her head. The blurred memory of escaping slowly gained clarity. What was the reson she needed to escape?

Her vision filled with hues of red and purple. Cold wrapped her body like a blanket. Closing her eyes, she hoped it would go away. Instead, her heart sped up, softly at first, then growing into a loud boom in her chest as she gasped for air. With a shiver she saw her breath. The event seemed distant and unreal, but the sensations pricked her skin in the present. She had to make it stop, but how? It ran from her like a fading dream with nothing left to prove her memory of the horror existed in reality at all.

Alone with only fear and confusion, she walked over to the window and looked out. All appeared well. Looking down at her tight clothing, she opened the closet door and pulled out a grey three-piece pantsuit with a pink silk blouse.

At least I have good taste in clothes. A loud rumble came from her stomach, and the noise drove her into the kitchen to find something to feed herself as well as the emptiness in her spirit. As she ate, a vague memory crept into her mind.

It was almost a romantic memory. A handsome man held out his hand. She placed her hand in his and smiled at him. His green eyes sparkled like a cartoon, and the glow hid his face from her. She felt his touch when he pulled her close to him. The touch quickly turned into a tight grip. Pushing against him proved fruitless. A squeal came from her lips, he let go and faded away.

She sighed and put the cracker box away in the cabinet with the glass front. Pushing the cabinet closed she saw a reflection in the glass. It was a horrid face. Worse, it was familiar. She shuttered and let out a little yelp.

She needed to talk to someone fast. "Marcy!" she called out. No answer.

Like a concrete wall, Marcy kept Christine stable. It wasn't like Marcy to ignore her. She decided to call someone else, but who? She'd been raised as a ward of the state and had no family. A nauseating sickness filled her stomach. Running for the toilet, she barely made it before she filled the bowl with vomit. She rested on her hands and knees in front of the toilet for a while, having never felt anything like this before. She rose from the floor and cleaned herself up along with the bathroom. Moving to the living room, she plopped herself in a chair and cried.

Zay unlocked the door to his office cautiously. He entered and saw Ronnie sitting at the desk on the opposite wall.

"How long have you been here?"

"About an hour. We got through early. Since I can't quit thinking of our problem, I decided to come here and do some work. I've been reading your notes on your experiments. This is weird stuff, you know?"

"I know, the God part comes from my dad and the rest from my research and my experiments. Both are weird," Zay said.

"Is he a scientist too?"

"No, actually he's a farmer. I spent last weekend with him."

"Must be one smart cookie."

"He is, but not with education. He only completed third grade. Life gave him a doctor's degree in common sense." Zay shrugged. "And his one goal in life is to teach me." Zay moaned thinking of his dad's free advice given often.

"How do you think he came to this conclusion?"

"Which one?" Zay asked.

"The demon spirit in man?"

"Probably the Bible and the book of Enoch."

"I don't like the Bible. I only read it to be prepared for assaults by Christians." Ronnie realized what he had said.

"Why?" Zay asked.

"If a Christian attacks me, then I can show them how stupid their Bible really is." Ronnie huffed.

Zay chuckled remembering his conversation with his dad about homosexuality. "Ronnie, how many Christians have attacked you?"

Ronnie cocked his head and put his index finger under his chin. "I can't think of any."

"Probably because they really don't care if you're gay or not. And that's a poor excuse to read the Bible."

"Then why do Christians get so huffy about it?"

"Again, how many Christians have you seen get huffy?"

Ronnie raised his hands in the air and shrugged. "Why do you read the Bible?"

"I don't," Zay said continuing his work.

Ronnie squeezed his lips together and made a small hum sound. "Are you a Christian?"

Zay stopped working, turned toward Ronnie and gave the most honest answer he knew, "I don't know."

Ronnie picked up the notes and read some more. He spotted something and said with his back to Zay, "I don't remember reading this."

"What?" Zay asked.

Ronnie put the notes in front of Zay.

"Oh," Zay said. "People don't talk about it because it's so weird. Mostly, church people work at denying it. It's found in Genesis six where the sons of God mated with the daughters of men and had children with them."

"There's a whole lot of 'wow' in that statement." Ronnie said.

"The Bible even says in Jude six and seven that they're angels who did not keep their own domain but abandoned their proper abode. They're kept in eternal bonds under darkness for the judgment of the great day. Just as Sodom and Gomorrah and the cities around them indulged in gross immorality and went after strange flesh, they are exhibited as an example in undergoing the punishment of eternal fire."

"For someone who doesn't read the Bible, you sure know a lot of Scripture," Ronnie mused.

Zay chuckled. "My dad and I discussed those verses last weekend. I guess I was prepared, like you said."

Ronnie made a small chuckle, but he walked over to Zay and looked him square in the eyes. "Is that saying I'm going to hell?"

Zay didn't flicker at the seriousness of Ronnie's question. "Read the next verse."

Ronnie retrieved the Bible Zay kept in the storage closet and opened it to Jude eight, "Yet in the same way these men, also by dreaming, defile the flesh, and reject authority, and revile angelic majesties."

"I'm not getting this."

Zay saw the perspiration on Ronnie's lip. He stopped his experiment, took him by the arm, and led him to the couch. They sat down. "Ronnie, it's saying that homosexuality destroys your body because it is the worship of a deceptive and evil god."

"What's the god?" Ronnie asked.

"The homosexual agenda," Zay answered. "Besides, I thought you didn't believe the Bible."

"I didn't say that. I said I don't like it, and this is one of the reasons why." Ronnie wiped the sweat from his forehead. "It scares me."

Zay felt great compassion for his assistant. He took the Bible from him and said, "You have to read the whole thing to have understanding, at least that's what my dad says. So, let's read the whole thing."

The two read quietly together when Ronnie pointed to verse fifteen, ". . . to execute judgment upon all, and to convict all the ungodly of all their ungodly deeds which they have done in an ungodly way, and of all the harsh things which ungodly sinners have spoken against Him."

"It says all ungodly deeds," Zay explained. "Maybe you need to discover what ungodly deeds means."

Ronnie nodded. "How?"

"A good Bible dictionary," Zay answered. "Now, come on, we have work to do, and we'll be judged in dollars and cents."

Ronnie let out a deep sigh and went back to work. A few minutes later, he asked Zay another question, "How do you know that happened?"

"There are other theories about that verse, such as all the daughters of Cain were evil, and all the sons of Seth were good. But then what do you do with the verse in Jude? Dad tells me there's another Scripture proof in second Peter chapter two."

"Does any of this have to do with our creature?" Ronnie added. "Our creature has definitely left his proper domain."

Zay picked up a beaker from a heater without a glove. It contained the cell clump from the dragon. Without warning, he slammed the glass beaker into the tiled floor, shattering it over the lab with a loud crash.

Ronnie jumped and turned toward him. "Hey man, what happened?"

"I'm sorry, I just did a stupid thing, picking up a hot beaker with no protection."

"We weren't paying attention to the experiment and went off in fantasy land with the Bible." Ronnie tightened his lips.

"You're right; we need to focus." Zay put his hands under the cold water. It would sting for a few minutes, but he wasn't burned bad. He pointed to the stack of papers on his desk with his good hand. "That paper written by Marcy says the exact same thing. We can't ignore it. Our dragon is a distortion of God's creatures."

Ronnie tossed the dust pan full of broken glass into the trash can, pulled another beaker from the cabinet, and handed it to Zay. The world returned to a normal rotation in the lab.

"Okay. Back to the topic. What does this Bible stuff have to do with our creature in the basement?"

"Have you ever heard of a satyr?"

"No."

"The literal definition is 'hairy goat.' But it's a creature that is part goat and part human."

"Is that possible?" Ronnie wrinkled up his nose.

"It's been done with cattle and human DNA to develop human antibodies. It's also been done with goats and spiders."

"Ugg." Ronnie shuddered. "Why?"

"Spider webs are strong because of the filament the spiders use to make their webs. But it's not practical to milk spiders to get that thread for products. So, by mixing the goat DNA with spider DNA, the goat's milk produces spider threads. It can be strained from the milk and used to make bullet-proof vests."

"Wow! So, it's not necessarily bad?" Ronnie exclaimed, leaning over the lab desk.

"The heterokaryons or a multinucleate cell which contains nuclei with different genetic material is usually formed in an experimental fusion of two genetically different cells, or cells with more than one nuclei form the hybrid cells." Zay started to explain the process of mixing DNA.

"To what end?" Ronnie sat down and rested his chin in his palm. He had a pen in the other hand to make notes.

"It helps to map out the human cells. The parental nuclei remained distinct and retains a full set of chromosomes."

"Still not getting the connection between the Bible stuff and that creature's DNA study."

"In the Bible, it says angels mated with human women and had children with them. Ever hear of the book of Enoch?"

"No, but you've got my attention."

"It was among the scrolls found at the Dead Sea, it's also mentioned by Jude and Peter in the Bible."

"What does he have to do with the blending of mice and human cells?

"Enoch tells in 7:6 how the children from this union of humans and angels created huge creatures, up to 450 feet tall."

"You gotta be kidding!" Ronnie exclaimed.

"It says 300 cubits and a cubit is 18 inches. So, do the math."

Ronnie scribbled on a piece of paper. His mouth dropped open and his eyes were wide. "That's right, it took a gang of farmers to feed them. I wonder how many of them there were?"

"It doesn't tell that, but it does say they ate all the food, and when the people didn't have enough to feed them they ate the people."

"This sounds like a fiction novel." Ronnie snorted.

"I know."

"What about the animals? Did they eat them too?"

"Probably, but they also used them for sex to create larger animals for food."

"Maybe dinosaurs."

"Or dragons?"

"And now we have our hybrid cells?" Ronnie surmised as he stared past Zay.

"Hey what's going on in that brilliant mind of yours?" Zay asked him.

"Follow me. A giant that is half human and half spirit mates with an animal, say an elephant. What is the product?"

"An elephant with human ears and a demon heart?" Zay smirked. "I don't know. What do you think?"

"I think we have the beginning of our monster. He's part goat, dragon, and human. We can't see the spirit part."

"That's the part that can come and go. Yet, there is no sign Phobus has that ability."

"If he has that ability, why is he able to come and go now but has been stationary for the last eight years? Or" Zay stopped talking and stared up into space, mumbling.

"Something has changed or—"

"We see glimpses of something else." Zay's mind raced at the thought.

Christine decided to go see Dr. Greenstein. As she rose to grab her car keys, Phobus heard her thought. The monster roared and rejoined her. Dr. Greenstein didn't know Christine was not in the pavilion; playtime ended. No matter how much fun the sound of a rapid beating heart from fear gave the monster, Christine served as the monster's mobility. Without her, he couldn't play these fun games. With the swiftness of the air, Phobus rejoined Christine. He had left her when she almost saw an image of his master in the reflection of a glass cabinet. Phobus made a note to be more careful.

He could still hear the growl of Belial, "Do not let the humans see me!"

Christine picked up the keys from the coffee table. Phobus slapped them from her hands.

She bent over to pick them up.

Phobus kicked her.

She fell on her face.

Phobus put his foot on her back.

Christine tried to get up but felt paralyzed. She crawled toward the phone and pulled the cord till the phone fell on the floor. She dialed the only number she knew by heart, Dr. Greenstein's office.

Phobus sat back and watched Christine struggle. *This should be fun.*

Abby Greenstein picked up the phone. Before she could answer, she heard a desperate voice on the other end.

"Who is this?" she asked.

"Christine. Please help me."

The line went dead. Abby called the pavilion and asked the staff to look in on Christine. They returned with a report that she was sleeping soundly.

Abby pondered the strange call. Then dismissed it.

15

A Map

Who is the wise man that may understand this? And who is he to whom the mouth of the Lord has spoken, that he may declare it? Why is the land ruined, laid waste like a desert, so that no one passes through? The Lord said, "Because they have forsaken My law which I set before them and have not obeyed My voice nor walked according to it but have walked after the stubbornness of their heart and after the gods as their fathers taught them."

---Jeremiah 9: 12-13

FOUR STORIES BELOW the lab sat the most horrid abomination any man ever saw. A super-strong monster devoid of emotion, ruthless, without pity, uncaring, callous, and something else that could not be seen, only sensed; a spirit of immeasurable evil.

The opening of the ground floor lab door made a creaking noise that brought a chill of foreboding each time it opened. A familiar sound to the workers in the lab. Nonetheless, useful as a warning to hide evidence of a project not sanctioned by the university or the grant . . . namely, the monster in the basement.

Zay's thoughts rattled through a dark tunnel like a speeding train with no intent of slowing. Even the grating squeak of the door didn't slow him. With no fear of exposure, he continued in his quest, thinking it's Dr. Winegren joining him in the examination of the genome map he completed. He spoke without turning to see who actually entered the lab.

"I still can't understand this creature's origin."

"You sound puzzled." came a female voice. Zay turned, thinking one of his students broke protocol and wandered into the lab unannounced and uninvited.

"What?" Zay exclaimed.

The young woman had a slight tilt to her head with her eyes looking up, similar to Princess Diana. She shared a similar beauty with the Princess too.

Zay pressed his lips together and nodded. His worst nightmare stood at the door; an unannounced female. He didn't know what to say. He didn't relate to girls well outside of the classroom. She displayed a seductive smile beneath her blonde bangs.

The eyes belied her innocent looks; they were cold and calculating, cruel and fearless.

Initially, Zay's mind was awash with confusion, fear, and then recognition as the yellow eyes focused on him.

She stopped, and her body muscles rippled like a cat about to pounce. A grin crept across her face and spread from one side to the other, revealing the sharpened spear-like teeth of Phobus.

"You recognize me." The image of Christine faded into the image of a creature spending its life in perpetual shadow. It slithered and oozed in and out of situations unseen while actively working as a catalyst to bring about its own maniacal desires.

Zay knew this was not Phobus because he didn't possess those qualities, even though the image before Zay bore the same distortions.

His stress levels elevated to anger which could serve to keep his true thoughts hidden from the prying mental probe of the unseen dragon.

"You're hiding something?" the creature remarked.

"What do you want?" Zay barked at it.

"You humans are so stupid and easy to manipulate. I can get whatever I want with either lust or fear, both of which are my specialties."

Once he regained his wits a bit, Zay asked, "How do you do it?"

"Do what?" The dragon asked while stomping around the room.

"Get into a human body?"

"Illusion my boy, illusion. What you really want to know is, why am I here."

Zay nodded.

"I need to know about Patti."

"I don't know a Patti," Zay answered.

"Then find out. I'll be back tomorrow, and if I don't get answers, I'll have a little surprise for Ms. Marcy Odom."

Zay froze at the threat. At that moment the squeak of the door sounded, and a firm voice spoke. "Young lady, what are you doing here?" Dr. Winegren scolded.

"I need information," she fluttered her voice and eyelashes.

"You need to leave now."

With that statement, the woman made a disgruntled sound and pulled her purse close to her body. "You know, I'll be back." She glared at Zay for a moment, then turned to leave.

Once she exited the lab, Dr. Winegren closed the door and locked it. "What were you thinking, letting that thing in here?"

"What did you see?" Zay asked.

"I saw a blending of a dragon and a woman. I didn't want it to know I could see the monster, which by the way, was not Phobus."

"It just walked in."

"Now you know why I lock the door."

"Will a door stop him?" Zay muttered under his breath.

Dr. Winegren shrugged his shoulders, "I don't know."

"What have you found?" Dr. Winegren asked as he stepped closer.

Zay picked up some papers containing the latest genome mapping from both Phobus and Christine and handed them to Dr. Winegren. "This."

Dr. Winegren sat down and read the paper. When he finished, he looked up at Zay and asked, "Was that Christine?"

"I think so."

Ronnie stepped into the room just as Dr. Winegren asked the question. "Who?" he asked.

Dr. Winegren extended the paper to Ronnie. "Looks like we have more work to do."

"Are you sure about these results?" Ronnie asked Zay.

Zay nodded. "Just finished them right before Phobus or whatever waltzed in here like a VIP guest."

"What?"

"He's using Christine's image for mobility."

Dr. Winegren said. "Christine is the thing's mother?"

"There is a definite connection between Christine and Phobus since the mitochondria only come from the mother."

Ronnie ran his fingers through his hair, "You know this is getting more and more weird. There's no way Christine could be the monster's mother."

Zay crossed his arms in front of him and stared at Ronnie. He put his index finger on his chin.

"Boss, your thinking is taking you away again." Ronnie smirked at him.

"He's in deep thought," Dr. Winegren said as he rose and walked in front of Zay.

Without warning Zay snapped his arm down and clapped his hands. "She asked about Patti."

"Patti who?"

"I don't know, but I know someone who might."

Christine awoke in her car. A tear crept down her cheek. Using a tissue, she wiped her face, wondering why she cried. Instead of memory, a blank beige wall faced her. She shrugged, noticing forty-five minutes of her life had disappeared—if one could call it a life when it had more holes than Swiss cheese.

Inspecting her surroundings brought the sensation of being lost . . . again. It's a lonely feeling, being deserted and slowly disappearing without being missed.

Christine pondered calling Dr. Greenstein again, but the last time had been . . . embarrassing. Until Marcy could be found there was no one to help her. *Where the heck are you, my friend? I need answers.* Heading toward her next appointment, she pulled her car onto the street and turned toward the office of Dr. Robert Burton, Obstetrician.

Phobus senses accelerated since his mentor allowed him to escape from this grotesque body and the physical bounds of the cell. He settled his dragon head on the rug, closed his eyes and pondered a riddle.

I'm not God and I'm not Satan,
but merely a strange homosapein?
I'm broken, and I burst with pain.
How did I become an eyesore?
Am I redeemable?
There is no god to help me
This means, I must find myself, by myself.
Still, I am feared.

And in that refrain,
I bear my pain.

Ronnie fell across his bed, laying on his stomach and stared out the window. The view overlooked the campus from his fourth-floor dorm room. The magic of the lights mingled with the landscaped trees and star-lit sky gave him a sense of an exotic vacation.

He rolled onto his back and looked at the ceiling. It was still there. The little secret he found the first day he moved into the dorm. He never spoke of it but often spoke to it. Spots like water damage with a secret in plain sight. The picture popped when he relaxed his eyes and allowed the dots to meld together forming a three-dimensional scene.

Ronnie smiled at the magnificent maroon dragon with wide-spread wings. The tips of the wings spread across the entire secret painting. Slipped under one wing stood a majestic, solid-white horse with head held high and rippling muscles. He held his left leg up as if ready to prance out of the picture.

Those who took the time to let their eyes go out of focus and their mind go blank could see the dragon and horse. A streamer floated in the air even with the horse's neck. It bore the words, "Let no one shame you."

He leaned back and looked at the dragon. "I'm the horse, and the dragon is my protector." Ronnie could see a slight smile on the dragon lips, revealing spear-like teeth and fangs. The picture turned into a moving picture.

The dragon's head curved down and wrapped around the muscles of the horse. The horse looked strained. The dragon looked at Ronnie and winked.

Ronnie yelped and jumped up from the bed.

A student from across the hall burst through the door. "What's going on man?" He yelled.

Ronnie looked at him with a blank mind. "Nothing. Why?"

"I heard you scream like you were terrified." The boy said. "Look at your hands. What happened?"

Ronnie looked down at his raw, red, blistered hands with no flesh left. "I don't know."

"They're burned. Come on, let's get you to the infirmary." He wrapped a white cotton tee shirt around Ronnie's arms and hands.

Ronnie looked up. The horse lay at the dragon's feet—barely alive.

16

Messages

> The LORD made known to me and I
> knew it; You showed me their deeds. I was
> like a gentle lamb led to the slaughter and I
> did not know that they had devised plots
> against me.
>
> ---Jeremiah 11:18-19

LEAVES OF RED and brown swirled with the soft
gentle breeze, whispering words of comfort. Zay took a
deep refreshing breath of the crisp air. His body shuddered
with the release of tension. He stood on the steps of the
science building watching the slow change in seasons from
green to brown reflecting the darkness his soul felt coming.

The evening meant hunting. It kept the budget for
large animals under control. He didn't have to offer any
explanations for the condemned shelter animals, although,
he did have to account for the cost of a two-thousand-
pound bull and delivery.

The fear of a monstrous creature roaming and seeking his own source of meat weighed heavily on Zay's shoulders. Since recent incidents hinted to Zay that the creature did roam. He had no assurance the monster wouldn't seek livestock or humans for his own selfish appetite. The monster displayed no self-regulation, and its demands increased as its intelligence emerged with a mind keen on seduction and trickery to gain its own desires.

When Zay slammed the van door shut behind the load of small animals, he let out the moan of a wounded man. "Lord, why?" The words were not offered as a question to a deity but rather as a curse.

"If this monster could burn Ronnie in his own dorm room, what other damage could he do and to whom?"

Closing the lid to the bin, he jumped into the van and hurried to the school parking lot where he switched back to his own vehicle and embarked on his second task of the evening—taking Ronnie to his sister's house for a bandage change.

Before Barbara removed the old dressings, she gave Ronnie a pill to numb the pain. Without the dose of codeine, the process of redressing the wounds would grip his entire body in a vice of pain, swelling, and ebbing like a wind-tossed sea. The wounds still oozed, but less than the day before.

Ronnie extended his unwrapped hands.

"It looks good," Barbara determined.

Ronnie chuckled at the evaluation. He was anything but good.

"Barbara, do you know anyone named Patti?"

She tightened her lips and nodded her head. "She's the witch that kidnapped me."

Zay's eyes opened wide. "Why would our dragon want her?"

"Like I said, she was a witch, and I use the term *literally*." Barbara emphasized the last word. "A dragon and a witch seems fairly normal." She laughed at the irony of a witch and dragon being normal.

Zay returned Ronnie to his room. He laid him down on his bed and placed a glass of water beside him. Ronnie muttered so Zay pulled up a chair and sat beside him.

"Look!" Ronnie pointed to the ceiling with his newly-bandaged hand.

"What is it?" Zay stared at a water-stained ceiling. "Do you have a leak?"

"No, it looks like it, but it's not. It's a picture."

Zay laughed. "It's an ugly picture."

"Just gaze without looking."

Zay laughed at the strange instructions, "Okay."

Time passed in a bubble while Zay stared mindlessly at the ceiling. Then it popped. "Whoa!" he exclaimed.

"You see it?"

Zay nodded with mouth agape.

"What do you see?"

"A . . . a . . . dragon!" Zay stuttered.

"Anything else?"

"A horse and a boy."

"That's the dragon that did this." Ronnie held up his hands. "Is the horse alive?"

"Hard to tell; it's lying on the ground with the dragon's foot on top."

"That's what I see too. It changes," Ronnie stated.

"Why?"

"Messages."

"So what message is this?"

"At first I thought I was the horse but not anymore."

"How come?"

"My classmate across the hall saw the dragon burning me. He also saw the horse protecting me from the blast of dragon fire."

"From a picture?" Zay said as he stared at the 3-D picture above him.

"He saw the dragon and horse for real."

"Did you see it?

Ronnie shook his head.

"What did he think?" Zay asked.

"He said the dragon turned away from me and spoke to him. I think the dragon would have burned my whole body if he hadn't come in."

Zay stood up and paced a bit. He turned back to Ronnie and noticed the pain pill had pulled him into a deep sleep. He walked across the hall and knocked on the door.

The door opened, and a bandaged young man stood in front of Zay, "Dr. Troye?"

He recognized the man from one of his classes. "What happened to you?"

"A little burn, I'm okay. Come in."

"I need to know about your burn and Ronnie's." Zay pointed toward the door. The young man named Jacob offered a chair for Zay, and he sat on the edge of the bed. "Ronnie's your lab worker, isn't he?"

Zay nodded.

"He's special to me too." Jacob eyed Zay.

"How so?" Zay asked.

Jacob took a deep breath before he said, "He's the soul that plays like me, fights like me, has a determination like me and—"

"And?" Zay prodded when Jacob stopped.

"He's my boyfriend," Jacob said softly.

Zay adjusted himself in the chair.

"I see. Were you with him when . . . the burns happened?"

"No, I heard him screaming, I ran over there, and I saw—"

"Saw what?"

"Please don't think me crazy."

"Don't worry about that. I have a first-class reservation on crazy." Zay smiled at him in an attempt to calm him.

"I saw a dragon blowing fire on him. He held his hands up in front of his face. I grabbed Ronnie and took him to the floor. That was when I got burned too."

"Have you seen the dragon since?"

"No, but I will never forget that voice that growled at me."

"What did it say?"

"Find Patti."

Jacob stared at Zay for a few minutes before he asked, "Do you know what it means?"

17

Findings

> Thus says the Lord, "Let not a wise man boast of his wisdom, and let not the mighty man boast of his might, let not a rich man boast of his riches; but let him who boasts boast of this, that he understands and knows Me, that I am the Lord who exercises lovingkindness, justice and righteousness on earth; for I delight in these things," declares the Lord.
>
> --- Jeremiah 9:23-24

"LET'S EXAMINE THE facts we know." Zay pulled up a chair and grabbed the charts the two men had been keeping.

"Okay."

"We've found genetic markers in the epigenomes."

Ronnie nodded.

"We know these epigenetic underpinnings reveal evidence of behavior-based genes being passed from one generation to the next. This inheritable genetic change can influence the next generation with sex-specific behavior and gene expression in the brain."

Ronnie stared at Zay with a blank expression.

"That means we next apply our model of sexually antagonistic epimarkers to the human homosexual phenotype," Zay added.

"I'm still a student. Can you dumb it down a little?" Ronnie asked.

Zay laughed. "It means we need to use the same research that has been done looking for the homosexual gene. There are studies that say it exist, yet it can't be found.

"We have a similar situation; we test on a creature out of the norm. What made him half one species and half another? What makes one person say they are homosexual, and another person say it's an abomination."

"I think I'm beginning to understand what you're saying."

"Yes, I think that's where I'm going with this. Instead of testing for the norm, we test for the abnormal."

"Oh, so we are looking for non-existent genes in a fantasy creature that doesn't exist?" Ronnie wrinkled his brow and smirked.

"In a way, epigenetics is a method of reading between the lines." Zay stood and paced across the room as he spoke. "My tests show the markers can be modified by supplements, medicines, food, and environment."

"Can they be inherited?" Ronnie asked.

"That's a good question, and a good test." Zay scribbled a note.

"What about our dragon, did behavior cause him to be so ugly?"

Zay rose and started his pacing routine as he reasoned out loud. "The only possible homosexual gene can only be imagined by the information found in these epigenetic markers, and they can be changed by attitude and behavior, as well as food and drug changes."

"Are you saying our dragon is a homosexual?" Ronnie queried and sat down.

"In a way, yes, he is the combination of DNA that never should have been put together, much in the same way the Bible says two men or two women should not be together intimately."

"But shouldn't sexuality be a personal decision?" Ronnie asked.

"Let's go with the Bible thesis, God gives man the freedom to make his own choices, but He didn't give man the freedom to remove the consequences of his choices."

"Then homosexuality is a choice? I disagree," Ronnie said flatly.

"It doesn't matter whether you agree or not, the Bible states it's not to be, just as it declares one is not to be an adulterer or a thief or a murderer or a plotter of evil against another person. The law is stated; the individual has the choice to follow the law or not."

"You're saying homosexuality is like a thief or murderer?"

"Yes, but there's more."

Ronnie sighed and sat down on the couch, crossing his arms across his chest.

"Every person has it within themselves to be homosexual, or a thief, or murderer. They often don't make the decision to do so, but circumstances dictate the decision."

"Is this from the Bible or the genome study?"

"Both." Zay chuckled. "One follows the other. The inclination to be a homosexual is within every human being, just like the tendency is there for every man to be tempted by a beautiful woman."

Ronnie smiled as he watched Zay reason out the findings of his research. "This world is filled with things and events that cause people to make decisions. Whether those things are right or wrong, the circumstances, environment, physical and mental condition in a person's life at a given time play a role in one's life decisions."

Ronnie stood up and joined Zay in the slow pace. He pondered the ideas Zay espoused from the Bible and from science. "

"Explain how the epigenomes give you this insight."

"The changes are determined to help an organism survive, but when trauma occurs the markers may cause survival to occur in an unnatural way."

"Example."

"Trauma such as the loss of a father at a young age." Zay stopped and looked directly into Ronnie's face.

"I'm hearing you say things can change and cause someone to choose to be homosexual to survive? Or make a dragon a half goat?"

"Yes, that's it exactly." Zay answered.

"And that change helps one survive through extreme circumstances or trauma?"

"That's right."

"Not sure I get the connection," Ronnie muttered.

"Let's go back to the Bible. God made marriage so man would not be alone. He gave him a helper different from him so she could help in areas he needed help. For example, companionship and sexually."

"Okay?"

"It's like the homosexual tendency in males is considered to be due to reduced male hormones in pregnancy, and that leaning is fueled by the worldly influence to behave outside the normal genetic information."

"So, homosexuality can be inherited?"

"That's part of the study," Zay answered.

Ronnie stopped pacing. "Do you think this thing is a homosexual?" he queried Zay.

"No . . . Maybe . . . I'm not sure," Zay answered. "It presents the same image of a homosexual, so I think the best scientific inquiry would be to go with the homosexual genetic evolution theory. It gives us more insight into the origins of this thing and its purpose."

"What is that theory?"

"That homosexuality is inherited by changing genes from one generation to the next. The strength in the model is the ability to make a theory which is not absolute, but it is testable."

"So what test do we do?" Ronnie asked.

Zay paced the room a couple of times with his head down expressing an occasional "Hmm."

"Maybe we need to discover why he calls himself an abomination," Ronnie said.

"You're right. Whatever he considers an abomination may be a clue to the epigenetics in its history." Zay raised his head with the authority of knowledge.

Zay went to the storage cabinet where he kept his books and journals. He pulled out a file full of papers. "Do you remember the paper Marcy Odom wrote?"

"Yes, it was off the wall but interesting."

"We need to reread it."

"Better yet, why don't we talk to her?" Ronnie queried.

"I would love to, but I can't locate her. I have offered her a lab assistant job with us, but I haven't heard anything. I'll keep looking. In the meantime, I think we have another piece of our resident puzzle," Zay concluded.

"I'm getting confused." Ronnie sat down. "What have we learned?"

"Possibilities. Nothing can be proven since the epigenomes come and go."

"Why do they do that?"

"Survival?"

"Are you saying homosexuality is a means of survival?" Ronnie mused.

"Could be, just as stealing a loaf of bread by a hungry orphan is survival."

Ronnie angled his head to one side and pursed his lips.

"Is that thing merely trying to survive?"

"I don't think it has the power to reason and make decisions; it lives by instinct. I think its origin is the real problem. Was it born of a human woman?"

18

Patti

> But they are altogether stupid and
> foolish in their discipline of delusion —their
> idol is wood? Beaten silver and gold, the
> work of a craftsman and of the hands of a
> goldsmith; violet and purple are their
> clothing; they are all the work of skilled men.
> --- Jeremiah 10:8-9

PATTI PAULSEN STROLLED through the old mansion. The oversized, mullioned windows rose from the floor like a cathedral. With the dusty, thread-bare, emerald-green, bishop-sleeve velvet drapes removed, every room lit up with sunlight. The weathered oak floors reflected the light well into the evening hours.

The dark illusion no longer existed. The reality gave way to a warm, comfortable home in the place of hidden dirt, scurrying pests, and ancient, pretentious décor. Scrubbing the house of horrors cleansed Patti's spirit as well as the house. For the first time in her wicked-witch life she felt free. Soon, all evidence of the past activities would be removed, and the house could be sold. Maybe a real family would live in it and bring some happiness to the majestic walls.

She raised her glass of red wine to the portrait of the woman she had called Grandmamma, or Madame Lilith. "Thanks for the inheritance, Granny."

She toasted to a mere painting, yet it could cause all the deep pain within her heart to come rushing out her eyes in tearful regrets. Patti stared at the ghostly reflection of the monster who stole her from her loving parents and raised her in a house of horrors—this house.

She gazed at the painted image of a perfect woman whose only flawlessness was the practice of all things evil. Patti wanted her time back with her mother. She wanted to feel the arms of Paps holding her when she felt frightened. She wanted to see the love Paps spoke about when he spoke of her mother. How she longed to be free of the image of wickedness in the woman dead to the world and forgotten by all except her victims.

"No more!" With a smirk on her face, she tipped the glass and took a deep drink, then she ripped the portrait to shreds with a box cutter knife, laughing with each gash. She threw the pieces into the fire place and lit it.

Watching the portrait burn, Patti settled onto the settee to watch the last ember devour the ugliness that had plagued her every breath. Physically spent from the emotion spilt in the destruction, she sighed. The next chore required her full attention, but it would be the last. Then she could sell the place and move on and retrieve the good in the years left to her.

Lying in wait behind the basement door lived the most painful of her memories—the lab of Lapetos, Madame Lilith's butler. In that dark chamber lay the atrocities of experimentation and the inventions of a sadistic mind. As much as she wanted to hire people to do the job, the risk of curious and talkative workers ranked high among her fears. With the help of Cook and Michelle, they would face the hall of horrors.

With a heavy sigh, she unlocked the heavy door to Lapetos's lair. The smell hit her first. It smelled of chemicals and rot mixed together. *Oh Lapetos, you were a friend and a mad man.* She took a few more steps down . . . down . . . into an abyss of mystery and nightmares. A place where many lives both ended and started. None were good.

Patti looked around the lab and noticed the small cell she called home during her childhood. It was a dark unforgiving place with nothing but a rusted frame and thin worn mattress. Madame Lilith's form of training. It must have worked since Cook, Michelle, and Patti remained.

After a few hours of cleaning the lab, Patti suggested Cook go prepare them some dinner.

"Come on upstairs," Patti said to Michelle. "Let's see what Cook has prepared for us."

Patti went directly to the kitchen and sat at her table without hesitancy. The three women crowded each other because they needed each other's touch and warmth in the midst of this great change in their lives.

"Do you have plans?" Patti asked Michelle.

"Oui, Madame." Michelle hurried to answer Patti.

"First off, you are free to leave whenever you want, but if you want to stay and help me, I will pay you a fair wage," Patti promised the shaking young girl.

She smiled and said, "Thank you, Madame, I will help you."

"Don't call me that; my name is Patti," she scolded, remembering Michelle's service to Lilith had also started in the dungeon as well as Cook's. Everyone remaining in the house started as a victim. Now they were free, and they didn't know what to do, including herself.

Patti returned to her bedroom. She needed a plan; she needed a friend; but most of all, she needed Paps, the only man who truly loved her for herself. The thought of Paps brought up his friend, Michael. The man she both hated and loved. He freed her from Lilith when he rescued Barbara Troye Holloway from her marriage to the demon, Jorgphat.

She crossed the room and looked out the window. The neighborhood was deteriorating. She remembered the few times she'd been allowed to venture out into the neighborhood as a child. Lapetos held tight to her hand, which made her feel secure. The houses were beautiful, stately mansions with manicured yards and children and dogs playing in them. She smiled at the memory. She looked across the street, and her smile faded for that had been her first job.

Lilith told her to become friends with the little girl who lived there. She did, and she loved Emily. She remembered how excited she was when Emily would come to dinner, that is, until that fateful night Lilith took her downstairs, and she occupied the next cell. Emily died within days, her little heart couldn't take the separation from her parents and siblings, and her body couldn't endure the abuse. Patti never made another friend after Emily's death. She steeled her emotions and did her job. Barbara Troye served as her last victim.

After visiting Michelle, the three came back to the kitchen where Patti and Cook drank a cup of coffee in silence.

"Do you feel better?" she asked them.

"Yes, ma'am, thank you. What do you want us to do now?" Cook asked.

Patti asked Cook to join her in the lab. She opened the door to a storage closet and waved her hand around at the contents. "What do we do with it?"

Cook's hand went over her mouth as she gazed at the glass jars filled with fetuses of different gestation periods.

"What did *he* do with them?" Cook groaned.

"Made monsters or sold them to people who make or study to make monsters," Patti said as she stroked her hair.

"Why?"

"He wanted to make a superhuman with the mind of a human but with the characteristics of certain animals. You know, like the cartoon character Spiderman."

"So, did he succeed?" Cook ventured to ask.

"Only in creating monsters."

"Where are they?"

"Dead."

"All of them?" Cook asked wide-eyed.

"One got away," Patti moaned.

"Where is it?" Cook asked with wide eyes and a shaky voice.

Patti shook her head and looked around the room. She cupped her hands over her mouth and with a search for strength finally gave Cook the answer that caused sweat to drip down her face. "I don't know."

19

A Worried Mother

> If you will not listen to it, My soul will sob in secret for such pride; and my eyes will bitterly weep and flow down with tears, because the flock of the LORD has been taken captive.
>
> ---Jeremiah 13:17

RONNIE HEARD THE ear-splitting howl, along with the rest of his class. The room reverberated with the sound. Ronnie continued on as if nothing happened, but his heart raced. The sound could reveal the secret of the biology lab. The noise stopped, and the class settled back into their test.

The creature grew more restless and dangerous as time passed. His pacing echoed through the science lab like gunshots. His roars sounded like earthquakes, which was the common explanation used to describe the sounds. It created havoc every day, with each day growing worse than the day before.

After class, Ronnie hot-footed it to the lab. There he found his mentor and friend struggling to block the sound with more foam around the door leading to the basement.

"It must be deafening in the dungeon," Ronnie said as he entered the room to keep from startling Zay.

When Zay turned and faced him, he almost gasped at the haggard look in Zay's face. "How long have you been here?" he asked, pulling a bottle of orange juice from the refrigerator with his bandaged hands and handing it to Zay.

He drank deeply of the sweet nectar, letting it revive his spirit and heal his body. "I don't know."

Ronnie gazed at Dr. Troye, who paced the room with his hands on his hips and his lips moving in a solo conversation. After a few minutes he turned to Ronnie and nodded. Then he expressed the thought which captivated him.

"It's not alone."

"What?"

"I saw the other dragon in there with him."

"What does that mean?"

"I wondered how Phobus could escape and why he started now, but I think he has help." Zay gulped the rest of the orange juice and wiped his mouth with the back of his hand. He sat down and motioned for Ronnie to join him.

"What happened?"

"I've gone as far as I can go on mapping that thing's DNA," Zay said. "I need to identify it, stop it, change it, but mostly get rid of that abomination."

Ronnie moaned and turned his face away from Zay.

"You okay buddy?" Zay asked him.

"It's that word, every time you use it, my stomach ties in knots."

"What word?"

"That *A* word."

"Abomination?"

Ronnie groaned louder and doubled over. "It literally hurts me."

"Why?"

"I don't know, but the creature told me I was as much of one as he is."

"Don't listen to him. His whole game plan is to confuse you."

"I know, but ever since then, the word hurts. I think I know why." Ronnie straightened up and stretched.

"Why would a word hurt you like that?"

"It's the word the Bible uses for people like me."

"What?" Zay wrinkled his brow as he raised his head.

"Gay."

"Oh."

"That's all you're going to say?"

"Yes, let's get to work. I found some new research," Zay muttered.

"What kind?"

"Ronnie, look at what we have in our basement. He is neither goat nor dragon; it's a mess, and we're looking at his DNA. Do you think you're messed up like that thing? You want to find some weird stuff in your DNA too?"

Ronnie laughed at Zay and patted him on the back, "You're funny, my friend." Then he became a bit more serious as he whispered, "What do you think you'll find?"

"I'm looking between the lines now. At the science called epigenetics."

Ronnie laughed. "Don't make it up. If it's not real, I want to know the truth."

Zay didn't respond but continued to pour over his crude drawings.

Ronnie pulled out the guide sheet and read through Zay's notes to catch up.

Zay stopped reading, looked up at Ronnie and took a deep breath. "Ronnie, why do you think you're gay? Outside of a possible gene? I've heard you talk about that girl Marianne. You called her the love of your life."

"She broke my heart," Ronnie moaned.

Zay stood up and walked across the room. He opened a cabinet, pulled out some test tubes, and returned to the lab table. He looked at Ronnie and in a firm voice responded, "No she didn't."

"You sound sure."

"The teacher who embarrassed you both is the one that broke your heart. You both felt so much humiliation, you never spoke to each other again."

"I guess you're right. I guess my heart really broke when my dad died in Vietnam."

"Do you remember him?"

"A little. I was five the last time I saw him. We were at the air base as he was deploying. Then fourteen months later, we picked him up in a flag-covered box." Ronnie stared at the corner of the room reliving his memories.

"Is the group helping?"

Ronnie shrugged his shoulders. "I think so; at least there are others like me."

Snarling booms raised from the basement and interrupted their conversation.

"I guess I better get to the pound and gather up the animals slated for euthanasia," Zay said.

"I'll go." Ronnie interrupted.

"Can you drive . . . you know with your hands?"

"Yeah, I don't feel any pain and Mrs. Holloway wraps them solid. She left my fingers free yesterday. Didn't realize how much I missed them."

Zay smiled. "Thanks, it's getting harder to bring those mutts in here."

"So, why do it? Let the thing starve to death."

"He won't starve." Zay emphasized the implications of the statement with a raised eyebrow.

"Okay, at least we can control his diet. For now," Ronnie said as he exited the lab to go to the local pound. Zay picked up the phone and dialed the *Used Cow Factory*. Before he could complete the number, a loud knock came on his door.

"Mr. Doctor," The female voice on the other side called. Zay opened the door and saw a fiftyish woman standing there out of breath.

"May I help you?" he asked without letting her in the lab. Instead he stepped out into the hallway.

"I'm Elena Odom," she said.

He nodded, waiting for her to explain her presence.

"I'm Marcy Odom's mother. Please help me; we must rescue her," the woman said in a breathless voice. She grabbed Zay by the arm and started pulling him.

He pulled away from her.

"Please, don't delay, she needs out."

The desperation of the woman reminded him of his own mother. "Tell me, what's wrong." He led her into his office next to the lab and motioned for her to sit.

She wouldn't. Instead, she stomped about the small room growing more agitated. "You have to help her. Come. Come," she kept saying.

"I need details," he said, attempting to reach through her agitation.

"She's in the psychiatric pavilion, and they think she's Christine!" she blurted out in a loud voice. "Get her out!" she screamed at him. "Now!"

Zay slumped on his desk. "What are you saying?"

"Christine escaped and left Marcy in her place, she's been in there for two months, and nobody will help me."

"Did you talk to her doctor?" Zay asked, wanting to go through proper channels.

"Yes, he's no help. He gave me pills. Only you can help me now."

"How do you know Marcy is there?"

"I saw her. I talked to her. Nobody will believe her. She's locked up like a criminal." Tears streamed down the woman's face, and she finally sat down on the edge of a chair. "Please, help me get her out. She said you were a good and fair man."

Zay stood and removed his lab coat. "Give me a minute."

Mrs. Odom nodded.

"I think we must be careful," Zay cautioned Mrs. Odom.

"Why?"

"I think if we go rushing in there to get her out, we'll make more problems for her." Zay ran his fingers through his hair. "But trust me, we will get her out of there." He escorted her out of the lab, leaving her little time to respond.

She nodded and walked out the door.

Zay slammed the door in her face and locked it behind him. He went downstairs to Phobus's cage.

The monster was sitting there on his haunches. "Don't you dare let her out or you will discover what I can do." He snarled at Zay when he opened the door. Zay saw the image of the greater dragon standing behind and mouthing the words Phobus spoke.

He didn't answer. Instead, he backed out of the door, slammed it shut, and let out a breath of cold fear. He needed a plan. One that could prove to be sure-fire to accomplish Marcy's release and Phobus's containment.

What could Phobus do? Was the threat real? He stood outside his office door, attempting to catch his breath. He could be certain Mrs. Odom would do whatever necessary to release her daughter from a prison. And the spirit behind Phobus would exercise his abilities to keep her in. He had no time to lose before Mrs. Odom did something wild. At the same time, he needed to keep Phobus from doing anything disastrous. But then he had to ask himself who was more fearful—a desperate mother or a lying monster.

20

Escape

The word of the LORD to Jeremiah in regard to the drought; they set on the ground in mourning, their nobles have sent their servants for water, they have come to the cisterns and found no water, they have returned with their vessels empty; they have been put to shame and humiliated, and they cover their heads...our iniquities testify against us.

---Jeremiah 14:1-7

ZAY HELD MARCY'S hand. How did no one see the difference between her and Christine? Then he wondered if they couldn't for some reason. Marcy's brunette hair and dark skin stood in stark contrast to Christine's blonde hair and fair skin.

"I'm so sorry," he whispered to her. He held her head as she rested it on his shoulder.

She wept for a moment. "How do I get out of here?" she finally asked quietly.

"I don't think you do, not yet anyway."

"You can't leave me in here. I have terrible nightmares."

Zay attempted to comfort Marcy. After a while, he asked her the question which needed an answer. "Tell me about the nightmares?"

"In the dark, I see a jaw filled with razor-like teeth, and labored breathing from the jaw fills the room with the stink of a thousand skunks. It's red with a purple gleam. It's actually pretty if you get past the teeth and the stink. But how can I call it a nightmare if it is still present when I'm awake?" Marcy's eyes turned toward the ceiling in the left corner of the room.

The description didn't match Phobus, but it did match the image he had seen behind Phobus.

"Do you remember the paper you wrote about the AGCT genes in the DNA strand?"

"Yes."

"I think you may have uncovered a secret that may destroy the creature," Zay said.

"How?"

"Not sure yet, still working with it. But you keep up the research."

"How can that control a dragon?" Marcy squeezed his hand.

Zay revealed the threat Phobus made before he came over here. "He's afraid of you or at least afraid of you being released."

Marcy sat up. She stood and walked around the small room to her wardrobe. She looked in the fake mirror made from a single sheet of polished metal, and warped. Marcy moaned at her distorted reflection.

"I helped bring this horror into our lives. I loved watching the shows about vampires and witches and dragons—"

"Don't list your failings; focus on your strength. For starters, your faith in God."

"Do you have faith?' she asked Zay.

He rubbed his face. "I try."

She sat back down on the bed beside him. "It's hard to have faith when you've been abandoned."

"You're not abandoned. You're imprisoned because the monster knows you have information which will help us destroy him."

"How, can I destroy a monster?" She moaned and sank her head into her hands, letting her long hair fall over her face.

"Knowledge makes slavery to a lie impossible." Zay pushed her hair back out of her face and raised her chin so her eyes meet his.

"But why must I stay here?" Marcy groaned as she leaned on Zay's shoulder again. "I've been here two months. and in another week. I'll truly belong here."

"As long as you're in here, the monster feels safe from your knowledge. You have a perfect opportunity to do some study and work in here without his awareness."

"What about his nighttime visits?" Marcy asked. "He'll see what I'm doing."

"Good point." Zay paced the room. "I know, I'll bring work to you every morning and come get it every night."

"That's an awful lot of traveling."

"I don't mind," Zay said, patting her hand.

Marcy blushed and gave him a coy smile.

"I have requested you as a student assistant in my lab."

Marcy's smile faded, and in resolution she answered, "Really?"

"You can help me unravel a monster's DNA."

"Okay, sounds like a plan. Can you tell my mother? She's frantic."

"First thing on my list when I leave here." Zay smiled and carefully let go of her hand. He handed her his briefcase. "I think I have everything you need in here to start. I'm using this time to look for a gene or a gene sequence that might give some insight into behavior. It's called epigenetic."

"Why is that important for the demise of a monster?"

"Maybe it isn't, but primarily I'm looking to see if there is a possibility that socially deviant behaviors may have a genesis in the digital code of DNA."

"Hmm, for Ronnie?" she mused.

Zay smiled. "Among others."

"Are you praying for him?" Marcy muttered.

"I don't have much faith in prayer; I prefer science."

"You know the Bible has a lot of science in it, don't you?" Marcy asked him.

"My dad keeps telling me that, and often he can even prove it, but I guess I don't have any faith in the unseen."

"And yet, you see a dragon spirit behind a dragon?"

Zay ducked his head and laughed. "Point made."

"I think you may find more answers in the words of a Bible than in a genome study."

"This coming from a girl who loves vampires and ghosts." Zay snickered.

"Well, they are both in the Bible." She smiled.

Zay put the teasing aside, sat down in the one lone chair in the room, and rested his chin on his fingers. "Ya know, Marcy, that may be the source for our other dilemma too."

"Bring me my Bible, and I'll research both sources, scientific and spiritual," Marcy said. "Include some notebooks and pens for taking notes." She winked at him. "A good scientist keeps good notes."

Phobus roared!

Christine moaned.

Patti Paulsen shuddered.

The spirit realm shifted.

An unseen but ever-present red dragon spread his wings and lifted his head. With a blast of fire from his mouth, he announced to the spirit world, "It's harvest time!"

21

Facing Fear

O Hope of Israel, its Savior in time of distress, why are You like a stranger in the land or like a traveler who has pitched his tent for the night? Why are You like a man dismayed, like a mighty man who cannot save? Yet, You are in our midst, O LORD and we are called by Your name; Do not forsake us!"

---Jeremiah 14:8-9

RONNIE FELT THE shadow more than saw it. "What was that?" he asked.

Zay shrugged and searched for the source. Suddenly, he found it. He froze in place.

Ronnie noticed the strained expression on Zay's face in the dim light. "Dr. Troye." He touched the cold face of his boss. Shallow breaths tickled his hand. He yelled at Zay.

Sweat droplets streamed down Ronnie's face when he followed the direction in which Zay stared.

Coming from a cloudless early morning sky a large shadow covered them. The dragon held Dr. Troye prisoner.

"Go Away!" Ronnie screamed.

The reddish-purple scales reflecting the dim light mesmerized Zay. Instinct wanted to embrace it. Fear wanted to kill it. The reptilian-like face with huge spikes protruding from its head produced paralyzing fear.

Zay wanted to speak, but the dragon took his voice. Through his thoughts asked the creature, "What do you want?"

"I want you to stop meddling in my business."

The creature stared directly into Zay's eye with wicked intentions, causing Zay's brain to fall into stupid mode. He muttered syllables and searched for words to argue or defend himself.

"You're a monster." Zay stated the obvious.

The creature raised his head and laughed. "Call me what I am—an abomination." The dragon answered. "Because I'm dangerous!"

"Who are you?" Zay managed to ask. This dragon bore little resemblance to Nisroch, the dragon his family fought on their family farm. Compared to this dragon, Nisroch was a kitty cat.

"I am known as Belial."

"Worthless?" Zay smirked to himself.

Belial roared.

Zay put his hands over his ears to block the unearthly sound.

"I'm worthless not harmless."

Zay's whole body trembled fearing the monster would rip him to shreds. He could feel Belial probing him with his sharp claws and his writhing tale.

The monster's head jerked, its lips parted, and it extended it's long tongue toward Zay. It came within centimeters of his face.

Zay squinted his eyes, both wanting to see what the tongue would do and also to block out the horror of the rope-like tentacle swaying in front of his face.

"You know Him?" Came the harsh voice of the monster.

Zay responded with a shout, "Yes, I know him."

Belial pulled the tongue back, raised the spiked head to the sky, and roared.

Zay felt confused. In one second the monster is ready to eat him, and in the next, he lets him go because he knows Ronnie?

"You don't even know what he does for you." Belial roared and releases a plume of fire. Then with the sound of a rock avalanche, the creature flew away.

Zay stared at the hideous monster until it disappeared from sight. Even with the monster gone, He could hear the words it planted in his mind, "I am Leyla which means 'terror of the night.'"

Tentacles of fear wrapped around his spirit as the adrenaline rush of facing a dragon crashed down on him.

"What happened?" Ronnie asked.

"I think I just encountered that dragon on your ceiling. He's a lot bigger in person."

"Who do you know?"

Zay wrinkled his brow. "What?"

"You said, you know him. Who do you know?"

"I thought he meant you, but then he said I don't know what he does for me. What were you doing?"

"Nothin'."

The sun hid on the edge of the Eastern horizon, so the two brushed themselves off and got back into the car.

"Do you think it could have been talking about God?" Ronnie asked.

"Could be. I'm sure if there is a God that thing knows about Him." Zay's brain survived the trauma of fear and now returned to the analysis of the event, like a good scientific brain should. "You know if God is the Creator, that means He created that thing."

"I guess so." Ronnie leaned back against the car seat.

"Did the monster see God in me?" Zay trembled at the thought. "Is that why he pulled away?

"Maybe. You may be questioning God, but you still have faith in Him."

"How do you know that?"

"I work beside you. I hear your thesis. I see your experiments, and I read your notes."

"The answers are in science. The Bible is an ancient resource."

"Okay," Ronnie answered with a smile.

"Our problem is we are doing origin science, not operational science. We have no experiments we can do to recreate the beginning of life."

"On the other hand, you do have physical evidence in your basement," Ronnie reminded Zay.

"You know this DNA research needs an intelligent design," Zay answered.

"How come?"

"The information in the single nucleus of a cell means there has to be someone or something putting that information there."

"What about Darwin's theory?" Ronnie reminded him.

"His theory is about sustaining life; he didn't address the origin of life." Zay sighed. "We have nothing except faith. Do you think that monster was telling me I didn't know what God does for me?"

"It fits better, 'cause I wasn't doing nothing, 'cept, crying."

Zay laughed at Ronnie. "I guess it helped."

"I don't think God does anything for me. He took my dad and made me a freak like our basement resident." Ronnie moaned.

"I just saw a new possibility, and it frightens me," Zay blurted out, changing the subject.

As a scientist the genome project held fascination for Zay, but it also consumed his every thought. Last week's discovery in Phobus's sample connecting it to Christine's DNA left him feeling bewildered, and this encounter with Belial augmented that feeling. If God could create such monsters and be a good God, and science couldn't destroy the evil, then . . .

A question formed in Zay's mind which frightened him as much as the monster, "Does science reveal God?"

22

Idols

> For My eyes are on all their ways; they are not hidden from My face, nor is their iniquity concealed from My eyes. I will first doubly repay their iniquity and their sin, because they have polluted My land; they have filled My inheritance with the carcasses of their detestable idols and with their abominations."
>
> ---Jeremiah 16:17-18

THE DECISION FOR Marcy to stay in the psychiatric ward at the hospital proved difficult for her. However, her secret work on the genome project sped up the exploration and her Bible study revealed some secret truths to her about the dragon.

The threat from Phobus must be taken seriously. Marcy's residence in the psychiatric ward remained the only solution until enough information could be gained to control or destroy Phobus. The travel back and forth from the hospital grew tedious, but it gave Zay opportunity to spend time with her. Her discoveries both amazed and delighted him.

Marcy shared his love of science and his curiosity. He almost hated to see her go home, fearful he wouldn't be able to see her as much. At least she accepted the offer to work in the lab with him as a student.

The trip today was less science and more theology. His encounter with Belial burdened him with questions. When Zay entered her room with wrinkled brows, his thought processes were on overload.

"Marcy, there's another dragon."

"I know."

"I don't mean just another dragon; I mean a fiercer dragon—like the devil."

Marcy shuddered and said, "Paul did say in 1 Corinthians 10, a demon spirit is behind every idol." She melted onto the bed with all color draining from her face. "I just realized that the enemy in your battle won't be found in genome research. It'll be found behind the idol of the deformed dragon."

"What can we do?" she asked Zay.

"I need your help. This battle is supernatural and I don't have enough knowledge." Zay said. He pulled a file from his briefcase. "Here's some of my dad's notes. I think they'll help us."

Marcy nodded, took the notes, and scanned through them.

"They are about the book of Jeremiah," Zay said.

"Jeremiah was God's mouthpiece to the king. He gave God's direction to the king." Marcy responded.

"They why did all these bad things happen to the people then?"

"The king didn't listen, and the people worshipped the dragons."

"What were those dragons?"

Marcy tipped her head down and looked up at Zay, "Really, you want to ask that question." She waved her arm around the room. "What am I doing here? How did I get here and what are you doing here?"

"Are you saying the dragon in the lab and the other one in this room are the same as those dragons?"

"Pretty much."

"Where are you getting your information?" Zay asked her and sat down on the bed beside her.

"The articles and books you bring reveal a lot, but I am getting most of the information from the Bible study. Dragons are deceivers. They want to lure people into their lies. They present themselves as powerful, knowledgeable and semi-caring gods. You know like the gods in mythology."

"Are they the same?"

"Maybe, I don't know, but the gods led the people to build images or idols of them. Solomon's wives put them all over Israel. The worship of these gods promised wealth, prestige and power to the people. It was easy for the people to follow their rules."

"I didn't know the pagan gods had rules." Zay pondered as he stood and crossed the room leaning against the wall.

"The gods demanded the sacrifice of their children and offerings of food."

"That's really harsh. Why would people do that?" Zay wrinkled up his nose.

"Why do people get abortions today?" Marcy asked and returned the bed and picked up her notepad and pencil.

"Look at this." Marcy handed Zay the tablet. "What do you see?"

"I don't know, its all distorted."

"Yeah. Did I draw it that way or are you seeing it distorted?"

"I'm missing your point." Zay handed the pad back to her.

Marcy continued, "God gave clear guidelines to know the difference between the one true God and the dragon or false gods."

"What were guidelines?" Zay asked.

"God wrote a law and gave it to the people, we call it the ten commandments." Marcy smiled.

"I know that." Zay winked at her.

"But did you know that Leviticus is the explanation of that law to the priests and Deuteronomy is the explanation of the law to the people by Moses?"

"I guess I never read those books." Zay sat down in the one chair in the room and crossed his legs.

"God gave the law in Exodus, the angels gave the explanation to Moses in Leviticus and then Moses gave that to the teachers and the people in Deuteronomy."

"That's pretty much the same system we use at the university." Zay chuckled and uncrossed his legs. Leaning into Marcy. He loved these moments of discussion. Her curious mind retained most everything she studied. He loved it. She would make a wonderful lab assistant and wife. Zay smiled at the random thought. He made a mental note to move things along and get her out of this place as soon as he could manage. He smiled at Marcy as she fluffed her pillows to make herself a seat on her bed. Zay leaned back and waited for more enlightenment. The lab would wait.

"Did you know in the book of Judges it says in one generation, the people forgot God and His works. After Joshua and all the elders died, they fell hard into worshiping the dragon/gods."

"One!" Zay raised his eyebrows.

"Remarkable how quickly we forget. God kept begging them to turn back to Him, but they went deeper and deeper into idol worship." Marcy responded.

"Why?" Zay couldn't help himself, the question banged at his thinking.

"We can only answer that from Jeremiah 17:9, the heart is wicked."

Zay smiled and let out a whimper of a chuckle.

"What's funny?" Marcy smiled at him.

"I'm thinking about students who excuse their behavior by saying 'the heart wants what the heart wants.'"

Marcy chuckled too.

"It's still hard to understand why the people of that time didn't listen."

"Do we do any better? How many people do you know who seriously study God's Word today?"

"Not many."

"We don't listen either. We have God's laws written before us, and He even gives us the reasons for the laws, and still we won't listen."

"What reasons?" Zay exclaimed in surprise.

"John 10:10. 'I came to give life and give it more abundantly,' but in Deuteronomy twenty-eight, God lays out the blessings of following his guidelines and the curses if one doesn't. You could call it, 'How to live well and succeed.'"

"He doesn't have a set of rules you have to follow to be a Christian?"

"Only one thing you must do to live the Christian life."

"I doubt that, but go ahead, dazzle me." Zay smiled at Marcy, thinking she wouldn't have an answer.

"Trust Him."

"I trust Him, after all He is God."

"How do you show your trust?" Marcy probed and Zay squirmed in the chair. He started to stand but tripped over Marcy's shoes and lost his balance and stumbled to Marcy. She reached out and grabbed him helping him regain his balance. Zay looked at her beautiful serene face in spite of the horrors she experienced in this place. He had an urge to kiss her but knew it was inappropriate and restrained himself. "Sorry," he muttered.

"If that's all then why are we taught that certain behaviors and acts like homosexuality are *sins* and will send us to hell?"

Marcy laughed at Zay and squeezed his arm as he walked away.

Zay liked it but didn't acknowledge the gesture.

"Look at Deuteronomy thirty, It starts out saying if you listen to and obey the things God commands— "

"Aha!" Zay exclaimed and pointed a finger at her. "There it is; it says commands."

"You are so funny." Marcy slapped him on the arm. "You've been in church your whole life and still don't get it. That should show you why the people didn't listen; you don't listen either."

Zay felt stupid about something he thought he knew so well. His admiration for Marcy grew. Zay didn't like being the submissive one in this conversation, but Marcy clearly had the broader knowledge and understanding. He decided to take this conversation as far as it would go. He wanted to hear more, but Marcy rose from the bed and led him to the door. "It's time for you to go. Read all of chapter thirty, especially the part where God says, 'Hey you idiots, I didn't make this hard.'"

"God calls us idiots?"

"Only the ones that don't listen. Check out Deuteronomy thirty verse eleven."

"I think you just called me an idiot," he joked with her.

"Yeah, I did, but if you look at verses fifteen and sixteen in that chapter, you'll find the answer."

"I can't leave until you explain this to me." Zay sat back down in the chair and crossed his legs, steepling his fingers.

"Okay, in verses fifteen and sixteen, it says, "See!" It tells you He isn't hiding anything from you. It's there in plain sight for you to see."

"See what?"

"He didn't make rules we have to follow in order to be His children."

"But he said *command*."

"Yes, He did. He said, 'I have set before you life and prosperity and death and adversity.'"

"What does that mean?"

"It means God gives us a freewill to choose to follow the directions for life, He doesn't command us to follow."

Zay snickered. "That would be nice."

"It is, you idiot." Marcy smiled at him sweetly when she said the word.

"Okay, I'm still an idiot. I need more explanation."

"He said, because I show you how to live both good and bad, I command you choose the good. Then He tells us how to choose good."

"That's the million-dollar question everyone wants to know."

"And this is why He calls us idiots—because He gives us explicit instructions, and we still don't listen."

"What are the instructions?"

"Love God with your whole heart, walk in His ways, and keep His commandments and His statutes and His judgments. Then you live and multiply, and the Lord your God will bless you in your life."

"Sounds impossible. His statutes and judgments are too hard."

"Okay, Mr. Idiot. Listen. Imagine you build a beautiful home, with a nice big backyard, a swimming pool, games and toys, and beautiful flowers and trees. It's a paradise."

"Okay, but what does this have to do with God's harsh commands?"

"You're doing the same thing the people in Israel did. You won't even listen to understand because you are so dead set against God, you don't want to hear anything good."

Zay dropped his head. "Okay, go on with your fantasy," he said.

"Let's say you have a family that enjoys this beautiful house and yard, but you know the neighbors have dogs that are beasts. So, you build a fence around your property to protect your family."

"Okay, I get that." Zay looked up at Marcy.

"You tell your small children about the dangers outside the fence, and you **command** them to stay inside the safe zone."

"Sounds reasonable."

"But then one day your child hears people on the other side of the fence, and your child wants to go play with them. You tell him no, it's not safe. You know they have several ferocious animals over there, and the people do not like children. You give your child a stern warning. Why?"

"Because I love him, and I want him to be safe."

"Well, Mr. Idiot, I think there is hope for you yet. Remember, God said this isn't hard."

"Okay, where are you going with this? The kid gets out and gets injured, right?" Zay said.

"Yes, he gets out, but he doesn't get injured. Instead, you go rescue him and the dogs attack you. The child runs back to the safety of your yard. He hears the growling dogs and your cries of pain. He cries and starts saying, 'I'm sorry, I'm sorry.' You make it back to the yard, wounded, bleeding, and barely alive. What do you do?"

"Good question, do I die, or beat the kid?"

"Neither, you grab him and hug him and forgive him and tell him, 'This is why I don't want you to go there.'"

Zay stared at Marcy for a while. "I don't get it? What does that have to do with God's harsh rules?"

"Were the father's rules harsh?"

"Yes, but the rules were to protect the child from harm." Zay answered and then looked up to the right side of the room, "It was the father's love that set the rules and rescued the children when they broke the rules."

"Yeah, you got it. It's not hard!"

Zay laughed. "Are you saying God tells us the commands to keep us safe? From what?"

"Yes, to keep us safe from the dragons. Didn't the dragon drop you because it saw God in you?"

Zay nodded.

"See, it's not hard." Marcy handed the open Bible to Zay. "Read verse 17 in Deuteronomy thirty, Remember this is Moses speaking to the people right before they enter the promised land of Israel."

"But if you heart turns away, and you will not obey but are drawn away and worship other gods and serve them, I declare to you today that you shall surely perish." Zay stared at the words.

"Read verse nineteen," she added.

"I have set before you life and death, the blessing and the curse. So, choose life in order that you may live, you and your children." He looked up at Marcy and scratched his head. "But if He is God, why did He set death before us?"

"It's the neighbor's dogs, you idiot. Why build your house next to those beasts?"

"What are you saying?"

"In order to have freedom of will, we have to have freedom of choice. Without the choice, we would be programmed robots. It's the love of God that allows us to choose to obey Him or a dragon. It is our choice how we live."

"So, is Ronnie choosing to be homosexual?"

"I don't know, but it appears to be so." Marcy answered.

Zay shook his head and pursed his lips in a thin line. "What about that commandment about not being gay?"

"What about it?"

"It's harsh."

"You mean like the commandments against cheating on your wife, overeating, lying, being jealous. Oh, just read the list in Read Galatians 5:19."

Zay turned over to the passage, read it, and said, "It doesn't say anything about homosexuality."

"Really? What are the first three words?"

"Adultery, fornication and uncleanness."

"What are those things?"

"Cheating on your wife, sex without marriage and. . ... I don't know what uncleanness means."

"What is the most unclean place in your home?"

"Duh, the bathroom."

"Why?"

Zay blushes and laughs at his assistant. "Why would the Bible mention . . . you know. . . body waste."

Marcy smiles at his reaction and her face turns a little pink. She drops her head before she speaks.

"It unclean. When a man has sex with another man what body opening is used?

Zay gasps, "it is talking about homosexuality."

Marcy nods and adds, "The Bible also speaks against homosexuality in every instance it speaks of marriage between one man and one woman."

"How so?"

"Because homosexuality is an insult to the intimacy of a marriage of one man and one woman, in the same way as adultery and fornication. These three things are mentioned first because they are the most shameful and harmful." Marcy rose from the bed and walked across the room and opens her closet. She sees the marks she made when she first entered this place.

"What's all that scratching?" Zay asked when he saw them.

"I marked off the days in the beginning when Christine trapped me here." She sighed and counted the marks. "I quit after twenty-one days, mostly because I was too drugged to keep up, but because I didn't want to know anymore. That's the way we are."

"What do you mean?" Zay rose from the chair and walked up behind Marcy and put his hands gently on her shoulders. He realized her body was thin and drawn. The marks became squiggles after the first few.

"I didn't know the rules here or anything, I kept trying to tell them who I was and they kept poking needles in me." Marcy whimpered and wiped her eyes. She closed the door and walked back to her bed. Zay leaned against the closet door. He didn't know whether to leave or stay and comfort.

"I know the meaning of shame." Marcy moaned.

"How?" Zay sat on the bed beside her.

"Ignorance." She said.

Zay nodded. "I think that is where my lab assistant is and he isn't locked up."

"What do you mean?" Marcy looked up at Zay who sat hunched over with his face in his hands.

"He's angry at God and he's homosexual."

"How does ignorance fit?" Marcy rubbed Zay's back.

"He doesn't know how he fits in this world. He's so full of anger, he can't see anything else but."

"If you read the whole list in Galatians five, you will see those first three acts lead to many of the other choices we make such as anger, drunkenness, being mad at one another."

Zay handed the Bible back to Marcy. "I guess I'm still Mr. Idiot, I don't get it."

"Like it says, It ain't hard, Mister. You choose whom you will follow and obey. If you choose God, you have life. If you choose any other god, it will be death of peace, joy and eventually life. The question is not if God made Ronnie gay, the real question is; what god is Ronnie choosing to follow?"

Zay rang the bell for the orderly to let him out. Before the orderly arrived, he asked Marcy one more question, "How will this help us with our problem?"

Zay arrived back at the lab, pulled out his Bible, and read a little. "Yep, God did call us idiots." He smiled as he remembered Marcy's eyes when she laughed. He forgot about the dragon downstairs until he heard the roaring. It must be feeding time again.

Throwing the dogs down the feeding bin bothered Zay less and less. He still hated it, but he didn't get as depressed anymore. "Maybe that's how the people felt when they sacrificed their babies to the dragon gods: Molech, Marduk, and Chemosh. But they were human babies. I'm throwing animals to that fire-breathing monster, and it cuts my heart into shreds. How could they do it?"

Zay pulled the last whimpering dog out of the van—a big mutt with a sweet face. He stopped and petted the dog, and he even bent down and hugged it. When he did, he heard a voice in his head whisper one word that shook him to the core, "Abortion."

Zay blew his nose and wiped his face. He reached down and patted the dog. Tonight, he would take the pooch to his sister's house.

He picked up the slides from yesterday. To his amazement, not all the evidence he explored last Friday appeared on the slide. "How?" he muttered.

Before he melted under the weight of his own fear, he repeated the words he read in the Scriptures yesterday with Marcy. "I know, O Lord that a man's way is not in himself." He didn't know what to do next.

"Help!" Zay pleaded with God. Phobus heard him and laughed with a deep rushing wind that was heard all over campus.

Ronnie came bursting in the door as if he were going to fall on his face. With breathless sounds, he uttered a few disconnected words, "What, it, loud."

Zay held his hands over his ears and twisted his face in pain. "I don't think that was Phobus," Zay muttered and sat down.

Ronnie nodded his head. "Are you alright?"

"As far as I can tell." Zay looked at himself.

The dog came up beside Ronnie with its tail wagging, and he petted it. "Did you hear about. . ." Ronnie choked up before he could finish his sentence. He looked at Zay who waited for the rest of the sentence.

"Hear about?" Zay prodded him to continue.

"The incident on campus last night?"

"No?"

"The second-floor windows of the administration building are broken," Ronnie said as he finally caught his breath.

"Anyone hurt?"

"Not sure."

"Doesn't sound good." Zay turned toward the door leading to the basement.

"Don't!" Ronnie shouted.

"Why not?"

"What are you going to do?"

Zay sat down, or rather fell into the nearest chair. "What are we going to do?"

"We gotta kill it and fast, before someone gets hurt." Ronnie answered and looked in the window of the door as if he could see the four stories down. He turned back toward Zay.

"It's violent and dangerous now."

"I think I may know a way."

Ronnie grinned when he asked, "How?"

"Look at this." Zay pointed to a microscope.

Ronnie leaned in and gasped. "How'd that happen?"

"I'm not sure, but do you remember our last experiment?"

"Yeah, we moved the AGCT genes around to see if we could change the genetic code to recreate Phobus in his original form."

"We failed."

"Obviously," Ronnie nodded.

"But look what happened?"

"The whole thing is dead."

Zay smiled and shook his head in all directions. He held up his arms with the palms of his hands facing upward. His smile took on a silly expression as Ronnie watched him while he processed the information.

Ronnie grabbed their notes and read aloud the processes they had used the day before. "Look at this. We put two sugars next to each other and two phosphates together. That's the slide we're looking at?"

Zay nodded and rolled his hands one over the other.

"It's dead. The whole cell died."

Zay clapped his hands and exclaimed, "Right! Now, will it kill the organism?"

23

Disturbed Genetics

Can man make gods for himself? Yet they are not gods!

---Jeremiah 16:20

MARCY PICKED AT the food on her plate. Freedom didn't taste as good as she thought it would. Christine's little fiasco put Marcy a full semester behind. Even with the weeks of helping Dr. Troye, she couldn't get herself together in the outside world. She had grown use to the forced routine and isolation. She stood up and took her plate to the kitchen. She put it in the sink and stared at it. *Wash it!* she told herself.

She turned on the television and pulled a blanket over her legs. An invisible wall of loneliness surrounded her. Rebellion against that wall raged inside her. Still, she refused to move back into her old apartment with

Christine. Zay found this apartment for her when he and Dr. Greenstein checked her out of the hospital.

The doorbell rang. Marcy jumped. She must have drifted off to sleep because the clang of the bell startled her. With her heart racing, she rose to answer the door. She pulled her robe together and tied the sash. She peeked through the peep hole.

Zay!" she exclaimed and quickly opened the door.

"I'm sorry to bother you, Marcy, but I wanted to check on you."

She ran her fingers through her hair and wished she had taken time to get groomed and dressed. She probably even stank since she hadn't taken a shower since she arrived home three days ago.

"That's nice."

"Can I come in and visit with you for a minute?" Zay asked with his head ducked down.

Marcy smiled, realizing this was not an easy task for him. He was a brilliant man but not good with people, especially those of the female persuasion. Things were different between them outside the hospital.

"Sure, I'm sorry I'm such a mess."

After Zay sat down, he fumbled with one hand lapping over the other.

Marcy struggled to find an appropriate position in the presence of a man she admired while dressed in stinky night clothes.

"Marcy. . ." he started but paused.

"Yes," she answered hoping he would continue.

"What happened?"

"When?" Marcy didn't understand his question.

"Back there at the hospital. How did you—"

"How did I get there?"

"Yeah." Zay looked up at her for the first time since his arrival. He let out a small gasp when he saw her. "Marcy, what happened to you?" He exclaimed in amazement at her disheveled appearance.

"Do you mind waiting while I get showered and dressed?" she asked him, hoping he would wait, knowing she couldn't talk under these circumstances.

"I have a small errand to run. I'll go do that and come back. Is that okay?" Zay offered.

"That would be wonderful." She escorted him to the door, keeping her distance from him. After he left, she ran to the shower, jumped in, and started singing.

The doorbell rang and this time it didn't startle her. She wanted to talk to Dr. Troye, and now clean, groomed, and smelling good, she couldn't wait to see him . . . in real life.

She opened the door, and he smiled at her.

"I brought us some donuts," Zay said as he handed the box to Marcy. "You look like you feel better now."

"I do, and I apologize. I've been moping around here ever since I got home."

"Why? I should think you would have been ecstatic to get out of there."

"I spent so much time in there and lost so much. I felt sorry for myself, and I don't know what to do with myself." Marcy took the donuts and set them on the table. She opened the box and realized they looked wonderful. She pulled out some plates and placed a couple on each plate. She poured two glasses of milk and set them by the plates.

"Shall we?" she said to Zay and pointed to the table.

He sat down, and Marcy sat down opposite him.

He took a huge bite.

She stared at him even though his mouth bulged as he chewed the donut. He was the most handsome man she had ever seen.

"What do you need to know, Dr. Troye?" She coyly asked him while taking delicate bites. It tasted delicious.

"I don't understand how you ended up in Christine's place."

"I don't think I can tell you."

"Why not?"

"It's bizarre."

Zay chuckled at the statement. "Try me." He smiled at her and touched her hand.

Marcy felt her heart speed up, and the butterflies in her stomach took away the desire for more donut. She smiled. "Okay." She would tell him anything he wanted to know.

Patti felt the shift in the universe a few days ago. She didn't know what brought it on, but she knew it could only bring trouble. For her own protection, she had to get rid of Lapetos's 'samples.' Which were aborted babies he'd obtained from the clinic near the university. The availability of the samples amazed Patti. Each one was labeled with the experiment in which it was used.

The sample labeled number five—Sanders—intrigued her. She didn't know the Sanders woman, but she knew number five was the one that escaped their clutches that rainy night at campus housing. She shook her head at the memory. *Why did I think that was a good place to dispose of the monster?*

She drained the samples of the preservation fluid and threw each one in the commercial blender she had purchased. Once they were no longer recognizable as human, she dumped them in the large drain, taking the solid pieces and putting them in the dumpster behind the butcher's shop. But she kept sample number five.

Christine doubled over in pain. She finally gave in and called the only person she knew that would help her without question.

"Hello," a sweet voice answered. Marcy.

"I need help."

"Why should I help you?" Marcy said in a guarded tone.

"No reason, but you're the only friend I have," Christine said between gasps of pain.

"You mean, had."

"What?"

"Why should I be your friend?"

"Okay, I understand, but right now, please help me."

Marcy softened in her tone. "What's wrong?"

"I don't know, but the pain is awful," Christine said.

Marcy hung up, called an ambulance, and gave them Christine's address. She had failed to ask Christine where she was, so she hoped it was the right place.

"Dr. Troye," she called out to Zay. "That was Christine, and she sounds like she's in a lot of pain. Do you want to go to the hospital with me? You may get some answers."

Zay nodded and picked up his hat. "Yes."

Zay and Marcy arrived at the hospital a few minutes after the ambulance. They were quickly directed to a room where Christine thrashed and moaned.

Marcy ran over to her and took her hand. "What happened to you."

"I don't know; the pain's getting worse." At that time Dr. Holloway entered. "She appears to be in labor."

The hospital staff quickly removed her. Daniel saw Zay and said in a soft voice meant only for Zay., "It's strange."

But Marcy heard it, and she and Zay went to a private corner of the waiting room.

"Marcy, do you know who the father is?"

"I don't know. Christine likes attention, you know. She never had a father and not much of a mother, and she's flirts with anyone."

Zay sat back and crossed his legs. He stared out the window.

"This is not the first time, you know."

Zay heard Marcy but had lost the context of their conversation, "First what?"

"First baby. She had an abortion a few years back. She said it was awful, and she would never do that again."

Zay looked up and saw Daniel coming toward them. His face went pale and his shoulders slumped.

"What's wrong?" Zay asked him as he stood and met him.

"I'm tired, it's been a long day, but Christine's okay."

Marcy nodded her head.

"You can go see her," Daniel told Marcy.

"Thank you, Doctor." Marcy headed down the hall, not sure what she was going to say to Christine.

Daniel sat beside Zay. He shook his head as he leaned over with his elbows resting on his knees.

"You know this story gets stranger as time goes on."

"Yes, your right, but what is the latest that has you bamboozled?" Zay asked.

"It was a hydatidiform mole."

"A what?"

"It's a rare condition."

"What caused it?" Zay leaned into Daniel and spoke in soft tones.

"Let's say, it's a blessing the fetus didn't develop. The lab is examining it now." Daniel chuckled.

"Let me in on the joke." Zay smiled.

"The excitement of the forensic team when they saw it, was similar to a child going to Disneyland."

"What do you think they will find?"

"I can't make any speculations on a piece of tissue, but I can tell you objectively what I saw."

"What did you see?" Zay changed his question.

Daniel ran his fingers through his hair. "The placenta is small, but I found some small fetal parts." Daniel leaned over on his knees and buried his face in his hands.

"Daniel, there's something you're not telling me," Zay responded.

"We'll talk later after I get the lab report." Daniel sat up and leaned his head back.

"Is Christine going to be okay?"

"Physically, yes. But I can't be as sure about her mental status. It will be a miracle if she doesn't suffer mental problems from this."

Marcy joined the two men in the waiting room and heard Daniel's statement. She raised an eyebrow and asked, "How will we know the difference between sane and crazy with that one?"

"Let's get you home," Zay said as he extended his hand to Marcy.

She let a small smile creep on her lips and accepted his hand.

Once Zay and Marcy arrived at her house, he turned toward her. "Is there anything else you can tell me?"

Marcy kicked the ground with her foot and swayed a bit. "Remember when I said there was something else in that room besides Christine when she traded places with me?"

"I remember."

Marcy looked around even though no one else was near. "It was a dragon but not Phobus."

Zay left Marcy's house and headed back to Daniel's office.

Zay faced Daniel as soon as he walked in the door. "Okay, it's just us. Tell me."

Daniel smiled at his brother-in-law. He wasn't one to waste time or mince words.

"It's called homozygous because it is formed from two sperm, and, of course, it doesn't make a fetus. That's what made this one so unusual that we found a small part of a fetus buried in the mole. Which would be impossible."

"What did you find?"

"A hydatidiform mole looks like a cluster of grapes, so finding parts of a fetus among the blisters is unusual, especially when it's formed from two sperm. This one wasn't human."

Zay leaned back in his chair and sighed. "Do you know what this means?"

Daniel looked at him and groaned. "Yeah, the thing in your basement wants to procreate."

"I'm not so sure it was the one in my basement." Now Zay moaned.

"What are you saying?" Daniel furrowed his brow and stared at him. "Do you have another dragon?"

"No, but I do think Phobus is nothing more than an image the real dragon is using."

"I don't understand." Daniel furrowed his brows.

"I'm not sure, but there is more to all these strange occurrences than Phobus."

"What makes you think that?" Daniel asked.

"Phobus has been in that basement for eight years, with no conversation, action, or anything." Zay was in his element of reasoning out loud and teaching all at the same time. "Why, did he start talking to us? How did he leave the prison and return? From where did he gain the intelligence to leave a message?" He stood and walked over to Daniel's bookcase and stared at the rows of books for a few minutes. Then turned back to Daniel and ask his final question. "Why does a messed-up dragon exist? What is its purpose?"

24

Research

> Now when you tell this peop0le all these
> words, they will say to you, For what reason
> has the LORD declared all this great calamity
> against us? And what is our iniquity, or what
> is our sin which we have committed against
> the LORD our God?"
>
> ---Jeremiah 16:10

MARCY'S FIRST WEEK in the lab kept her busy. She had lost a semester of school, but this lab job would help her recover. Dr. Troye entrusted her with highly secretive information. He hadn't let her see the creature in the basement. She didn't really want to see it; hearing it was enough.

She turned on the microscope to watch the DNA strand she had just removed. It started the transcription phase. Marveling at the machine working in front of her eyes, she sighed and spoke out loud, "Lord, your signature is all over our bodies."

"Yeah, in the form of beatings." Came the sarcastic tones of Ronnie entering in the room.

"I thought you were through with the semester?" Marcy said.

"I am, but I have to finish this week on my work-study program. For the next three days, I'll be by your warm side." He chuckled.

"That's good. I like having some company instead of being left with that thing in the basement."

"Have you gone down to see him?"

"Not yet." She shuddered. "I don't think I want to."

"Come on, consider it part of your education. Besides, this may be your chore next week." Ronnie pulled a large box on a furniture mover in with him. "The wheels help with the weight, but they don't do much for the wiggles." He grabbed a second cart and handed the rope to Marcy. "You can pull this one."

"What's in the box?"

"Phobus' dinner."

Marcy's hand went over her mouth with a gasp when she heard whimpers. "Puppies?"

"We try to stay away from puppies and go for the sick and old animals that'll be put down in a day. He won't eat them after they're dead, so we have to get them live. But today they only had an abundance of a mixed-breed pups they couldn't adopt out."

"Why not?"

"These pups come from a dachshund and a mastiff. They're freaks too."

"Oh!" Marcy moaned. "This just gets worse."

"I haven't gotten used to it yet, but it does get easier to do."

The two rang for the elevator. When the doors opened, Ronnie pulled the box inside and motioned for Marcy to join him. She did.

Once the elevator stopped on the fourth floor and opened, Marcy caught a passing glimpse of the creature. She squealed.

"Now you know why we call it Phobus."

"I've never seen anything so grotesque." She kept her eyes directly on him, even though fear crept up her spine. Her feet moved her backward in small steps until she hit the wall with her back. Putting her hands behind her she muttered to Ronnie, "That's not it."

"Not what?" Ronnie asked as he petted the condemned puppies.

"The dragon that came from our television," she droned.

Ronnie stood beside her. "How's it different?" Ronnie asked, pulling the condemned dogs from the crate and tossing the poor, frightened animals into a cage of fear.

"The dragon from the television . . . it looked . . . pretty."

Ronnie laughed. "If a dragon can look pretty."

Marcy raised one side of her mouth but never took her eyes off Phobus. She watched him gobble the pups two and three at a time.

"It's not hungry," she mused.

"Why do you say that?"

"It's a game." She raised her hand and pointed to his mouth, full of puppies squealing and looking for a way out. "He's not swallowing or chewing."

Ronnie gazed at the dragon's partially open mouth. Marcy was right. The puppies were actually playing with each other.

"Let's leave." Ronnie pulled Marcy toward the elevator.

Once they were inside Marcy reached to push the ground floor button.

Ronnie grabbed her hand. "Wait." He pulled out his small utility tool he kept on his belt, like a good Texas boy. He pulled a screwdriver from the protective sheaf. He then removed two screws from a metal plate on the side of the elevator revealing a small window in the wall.

"I installed this right after I came here. The thing scared the liver out of me, so I wanted a safe place to observe without being observed."

"Does Dr. Troye know about it?"

"Yeah, he said it was brilliant. The elevator keeps that monster from prowling around in our thinking while we watch its activity."

The two gazed through the concealed window. Phobus put his head down and opened his mouth. The puppies jumped out of his mouth, tales wagging and playful little yips coming from them. The dragon rested its head on his clawed feet and let the puppies crawl over its face and body. A couple of the puppies curled up beside the goat portion of Phobus and went to sleep.

"They're not scared," Marcy whispered.

Ronnie nodded and closed the flap. He pulled a small notebook from his lab pocket and took notes.

"What are you doing?"

"Remember the experiment we did where we removed some of information from one of the DNA genes?"

"Yeah, it was the RNA used during the translation process. There were intervening sequences in the RNA that were spliced out and the RNA segment left behind would translate to polypeptides."

"Remember our thesis?" Ronnie asked Marcy as he kept making notes.

"Self-healing. The RNA nucleotides were not all used. So, the damaged ones were not translated to the next DNA strand."

"Dr. Troye used that experiment to change the DNA instruction on Phobus."

"How?" Marcy stood up and wrinkled her nose.

"It was a bit of trial and error, but the ultimate desire was to change the monster's appetite,"

"To what?" Marcy wrinkled up her nose.

"Make it eat plants."

Marcy took another look through the window. "So, have you tested it?"

"I'm about to." Ronnie handed Marcy his pen and paper. "Stay here and keep quiet."

He grabbed the other cart he'd left in the elevator and pulled it behind him. He took it to the cage and lifted it, pouring a golden stream of wheat into the cage.

Ronnie quickly returned to the elevator. "Let's watch."

Phobus took little notice of the wheat at first, but when the dragon turned his head with its nostrils toward the stack of wheat, it sniffed. Raising his head, it nudged the pile of wheat then extended its tongue and touched it.

Ding Ding, the elevator started moving up, and the shaft of the elevator blacked out the window of observation.

When the elevator door opened, Zay stood there. He jumped when he saw Marcy and Ronnie scowling at him.

"What are you two doing?" He smirked and entered the elevator.

"I think it worked," Ronnie said and handed the notes to Zay.

Zay scanned the papers. "Did it eat the grain?"

"Don't know; the elevator was called." Marcy snarled with a smile.

"I'm sorry guys."

Once they hit the fourth basement floor, they all shushed, and Ronnie opened the window."

The creature nudged the grain, and while he was doing so, one of the puppies came up to Phobus and brushed up against him. In a flash, Phobus turned toward the puppy and wrapped his long tongue around the unsuspecting pup. Then in one movement, Phobus swallowed. Like picking raisins out of oatmeal, Phobus grabbed them one or two at a time, sometime taking time to chew a bit and other times swallowing whole. The three dozen pups were all gone in only a few minutes. The pile of grain remained. Phobus stood, raised his head, roared, and then with a blast of his nostrils spread the grain outside of the cage.

"I don't think he likes grain," Marcy said sarcastically.

Ronnie grabbed the empty grain cart and started out but Zay stopped him.

"Let's give it some time." Zay pressed the *up* button. "What did we learn?" he asked his two student assistants when they reached the top.

"The RNA may remove damaged genetic material, but that doesn't change the basic genetics."

Zay sat down at his desk and made some notes, occasionally looking at Ronnie's notes.

"We discovered the gene code can remove old or damaged code, but if it needs to be replaced, it's with the same code."

"Our endgame is to destroy the thing, remember?" Ronnie interjected. "Not repair it."

"Okay, back to the drawing board. Let's look at body defense mechanisms with the pox virus virulence factor," Dr. Troye instructed the two of them.

While they worked, Ronnie revisited one of Marcy's statements during their last failed experiment. "You said Phobus wasn't the dragon that attacked Christine."

Marcy nodded.

Zay raised his head and stared at Marcy. "So, what did you see attack Christine?"

"A huge red dragon, although it was beautiful, if a dragon can be beautiful."

"How was it beautiful?"

"It moved with precision and fluidity, not like the awkward steps of that thing or the putrid color mixing in his scales."

Zay didn't speak, he crossed his arms and put a finger to his cheek. He didn't take his eyes off Marcy but watched her turn the electron microscope on. They both watched the ribosome divide the helix into two strands. The right strand moved smoothly through the RNA, but the left took a little longer since it had to be read backwards.

She shook her head and muttered, "Amazing."

Ronnie and Zay nodded. "It's hard to believe that very action is taking place in every cell of our bodies every day."

"How can there be so much precision in the sustaining of an organism and it be an accident? There has to be an intelligent design," Marcy said in a slow drawl while watching the awesome fluid movement of a living cell.

Ronnie stepped up behind her. "Intelligent yes, but the Christian God, no."

"You thinking little green men?" She winked at him.

He pushed his hand through the air and rolled his eyes.

Zay glanced over at them. "You two think you can find the origin of life?"

"Yes, that's my job today, and I fully intend to complete it," Ronnie said with his nose in the air.

"You'd better. The semester is coming to an end, and you're running out of time," Zay reminded him.

"You think we can continue next semester?"

"I doubt it. Money's running out, and there isn't much interest in the genome study right now. Only people putting money into it is the pharmaceutical companies and the military."

"So, what happens to Phobus when the money runs out?" Marcy piped in.

Zay stopped and sighed. "I pray we run out of Phobus before we run out of money."

The day wore on with no new discoveries. Ronnie sat up straight and stretched his stiff muscles. Then he turned to Marcy and asked, "Would you go to dinner with me tonight?"

Marcy smiled at him and nodded.

"I didn't think you would say yes," Ronnie's voice raised a little with the surprise.

"Why not? Remember, I've been locked up for the last three months."

Ronnie lost his enthusiasm and responded with a quiet sheepish voice, "Yeah, I guess even I look good to you."

"Get over yourself. You do look good; you're just a little soft."

Zay rose from his chair. "I think I'll call it a night too. Would you mind if I joined you?"

"No problem," Marcy said. "The more, the merrier."

Ronnie scowled.

The trio found a quiet corner table at Chili's restaurant. They ordered chips and queso.

While nibbling on the appetizer, Ronnie asked Marcy, "What did you mean by 'soft?'"

She smiled. "I meant you're floundering. You have a brilliant mind with science, but you have no passion for it. It's your job, not your heart."

"How do you know?"

"I'm floundering too, but that three months locked up in a psychiatric hospital helped put some focus on my goals."

"You read me right," he responded.

"Marcy's right," Zay added. "You have the ability but not the passion."

"According to my PTSD group, it's because I didn't have a father growing up, so I grew up confused."

"Confused how?" Zay asked.

"My anger at my dad. Why did he leave me?"

"I thought he was killed in action in Vietnam?" Marcy prodded.

"He was, but why did he join the Army? Why didn't he rebel and go to Canada, like so many others? Why did he choose to leave me?"

Zay and Marcy stared at their co-scientist as he continued to rant about a useless war. He stopped, reached over, and took a tortilla chip. He filled it with queso, popped it in his mouth, and looked away from his dinner mates. The muscles in his jaw worked much harder than needed.

A quiet pallor covered the trio for the remainder of the meal. The waitress placed the ticket on the table. The three of them stared at it.

"Whose treat?" Marcy said. "I'm broke."

Zay picked it up and pulled out the money. He laid it on the ticket, then he asked the two of them. "What do you really know about the Vietnam War?"

"Not much, other than my dad died there," Ronnie huffed.

"Me neither," Zay said. "I remember watching the news reels on television, and I started crying. My dad spoke of the brave men fighting to keep us free."

"Did it help?"

Zay shook his head. "I let dad talk for a while and then through big alligator tears I moaned, 'I don't want to go fight a war.'"

"What happened then?" Marcy asked.

"My dad laughed a gentle, comforting laugh and assured me that young children didn't go to war." Zay stopped talking and looked at his hands as he wove his fingers together. "The war ended the same year I turned eighteen."

A melancholy mood overtook the trio.

"Have either of you ever heard of the Mt. St. Olympus?" Zay finally asked.

They both shook their heads.

"Operation High Jump?"

"No, what about them? Were they in the Vietnam War?" Ronnie asked, curious about this strange turn of conversation.

"No, it was a military exercise sanctioned by James Forrestal, the first secretary of the Navy under President Truman."

"What does this have to do with our conversation about Vietnam?" Ronnie asked with a controlled but agitated voice.

"Nothing, but I think it has something to do with Phobus."

"I'm not following your reasoning." Ronnie said.

"It's not much of a line, but I was thinking about how the Vietnam war lasted long enough that what I feared as a little child almost came to pass."

"Yes, and—?" Marcy probed.

"What if something discovered in 1946 could be sitting in our basement?"

25

A Killing Wound

> Many nations will pass by this city; and they will say to one another, 'Why has the LORD done thus to this great city?' Then they will answer, Because they forsook the covenant of the LORD their God and bowed down to other gods and served them'"
> ---Jeremiah 22 7-8

RONNIE SHIVERED WHEN he entered his room. The temperature outside was a Texas firestorm in the triple digits, but this room felt like a meat locker. He could even see his breath.

Flipping on the light switch, he noticed the air conditioner wasn't on. How could this room be so cold? He wrapped his arms around himself and headed to the bathroom. There, he shut the door and turned on the overhead heat lamp. After a few minutes, his shivering stopped. He took a shower, wrapped his robe around him, and walked back out.

Whoosh! The heat slapped him in the face like a tornado. He gasped for breath and stumbled toward the air conditioner, stubbing his toe on his dresser.

Once the refrigerated air filled the room, he felt his lungs sucking in air without pain. He stood in front of the window unit for several minutes with his eyes closed and raised his arms to get the air all around him. With the cool embracing him, he opened his eyes and sighed in relief.

There it was in front of him. The dragon from the ceiling picture in all its symmetry and regalia. Ronnie gasped and reached for the phone. He quickly dialed Dr. Troye, but the open maw of the creature in front of him dripped venom from huge fangs only inches from his face. Stunned by the enormous size of the creature, he dropped the phone.

Ronnie wrinkled his nose at the awful stench of the creature's breath. He opened his mouth to speak but no words came. Instead, the creature before him sank its poisonous fangs into his chest.

Ronnie cried out, "God, help me!" He gazed wide-eyed into the scaly, horned face of a monster until his breath left his body.

"What do we need to do?" Marcy asked Zay.

He stared at the slide on the electron microscope. His stillness and wrinkled brow bothered her.

The quiet of the lab gave a sense of being deserted. Even Phobus remained quiet.

A cloak of fear rested over them without cause. Still, it was a fear so dense it felt like something occupied the lab besides the two scientists.

Zay tried to bring security back to them. "You know we're ahead of the other labs?"

"Well, you are brilliant." She smiled.

"I don't think so; I sense something telling me what to do."

"What?" Marcy frowned.

"The red dragon behind Phobus. I think he tells me what to do."

"Looking at that slide makes me wonder how Phobus remains alive." Marcy moaned as she waved her hands in the air.

"He won't last much longer. Look at the deterioration in his DNA molecules since you injected the last set of modified AGCT cells into him."

"I noticed it significantly from this morning to this afternoon."

Zay nodded his head and cupped his chin in his hand. He looked at the door leading to the basement where Phobus stayed. "He sure has been quiet." He jumped up and started down the four flights of stairs. Marcy followed.

Once the two of them arrived, they saw Phobus laid out on the floor, gasping for breath.

"What's wrong with him?"

"Nor sure, but he looks like he's taking his last breaths. After eight years of laughing at us, why is he dying now?"

"Maybe, he served his purpose?" Marcy shrugged her shoulders.

Zay nodded. "Or our plan worked. By placing the sugars and phosphates in his genes next to each other, it killed his cells, killing him."

"Or—" Marcy stopped, unsure about how to proceed. "Maybe the red dragon doesn't need Phobus anymore," she finally choked out.

"You, me and Ronnie . . . we've all seen the red dragon." Zay said loudly as he tried to put the pieces of the puzzle together.

"Uh-huh, are we next?" Marcy stammered.

"I'm not sure, however, it all has to do with the image."

"What image?"

"There's one of those 3-D pop-out pictures in Ronnie's dorm room. It's a red dragon, a horse, and a boy."

"Are you saying the red dragon is just a picture?"

"No, it moves about freely, both seen and unseen. I'm saying it hovers over Ronnie day and night."

Marcy shuddered. Zay pulled her close to him and stroked her back. "I know, it's scary."

"What can we do?"

"We keep working on the dragon here. But I'm going to check on it. It's been strangely quiet. You want to come with me?"

"No, but I'm coming anyway." Marcy fell in step with Zay as he opened the cage door and cautiously approached the huge dragon head laying on the floor, resting on the old carpet.

"Hey buddy, what's going on?" He surprised himself at his tenderness toward the dragon. He almost—no—he did feel love for this creature that had been the focus of his life for the last eighteen months.

Phobus opened his eyes and spoke to Zay's mind. "I'm the aberration that detracts from the real thing." Then he raised his head slightly and opened his mouth. "See?"

"What?" Zay asked as he stared into the broad mouth of Phobus. Then he noticed the human teeth covering his mouth. The split tongue was gone, and in place was a normal, albeit huge, human-looking tongue.

"Find the lab; find answers."

"I am. It's upstairs," Zay reaffirmed.

"No, the lab that made me."

"How do I find it?"

"History." Phobus said aloud and then dropped his head on the floor. A last puff of smoke came from the dragon's mouth along with a moan of great agony.

Zay wiped a tear from his cheek. "Bye, buddy" he said out loud and stroked the fur of the goat body. He couldn't bring himself to touch the scales of the head.

Marcy stood outside the cage, listening. She too wiped a tear from her eye. "He left us a puzzle."

Zay turned away from the cage. This time, he didn't lock the door. "Somehow, his death and the image in Ronnie's dorm room are connected, but I don't have a clue how. This is a bigger puzzle than discovering the proteins in DNA and RNA."

As the two of them topped the stairs, Marcy voiced the obvious question. "What are we going to do with his body?"

Zay shook his head. "I don't know. Right now, I need time to process all this."

When they reached the ground floor, the phone was ringing. "It sounds urgent," Zay mocked.

"Dr. Troye? This is university hospital. Do you know a young man by the name of Ronnie Walton?"

"Yes, he works in my lab," Zay responded.

"He has listed you as his contact person. Could you possibly come and provide permission for treatment?"

Zay didn't answer, he stared at Marcy.

"What's wrong?" She asked as his mouth stood agape and his flesh turned pale.

"It's Ronnie," was all he could say.

Marcy kept quiet as he listened to the voice on the other end of the telephone line. "What happened?" she asked after Zay hung up.

"I don't know, but he's bad. His whole body is swollen. The doc says he believes it's some kind of poison, but he can't find the source. He's afraid to give him an antidote since he can't identify the poison."

"What are they going to do?"

Zay took off his lab coat and threw it onto the couch. He grabbed his coat and keys, leaving his briefcase behind. "Are you coming with me?" he asked.

"You bet." She followed him out the door.

Zay suddenly stopped and Marcy ran into him. "Michael," he said.

"What?" Marcy wrinkled her brow.

"Ronnie was going to a PTSD support group my cousin, Michael, leads for Vietnam veterans and families of those killed or missing in action."

"How does this help?" Marcy asked softly.

By this time, Zay returned to the lab and dialed Michael.

"This is Zay," he said when Michael answered. He quickly gave him the scenario about Ronnie.

After hanging up, he turned to Marcy. "He'll meet us there."

Marcy raised an eyebrow at the statement. Zay busily gathered a file and stuffed it under his arm.

Zay walked as fast as he dared in the hospital halls to get to Ronnie's room. As he entered, he saw the young man, swollen beyond recognition. He stood beside the bed with a blank mind and a wounded spirit.

"Hang on, buddy, you gotta' be strong," Zay whispered to him. He didn't know what else to do. Should he tell the doctor about the dragon or would that land him in a psychiatric room?

Michael entered Ronnie's room. Zay smiled at the apparition over Michael's head. A strong military man riding a muscled white horse. On his uniform flap it read Davis and the stripe on his sleeves identified him as a captain.

Captain Davis dismounted and walked to Ronnie's bedside. Ronnie opened his eyes, smiled and muttered, "white horse."

Davis shouted, "Holy, Holy, Holy, are you Lord Almighty!"

Michael prayed.

Zay groaned with agony.

Marcy put her hand on Michael's shoulder and joined in the prayer.

The light in the room saturated the patient and the swelling subsided. The poison injected into his body by the wicked one roaming the earth to devour anyone available seeped from his pores.

Zay watched and muttered to himself, "I guess dad is right. You are real."

26

Returning the Merchandise

He who dwells in this city will die by the sword and by famine and pestilence; but he who goes out and falls away to the Chaldeans who are besieging you will live, and he will have his own life as booty."

---Jeremiah 21:9

PATTI RAKED HER fingers through her hair. The destruction of Lapetos' experiments moved slowly. She kept looking toward the door, expecting law officials with battering rams against her door.

Cook noted her nervous fidgeting. "Madame, why you worry?"

"Don't call me Madame," she shouted. "You know this place is . . . evil."

"Yes, ma'am but no more."

"You think not? Look around us." Patti waved her arms in the air, stopping on the four residents in the nearby cages.

"They won't leave," Patti moaned.

"Where can they go?" Cook asked.

"Home."

"They don't know home anymore."

Patti turned back to the children watching her as they huddled on their thin mattresses in the cold concrete cells.

"Like me, you, and Michelle."

Patti moaned and raised her head. "What can I do?"

"Take them home?" Cook said in a soft voice.

Patti nodded. "I guess you're right, but right now we have to get rid of all this." Patti put her hands on her hips as she watched the blender turn tiny human flesh into goo. "It's vile," she muttered.

"Miss Patti, you go. I'll finish."

Patti looked at Cook and smiled. "Where do we go? Where is our home?"

"I'm going to a small town and open a restaurant."

Patti smiled at the thought of Cook's wonderful meals being served to the public. She looked at the pitiful waifs helping her clean the lab. With sadness in her voice, she said, "Maybe you will have jobs for them, real jobs where they can start over."

Cook nodded. Patti picked up the jar labeled Sanders and headed up the stairs. She stopped and turned toward Cook. "I think I'll put this place up for sale."

"Good idea, Miss Patti," Cook responded as she swept and mopped. She handed the oldest boy a drill and said, "Let's take those doors down and clean out those cages." The four residents nodded and smiled as they worked on dismantling the barred rooms they occupied—a first step to accepting freedom.

Patti opened the front door, carrying the Sanders fetus in a plain brown box. She gasped when a couple stood in front of her. The man held his fist in the air.

"Sorry, ma'am, I was about to knock on your door."

Breathing heavily, Patti gave a weak smile. "What can I do for you?"

"One of our former neighbors found her long-lost daughter."

Patti didn't understand their message, but it did make her heart race. She smiled keeping a calm outside demeanor. "That's nice."

"They said their daughter told them you helped her. We are . . ." The man hesitated and ducked his head.

"We're hoping you can help us find our son," the woman said, picking up his sentence. "He's been missing for three years."

Patti could feel her heart racing. She cleared her throat. "Maybe."

"His name is Scott, but we called him Scotty."

"Come in." Patti sat the box on the credenza in the hallway. The couple followed, and Patti motioned toward a couch for them to sit. She sat opposite them.

"Your Scott is here."

The parents leapt from their seats and turned their heads from side to side. "Where is he?" The father put his arms around his wife.

"He's afraid to see you," Patti intoned with measured calm.

"Why? We love him."

"He thinks he is unlovable; he's been through a lot."

"We don't care. We want him back in our family."

"What if he chooses not to be a part of your family?"

"Why would he do that?"

"Because he's different now."

"The mother buried her face in her hands. "I don't care. He's my son."

"Wait here." Patti went to the basement, closing the door behind her. Once she entered the lab, she called out, "Scotty."

The red-headed boy turned and look at her with dancing green eyes. Hearing his real name must have given him joy.

"I have something to tell you." Patti took him by the hand and led him out of the lab. "Do you want to see your parents?"

"I'm . . . scared," he stammered and shuffled his feet. "What if they won't love me anymore?"

"Listen, Scotty, they have been looking for you. They love you. I would give anything to see my father."

"So why don't you go see him?" Scotty asked.

"He died a few years back, but he was the only one who loved me as I am."

"Did he want to change you?"

"Yeah, and he succeeded."

"What do you mean?"

"I no longer do those bad things to innocent people." Patti smiled at him and stroked his face. He was growing into a man with peach fuzz on his face.

"What bad things did you do?" Scotty put his hand over hers and leaned into it.

"Scotty, I'm the reason, you're here. I'm the one who caused those bad things to happen to you."

Scotty looked up at her and wrinkled his brow. "You are?"

She nodded. "I'm so sorry. Please go to your parents. They love you, and they don't care what you've done."

Scotty nodded, and the two of them headed toward the living room. When he saw his mom and dad holding their arms out to him, he ran to them as hard as he could. The parents enveloped him and the three of them wept.

Patti watched and thought, *Oh Paps, if only I could have told you who I was, would you have embraced me?*

The reunited family walked out the front door of Patti's restored mansion.

The father stopped and turned to her, "Are there others?" he asked.

She nodded and held up three fingers.

"Do you know who they are?"

She shook her head and wiped a tear from her cheek. "They're afraid to go home."

"Why?"

"Because of the awful things we have all done."

The mother took her hand and said, "I'm so sorry for your trials, but there is nothing any of you could do to make your parents not love you."

"Even gross and terrible things done to their young bodies?" Patti asked.

"You were victims of evil, as we all are."

The mother's face had a softness of expression which Patti had never seen before. Patti wondered what made the difference between this mother loving her son and Lilith's harshness and constant demands. She sighed and whispered, "I wish I could have known my mother, I bet she was soft like that mother."

After they were out of sight, Patti picked up her box and headed toward the university lab and the office of Dr. Zay Troye. She waited in the parking lot until most everyone was gone. While waiting, she wrote a note and stuck it in the box.

Dressed in a delivery person's shirt Patti approached the science building. The door was open. She walked straight to the Bioengineering lab and office of Dr. Troye, where the monster of her making resided. There she set the box in front of the door.

27

The Source

> Here the word of the LORD, "Behold I am about to bring a calamity upon this place, because they have forsaken Me and have made this an alien place and have burned sacrifices in it to the other gods, and because they have filled this place with the blood of the innocent.
>
> --- Jeremiah 19:3-4

MARCY STUBBED HER toe as she reached for the door knob to enter the lab. She looked down and saw a box. She picked it up and set it on the work table. Then she proceeded with her day and picked up her work from yesterday.

When Zay came in, he tossed his coat over the box since he was carrying a large tub and a chainsaw.

"What are you going to do, Lumberjack?" Marcy sneered.

"Get rid of a body," he answered as if it were an everyday occurrence.

Marcy's face turned pale. She had forgotten about Phobus. She pulled on a protective apron like Zay's and followed him downstairs.

"You don't have to come if you don't want to."

"It's okay, I'll help."

The two silently rode the elevator with normal heartbeats and breathing. No sweat droplets trekked across their face. The first time they entered the dragon lair with no fear.

Zay sat the big tub beside Phobus' body. Already, the scales receded while the body swelled. He pulled a mask over his face and goggles over his eyes. He started the saw. Before he made the first cut, he patted the dragon and muttered, "Thanks for the help, you ugly devil. You sure boosted my career."

The goat legs came first and were tossed into the tub. Next came the separation of the reptile from the mammal. Zay shuddered. "What's going to come out?" he asked before he started cutting.

Marcy raised her hands in the air and shrugged.

The cut didn't happen easily. There was much resistance. Zay moved from one side of the long reptilian neck to other, hoping for a better angle. The huge chain saw would not penetrate the scales. A loud roar came from the head when Zay moved closer. Startled, he dropped the chainsaw without turning it off and backed away from the body. He pressed himself against the wall and held his hands over his ears.

Marcy was outside the cage, staring at him with her hands over her ears. She was shouting, but Zay couldn't hear the words above the continuing roar.

It wasn't Phobus. It was the wail of a dragon, a large living dragon. It even sounded as if he could have been mourning. After more than ten minutes of the continual noise, it stopped. Only the engine of the saw continued as it danced over the floor coming dangerously close to Zay's legs.

Marcy ran into the cage, jumped over the body of Phobus, and picked up the saw handle, tripping the off switch. "This has a safety on it. Why didn't it stop running?"

"I wondered the same," Zay answered and took the saw from her looking over the release arm which should have shut the saw off when he dropped it. There were nicks in the back of the reptilian body. Both he and Marcy stared at the bloodless corpse. Inside the cut open scaly neck of the reptile lay the image of the body of a small infant, curled in fetal position, with eyes closed and one arm missing.

Both Zay and Marcy heard a whisper in their heads. *Thank you.*

Then in a flash the body of Phobus went up in smoke, leaving the floor covered in ashes arranged in the words of a familiar phrase, *the planting of seed is singular, but the harvest comes in multiples.*

"What does that mean?" Marcy moaned.

"I don't know." Zay bent over and picked up a chunk of reptilian flesh. He threw it in the tub with the goat legs. "At least we still have some of his DNA."

"What now?"

"He's gone. We go back to work on our DNA and never speak of this to anyone. Do you understand?"

Marcy nodded.

When the two of them reached the lab, they shut the door without locking it. They pulled off their aprons now covered in goo from Phobus and threw them in the tub with the body parts. The aprons covered the gross contents of the tub.

They sat on the couch, under the only window in the room—the place where Marcy, Zay, and Ronnie brainstormed ideas.

Zay patted Marcy's hand. "Thanks for the help."

"I didn't do anything," she responded.

"You kept me from being attacked by a chain saw." Zay winked at her. Then he sighed and leaned his head back.

Marcy rose and poured herself a cup of coffee. She didn't sit on the couch but picked up a recent study, leaned against the desk, and began reading while sipping her coffee.

Zay drifted into a restless sleep after the adrenaline rush wore off. Marcy felt it too. She tried to read but the words weren't making sense. It was almost as if they kept changing. She kept seeing that phrase pop up in her paper.

At one time she noticed the sentence had an added phrase. *The planting of seed is singular, but the harvest comes in multiples; it's harvest time.*

She shook her head and the words went back to the scientific words of the study.

"What's wrong?" Zay groaned as he stretched and stood.

"This journal keeps changing its words."

He laughed.

"It isn't funny," Marcy scolded.

"I know, it's ironic. My mother had a book that kept doing that."

"How?"

"Not sure, but it was a book full of false ideas about an idol. The book was written long ago."

"Do you think this journal is writing about an idol?"

Zay walked over and took the journal from her hand. He read the page Marcy had open. "This is strange," he said, then he sat down in the chair next to hers.

"Are you seeing the words change?"

"Sort of."

"I read this article last night." He thumbed the book, checked the cover of the journal and scratched his head. "It's about—"

"hydatidiform moles, just like Christine's."

"Have you read this?" Zay asked, setting the journal down on the desk and refilling his coffee cup.

"Yes, it's quite interesting. No one knows what causes them. There are several different types, and they seldom have any fetal parts in them. One type has ninety-six chromosomes."

"Wow!" Zay exclaimed. "No wonder it's weird, when we only have forty-six total with twenty-three from each parent."

"That's the other part that's weird."

"What?"

"Some of them are formed when two sperm come together and try to fertilize each other."

Zay's mouth fell open and his hand went to his forehead. "Daniel said Christine's was formed from two sperm."

"You okay?" Macy asked at his reaction.

"Yeah, I'm okay, but think about that, Marcy."

"I have been. It's rather phenomenal."

"Two of the same cannot make a new."

"It's like the amylase in the DNA molecule. If you put the A and C together, the molecule dies."

"What is this DNA trying to tell us?"

"He created us in His image," she stated.

"Yeah, I get that, but this goes deeper."

"Not really deeper so much as plainer."

"Right." Zay turned and paced the room with one hand on his hip and the other under his chin.

Marcy smiled at his common habit.

"It's in our DNA."

"What?" Marcy asked while still staring into a microscope.

"Homosexuality."

"I thought you said it wasn't."

"I was wrong. It is. But not in the way we've been looking."

"Okay, explain." Marcy looked up at him and put her hand on her hip.

"The A & C Amylase are both Phosphates and the G and the T are both sugars."

"Yes." Marcy lengthened the word to state the obvious; they had learned this together.

"But if you put an A with a G and a C with a T, they don't form the helix, instead the whole thing dies, like Phobus. That's what we did to him."

Marcy's face brightened, and she pointed a finger in the air. "God made them live only as opposites."

"This DNA molecule is the blueprints of God's image, He placed in every single one of our cells."

Marcy fell into the same pacing pattern opposite Zay.

"Even in the tiny details, God is showing His plan," he said.

"For what?" Marcy stopped and looked at him.

He stopped pacing too and sat. "What an amazing God."

Marcy sat down beside him. He reached over and took her hand in his. He held it in an intimate motion. Then he turned her hand over and looked at it. "Look."

Marcy looked at her hand resting on top of Zay's palm. She took a deep breath. Her heart raced with the nearness of him.

"It fits. Perfectly. It's comfortable for both of us."

Marcy smiled and nodded.

"God made men and women different so they would fit together. They also thrive together and reproduce. But when the same come together—"

"They both die," Marcy whispered.

Zay and Marcy both leaned back on the couch. They stared at the box containing Phobus.

Zay pointed to the tub. "But—"

"That thing was not God's creation," Marcy said with sternness.

"No, it wasn't. It was the mixing of pieces of God's creation in order to make a new creature."

"Yeah, but why?" Marcy voiced her concern, certain Zay was thinking the same thing.

"And by whom?"

"The thing Christine gave birth to, did it. . ." She didn't know how to finish her sentence.

"Did Phobus rape Christine? Is that what you're trying to ask?"

"Something like that, but not exactly."

"Christine served him as an incubator for his own work. Her body couldn't hold the perversion and spit it out. I don't think she knows what happened."

"I saw it, and I don't know what happened."

"Marcy, what you saw was not Phobus."

She took a deep breath, squeezed Zay's hand and said, "I know."

Zay stood and walked to the worktable. He picked up his coat and took it to the wall peg where he usually hung it. He turned and looked at the box. "What's this?"

"It was by the front door when I came in."

Zay opened the box and retrieved the note inside.

Dear Dr. Troye,

I think I met you a few years back when you were with your sister, Barbara. You probably don't remember me. Which I hope you don't. But if you do, please do not try to contact me.

I am leaving this preserved fetus with you. It was used by myself and my uncle in an experiment in cross-breeding of species. We made a monster that ended up in the university lab. I don't know if you still have it or not, but if you do, this fetus is the tissue we used to create him. I thought it might be some help to you. If not, discard it in your own way.

Tell your sister I am not angry at her. In fact, I thank her for my freedom from Madame Lilith, but I am still searching.

Patti Pan Paulsen

Zay pulled the jar out of the box and stared into the open eyes of a five- to six-month fetus, identical to the image Marcy and Zay saw in Phobus. "Poor baby, you never had a chance."

Marcy stepped up beside him and stared at the baby in the jar. She could see one arm had been cut off. Then she gasped and pointed to the label at the baby's feet. *Christine Sanders.*

"What does that mean?"

Zay looked closely. "I think it means this aborted baby of Christine Sanders is the source of the tissue that gave life to Phobus. That's why the dragon came out of the television and claimed her instead of you."

28

Evidence

> And you will say to them, If you will not listen to Me, to walk in My law, which I have set before you, to listen to the words of My servants the prophets, whom I have been sending to you again and again but you have not listed; then I will make this house a curse to all the nations of the earth.
>
> ---Jeremiah 26:3-6

MICHAEL AND SHARON arrived at the hospital. Kneeling beside Ronnie's bed was Michael's war buddy, Sid. With furrowed brow, his lips moved with a few faint utterances. Michael put his hand on the man's shoulder. Sid opened his eyes and looked up at Michael, then he rose from the floor slowly due to arthritic knees. Michael helped him up knowing this prayer time on his knees required great physical sacrifice.

"It's been rough. This boy's suffering. A terrible dragon is beating on him. I ain't never prayed that hard before in my life. Even when I was in Nam." Sid groaned.

"What do you mean?" Sharon prodded.

"Stronger, and with a fierce, hate. I never felt so much hate." Sid answered while shaking his head.

Michael patted Sid on the back and said, "Go get something to eat. We'll take over."

The weary Vietnam veteran and spiritual soldier nodded his head, slipped his Bible into his pocket. "Thanks." He stroked Ronnie's cheek. "We won't leave you, little buddy, we won't leave you," he choked out, wiped his eyes, pursed his lips, and nodded once again at Michael before he left the room.

Michael touched Ronnie's head. He was cool. "At least he has peace for now."

The nurse entered the room as Michael made the statement. "They said it was a rough night in report." She injected something into Ronnie's IV.

"How is he being treated medically?" Sharon asked as the nurse made notes of the injection on his chart.

"We're throwing everything we can at it. He'll get some anti-venom later."

"Did he get some last night?" Sharon asked.

The nurse opened the chart and pulled her finger across the paper. "Yes, he received rattlesnake anti-venom."

"Do you think it helped?" Michael asked.

"Truthfully, I think it made it worse. I told the doc too, so I'm hoping he'll cancel the next one." The nurse answered.

Sharon picked up Ronnie's hand, the swelling lessened, but she noticed something different. The skin revealed scales, with reddish-purplish tones of burned skin. "Did you notice this?" she asked the nurse and pointed it out.

"Jeepers, what hit this boy?"

"Look like the serpent left more than venom," Sharon said.

The nurse looked at her with wide eyes. "That could explain a lot."

"What do you mean?" Michael asked as the nurse inspected the rest of Ronnie's body.

"Ever since he got here, we've been seeing and hearing strange things."

"Like what?" Michel asked.

"Roaring and red flashes. It's getting harder to keep staff on the night shift. I've been working doubles for the last three days."

"Has he been alone anytime?" Michael asked the nurse.

"Nope, nary a second. You guys have been here with him, praying. I think you're the only reason I come in. I believe in the power of prayer and seeing what this one is going through makes me a believer in the work of a devil too."

Sharon nodded. "Me too."

After the nurse left the room, Michael asked Sharon, "What do you think?"

"I don't think she found any more patches like the one on his hand.

"Sharon, look!" Michael exclaimed, pointing to Ronnie's face twisting in a mask of pain.

Michael called the nurse who came and examined him. She shook her head. "Must be a bad dream."

Michael took Ronnie's hand and bowed his head. He fervently prayed. "Lord, let Ronnie see the truth."

When the words of Michael's prayer reached the throne room of God an angel messenger named Davis swept Ronnie's spirit upon his horse.

Ronnie heard Michael's prayer and said 'yes' in the silent chamber of his mind. Davis rode up beside him on the familiar white horse and raised Ronnie from the bed onto the back of the horse. The horse bolted at a speed that could not be seen by human eyes and entered into the courts of the Holy One. Where the large red dragon called Belial stood in front of a high and lofty judges bench.

A bolt of lightning struck near Belial. It was Michael's prayer. Ronnie shuddered at the tremendous power of the lighting strike.

"The earth warrior Michael is a powerful enemy of the dragons. His skills have been honed with practice." Davis said to Ronnie when he saw him shudder. "Do not underestimate the power of prayer from an obedient saint." Davis pointed Ronnie to an area in front of the judge's bench. There stood his mother and a tall strong handsome man in his thirties stood beside her with his arm wrapped around her waist.

"Who is he?" Ronnie questioned.

"Your dad. Listen to him, while you can." Davis instructed.

Ronnie's dad smiled at him before he spoke. "I didn't want to leave you. Each deployment was harder than the last, but I was near retirement. I knew I would then have plenty of time with you."

"Why did you let yourself get killed?" Ronnie said with the sound of an accusation.

"That dragon came after me." his dad pointed to Belial.

"How?" Ronnie scorned.

"Near the end of the war, the 101st Airborne Division under the command of Ben Harrison carried out a supposedly covert operation to reopen a fire support base.

"We fought a no-win battle with ten North Vietnam soldiers to one U.S. soldier. There were seventy-five of us that fell that day before a blanket air-bomb ended the battle twenty-three days after we entered."

"You were a soldier; that was your job." Ronnie scowled. "I want to know why you took that last deployment when you didn't have to."

"I don't know how you know that, but that is partly true."

"He told me." Ronnie pointed to Belial.

"That was the last battle of the war, Nixon had already begun pulling troops out. We didn't know the North Vietnamese were watching us set up the base. I was coming home for good after that battle."

"Why didn't God protect you?" Ronnie looked at his dad.

Belial puffed.

Mrs. Walton stepped up to Ronnie. She took his hands in hers.

"Mom? Are you dead too?" Ronnie asked her. She smiled and shook her head. No I am in prayer for you." She answered him. "The Holy One invited me."

"I don't understand." Ronnie moaned and looked around the celestial court.

"I don't understand either. It is a privilege to be in the court of God and having the ability to plead for my son." She stopped speaking for a moment and looked up at the young face of her deceased husband. "It's a gift to see your dad again, even briefly."

"Have you been here before?" Ronnie asked her.

"Every time I kneel and pray for you, I enter the courts of God, pleading your case. But this is the first time I have been here with you and your dad."

"Mom, this is my dream, it's not real." Ronnie kissed her hands and smiled.

"No my sweet, it's more real than your body lying in that hospital bed. But this is not your final court hearing."

"I'm dreaming." Ronnie insisted and let go of her hands. He turned away from his parents and walked toward the bench. However, he couldn't reach it, with each step the bench moved further away.

"What's happening?"

"God is giving you more time. Your life hangs in the balance and that dragon wants to devour you. Your father and I are praying for you. We want you to know truth and trust what you learn."

"Like dad did, it got him killed." Ronnie waved his hand in the air toward his dad. He then noticed his dad looked to be about thirty years of age while his mother showed all fifty years of life in her face.

"Ronnie, he wanted to be with us as a family." Mrs. Walton began to argue, but Ronnie interrupted her.

"What good is a family if it's going to be broken?" Ronnie's voice choked as he held back the tears.

His mom nodded. She bent over and kissed Ronnie on the hand. She turned to his dad. "I dedicated myself to him afterward. I think I did him wrong."

"How?" his dad asked.

"I kept him in church because I thought that was where he would find men to be role models, like his father."

"Did he find a mentor?" Davis asked.

"No, but he did find a standard he would never be able to reach."

"The church people felt sympathy for us, and they really went out of their way to help us readjust."

His dad nodded. "That's the character of the church."

"Yes, but the problem in Ronnie's heart was invisible to us."

Ronnie smiled at his mother and nodded. "Everyone told me I was the man of the house. How can a five-year-old measure up to a war hero?" he asked his dad.

"A five-year-old seeking to be like a man he never knew, but one presented as being perfect in every way . . ." Ronnie continued his rant while his dad looked pensive.

"As he grew," his mother added, "I depended on him more and more for companionship, and my conversation always ended with my describing his dad as perfect." She dropped her head.

Ronnie listened with rapt attention. He had never heard these things from his mother.

"Did you know he claims to love another boy?" Mrs. Walton asked her husband. She added, "It's robbing him of life's joy. He's always angry and anxious."

Belial puffed again.

Ronnie waited for his dad's response. Then someone laid their hand tenderly on his face.

"His temperature is going up again," Sharon said as she felt Ronnie's head, and neck.

"What are you thinking about?" Michael asked.

"What makes a person think their homosexual? There isn't any evidence of permanent homosexuality" Sharon stated.

"What do you mean?"

"Like a person's color . . . that's permanent and out of their control, or like gender, or your genealogy. Those things are permanent and are part of the person. But homosexuality is something one does, not who they are."

"Something happens to the person. Kind of like that cursed little dragon you found" Sharon added.

"He wasn't supposed to exist, and yet he did. Why?" Michael rose from the chair and let Sharon sit. He moved to Ronnie's bedside.

"Because someone tried to be a god by building a god." Sharon answered.

"Sounds like a fool," Zay said as he walked into the room and greeted his cousin.

"It is and who would know that better than you, the keeper of the false god." Michael responded to Zay with a smile and a handshake.

"How's the patient?" Zay asked.

"Better, but not good, still needing lots of prayer," Michael reported to Zay. Ronnie opened his eyes and muttered one word, "Dad." He raised his hand to his chest.

A tear trekked down his dad's face. Ronnie reached out and took his hand. He dropped his head and felt his chest. His hand fell into the cavity of his chest.

A voice from behind the bench spoke to him, "Who will you choose to fill the empty space?"

29

Encounter

> Perhaps they will listen and everyone will
> turn from his evil way, that I may repent of
> the calamity which I am planning to do to
> them because of the evil of their deeds.
>
> ---Jeremiah 26:3

BARBARA AND SHARON ended their shopping trip with a hospital visit to see Ronnie and to take Michael home.

"How's he doing?" Sharon asked on the trip home."

"He changes," Michael said.

"I know you feel a responsibility toward him, but just remember that prayer is the strongest thing you can do for him."

Michael shook his head and smiled. He took Sharon's hand and kissed it. "I couldn't make it without you. You even understand how Ronnie is a son of a fellow veteran

"But you didn't know him." Sharon said.

"Doesn't matter," he replied. "All those who served in Vietnam are brothers and we have a responsibility to the families of those who didn't return." Michael had recited the phrase to her many times. His deep caring was one of the things she loved about him. She would never comprehend the depth of the bond that grew between men of war, and she would never doubt it. They stood together in life and in death.

Barbara drove into her driveway at the same time her brother, Zay, drove in behind her. When he got out of the car, he carried a box.

"Bring me a present?" she asked.

"In a way, but not in a good way. Needing your expertise."

Once the children were off to the playroom, Barbara fixed her and Zay a glass of tea and brought out a large tray of cookies.

"That's way too many for me," Zay said when he eyed the mound of cookies.

"Don't worry, I'm sure we'll have company as soon as we bite into them."

Zay smiled and saw three little boys playing with buckets of tiny toy cars.

"What are you thinking about?" she asked quietly.

"For the first time in weeks, I'm having good thoughts." He sipped his tea and reached for a cookie.

"What did Michael say about Ronnie?"

"The same. Still in a coma. The docs did determine the venom must be cobra, but not exactly. Of course. that confuses them even more."

Zay laughed. If they could see one of those sneaky serpents, they wouldn't be confused.

Barbara joined him. "How's your resident dragon?"

"He died," Zay said without expression.

Barbara nearly choked on her tea. "What? After all those failed attempts to kill him, he just died?"

"I think we killed him with gene manipulation. I got this box a few days ago, and I think it can prove what happened." Zay pulled the jar with the fetus from the box. He set it on the coffee table.

Barbara pushed it back into the box as soon as she saw it. "Not in front of the children. Where—"

"It was delivered to my lab . . . by a friend of yours." He handed Patti's note to her.

She read it and looked at Zay. "Do you remember her?"

"Not really, I was more excited about coming to school than I was about your friends."

"She wasn't a friend. She was the one who kidnapped me and arranged for me to be the bride of that demon. Michael saved me."

"Why would she have this fetus?"

"Zay, there was so much evil in that house; they probably did abortions as well as host parties for rich, sadistic old men and women."

"Did you notice she said they created Phobus."

"Patti was the one Daniel saw dragging Phobus. A man was with her too. Daniel and Michael thought it was Nisroch."

Zay leaned forward and got in close proximity to Barbara. "You mean, the dragon on the farm?"

"One and the same," Barbara assured him

"You know this makes sense and agrees with the information I gained from Phobus," Zay said. "I did some manipulation magic on his DNA and reinjected it into him. I can't help but wonder if I killed Phobus or if his handler killed him."

"Why would another dragon kill him?" Barbara asked

"Because he was no longer necessary to the plan."

"What plan?" Barbara set her cup on the coffee table.

"When Phobus's body turned to ashes, it spelled out that same old phrase you found," he informed her.

"You mean about the planting of seed?"

"Yep, that's the one."

"You said its body turned to ashes?"

"I was trying to cut it up to make it more manageable. He was a twenty-foot-tall dragon. You don't throw something like that into the garbage can."

Barbara laughed at the absurd sight. "No, you don't." She reached for a cookie and took a bite with a comical smile on her face.

"Mommy," came the sweet voice of her four-year-old middle child.

"Cookies?" Barbara gave each of the children a cookie.

"I told you as soon as I bit into one, they would hear and smell it."

Zay laughed, then he leaned back in his chair.

"How did Patti know I needed the fetus for my studies?"

"My guess is the dragon told her to bring it to you. The real question I see is which dragon?"

"One bigger and deadlier than Nisroch. Mrs. Waithe didn't get this bad when he bit her." Zay took a bite of cookie.

"Difference is, Mrs. Waithe was a praying woman who studied her Bible. She was full of anti-venom. He could only hurt her; he couldn't kill her."

"But he can kill Ronnie, if we weren't there praying and reading the Bible to him?"

Barbara tapped her nose and kept chewing her cookie.

The two of them sat there in silence, listening to the sounds of contented children down the hall.

"Ignorance doesn't protect them, but the love and prayers of their parents protect them," Zay pondered.

"That's deep. What are you getting at?"

"Ronnie."

"Who's protecting him?" she asked.

"You, Michael, and the group . . . and what about his mother?"

"But no father. He's an orphan."

"I don't know what to do to help him. What would a father do?"

"A father would know why the dragon bit him," Barbara answered.

"And a father would do everything he could, even let the dragon kill *him* rather than get to his child," Zay exclaimed as he remembered the lesson Marcy taught him. "I'm not going to be Mr. Idiot anymore."

"I don't understand that, but I won't argue with you." She smirked. "You may be getting some answers." She smiled when Zay grabbed a Bible from the coffee table.

He thumbed through different parts.

Barbara continued to wash dishes and left him alone.

"Barbara," he called out to her. "Listen to this. 'Moses lifted up the serpent in the wilderness, even so must the Son of Man be lifted up.' What does that mean? Did Moses lift up a dragon?"

Barbara rejoined Zay on the couch and patted him on the knee. "We have to take the whole Bible in context. You can't pick and choose."

"I don't pick and choose."

"Yes, you do, you pick the Scriptures you can mock, like that one."

"Well I was looking up John 3:16, you know, that famous verse we learned in kindergarten Sunday school." Zay smiled at his sister and started to close the Bible.

Barbara took it from his hands and kept it open. "If you go to Numbers twenty-one, you get the whole story."

They read the story together about the Israelites wandering in the desert after they left Egypt. Some of the people were complaining about the food.

Barbara chuckled.

"What's so funny?"

"Notice they are complaining about condiments."

"Yeah, what about that?"

"It's like us. We complain about the little things . . . like cucumbers."

"Finish the story before I lose my thoughts," Zay scolded her.

"They said, 'we hate this manna,' which was the food God provided them in the desert. It represented Christ as meeting all our needs. When they complained, God removed His protective hand from the natural elements of the desert, and the poisonous snakes rose from the dust and started biting the people."

"Because they wanted cucumbers and onions?" Zay wrinkled his nose. "See, this is why I have a hard time with the Bible. Why would a loving God punish them because they didn't like the food?"

"It wasn't about the food; it was about their rejection of His provision. They were longing to go back into Egypt and into captivity just to get cucumbers and onions."

"That's silly. Another reason I can't trust the Bible— sometimes it's just stupid." Zay rose from the couch and walked over to the window. He didn't like where this conversation was going. He wanted answers. Real answers. He wanted to help Ronnie, not learn a stupid Bible story.

Barbara ignored him and kept talking. "When the people said they hate this miserable food, they were telling God they didn't like His provision for them."

"So, it didn't taste good. Big deal." Zay grimaced.

"It wasn't about the taste; it was about rejecting God's provision. God was giving them a picture of Christ. Go back to John 6:32." She found her place and started reading again. "'Jesus said, it is not Moses who gives you the bread out of heaven (Manna), but it is My Father who gives you the true bread out of heaven. For the bread of God is that which comes down out of heaven and gives life to the world.' They said, 'give us the bread.' Jesus said, 'I am the bread of life, he who comes to Me will not hunger. . . For I have come down from heaven.'"

"So, Jesus is Manna?" Zay asked with a sneer.

"Now you're getting it."

"Their rejection of the manna was the same as rejecting Jesus? I don't get it." Zay threw his hands up in the air and plopped down in the chair opposite Barbara.

"God gives pictures, images, pieces of a puzzle to us throughout the Word. This is why we have to know the whole Scripture in order to understand it."

Zay leaned forward in the chair with his elbows resting on his thighs, his head facing the floor. "Sis, I don't understand any of it. But science I understand."

"And?" Barbara prompted.

"And my science study points to an intelligent design, which means an intelligent designer." Zay moaned.

Barbara smiled and picked up teaching her baby brother. "You see, God knows we are stubborn, and He also knows we are blinded by the dragons. He gives us pictures of His plan of redemption through Christ."

"So, the snakes coming up and biting the people was a picture?"

"Yep. It's only God's hand that keeps evil from harming us. When Moses prayed, God instructed him to make a bronze cross with a serpent coiled on it."

"That sounds stupid too. If it's a picture of Christ, why did he put the serpent on it?"

"Because it was Christ."

"Okay, you've lost it." Zay snickered. "I thought you were a Bible scholar."

"Okay, look at Psalm twenty-two." Barbara handed the open Bible to Zay. "Read it."

"That's weird. Another picture?"

"David wrote that hundreds of years before Christ was crucified," she said, "but God allowed him to see Christ's viewpoint of what was happening while He was on the cross."

"Okay, I need more clarification. This sounds like God rejected Him."

"That's right, because Christ became our sin and that sin had to be punished. He calls Himself a worm a reproach of men and despised by the people."

"Doesn't sound much like a Savior," Zay scoffed.

"Look further down. He says, 'I am surrounded by the bulls of Bashan, they open their mouths wide like a roaring lion, then he describes the dogs that have surrounded me, a band of evildoers around him.'"

"What is it saying?" Zay extended his open palms.

Barbara could see his frustration. "Dragons!"

"What?" Zay looked her in the eyes.

"Jesus was surrounded by dragons—evil roaring dragons—and you've seen them. Imagine being completely surrounded by them."

Zay shuddered and whimpered, "I . . . I . . . Sis, it makes my heart race to just think about one of those vile things around me, and you're saying He was completely surrounded?"

"Yes."

"But why?"

"So that we could look upon Him and see our rejection of God and what the dragons do to those who do not accept the gift of Jesus who was the manna."

Zay sat down and wept. "Sis, I've been dabbling in alternate lifestyles."

"I know." She patted him on the back.

"You do?" He wiped his face with the tissue she handed him.

She nodded. "Does that mean I'm the snake on the pole?"

"No, only Jesus could take the punishment. Only He could face the dragons. Only He has the power to defeat them."

"Are we doomed?" Zay sat up and put his hands on his head.

"Not if we look up at the serpent on the cross, the one who was destroyed, the one who took away the power of destruction and death from the dragon."

Zay picked up the Bible and turned back to Numbers twenty-one. "All who looked at the fiery serpent lived," He said.

"Fiery serpent . . . could that be a dragon?" she guided him toward the conclusion.

"I think it's a strong possibility, or maybe the bite of the serpent felt like fire. So, by looking upon the bronze serpent, the people were believing and trusting God's promise?"

"Now you see."

"So, when He says, 'whosoever believes in the sacrifice of Jesus on the cross' will be saved from the dragon?

"Yes. Now keep reading."

"God sent not His son to judge the world but that the world might be saved through Him. Just as the people in the wilderness were saved by the image of Jesus on the cross, so we are rescued by focusing on the image of God that we have through Jesus."

"I'm not sure I get that concept." Zay leaned forward to Barbara and focused his full attention on her.

"We still live in a world ruled by dragons, and we can't survive the torment they put us through unless we keep our eyes on Jesus who then reveals the purity of God to us. If we believe Jesus is God in a human body, we are spared the judgment of our rejection of God, but if we do not believe in Jesus as God, then we are judged by the dragons who already own this world and the people rejecting Christ."

"Sis, this is deep." Zay shook his head. "Are you saying that if I believe in Jesus, I don't have to give up my desire to be with Ronnie romantically."

Barbara ducked her head, "We fight dragons in many ways. They are deceptive, and their desire is to distort the image of God. You have to find the image of God before you can answer that question."

Zay put his forefinger and thumb to his chin in thought. "Jesus didn't die on the cross just to save us from our sins. He died on the cross to protect us from the evil of temptation that draws us to sin."

"I'm not sure I'm following you." Barbara slapped her hands together to remove cookie crumbs.

"Jesus is the weapon that stops the dragons from destroying us by luring us into wrong thinking which in turn causes wrong decisions. They tempt us so we will not see the right ways of God. Their deception looks better than God's ways and promises the things we want in this life, like power and money and relationships. That's why we follow their disguised lies and fall into their wickedness, which leads us to both a physical and a spiritual death. But trusting Jesus takes away the power of death."

Barbara leaned forward and said, "From the great dragon who is called the devil and Satan."

30

This is War

> When Jeremiah finished speaking all that
> the LORD had commanded him to speak to
> all the people, the priests and the prophets
> and all the people seized him, saying, "You
> must die!"
>
> ---Jeremiah 26:8

ZAY SET THE beaker on the work table, left the lab, and headed to the basement out of habit. The empty cage of a chimera dragon loomed deep beneath him in a hall of quiet. He turned on the radio for music to drown out the emptiness. He took a deep breath and let it out slowly. The stress of the last years flowed from him. Still, he felt the weighty absence of Phobus, especially as he took a tissue sample from the remaining pieces of carcass.

The ashes left from Phobus body formed words which haunted him; *the planting of seed is singular, but the harvest comes in multiples, harvest time is here.* In his soul, he yearned to understand it's meaning, especially the harvest comment. It hung over his spirit like a dark cloud.

The cage door shut behind him and locked. He reached into his pocket to get the key. It wasn't there.

"Looking for this?" Came a disembodied growly voice.

The key dangled in the air above his head out of his reach. He froze in place, and a bead of perspiration trickled down the side of his face.

"What do you want?" he asked the unseen dragon.

"Your cooperation."

"For what?" Zay calmed his racing heart.

At that moment, the elevator door opened with a whoosh of air.

"Dr. Troye? Are you down here?" Marcy called to him as she stepped off the elevator.

"Yes, I'm locked in the cage."

She unlocked the cage, and Zay offered a hasty thank you.

Marcy looked up at the key floating in the air. "Strange."

"Let's get out of here," Zay prompted and pushed her toward the steps. He didn't trust the elevator with that aberration in the room.

Once the two of them arrived at the top, Marcy stopped and asked him, "Why were you down there?"

"I wanted to get a sample of the ashes on the floor. You know, the ones with the message."

"Did you get them?"

Zay held up the paper cup filled with ashes. "Yep."

He set the ashes on the table, grabbed the beaker with Phobus' tissue, and added the amylase enzyme. Using the pipette, he removed the sample and placed it in the electron microscope.

"I'm looking at the T-cells."

"Why?" Marcy huddled closer to Zay to observe the microscopic view on the screen.

"The T-cells come from the Thymus in the medulla of the brain."

"I know. What do you hope to see?"

"I have a theory that since the T-cells control the bodily functions and fight off foreign objects—"

"You thought you might find if one part of the dragon was foreign to the other part."

"You're right, I ask the question if his goat body fought with his reptilian body." Zay explained.

"I think I found something," Marcy said. "I'm just not sure what it is."

"Share it with me."

"I'm looking at the T-cells; the TCF-1 is driven by dysregulation of the gene encoding the transcription factor LEF-1 which emphasizes the interdependence of the transcription factors that drive early thymocyte differentiation."

"Humm, I see. Sounds like whoever created that deformed little dragon, gave him cancer."

"I thought so too—to be specific, leukemia. I think it was added as a self-destruct sequence or it could be the result of the two species mixing in one body." She paused. "Reminds me of a Psalm."

Zay smiled. Marcy could relate the most mundane science jargon to God's Word. Most of the time he found it to be cute, putting complex systems and ideas in a simple verse. Other times it felt smothering.

Since his sister Barbara shared the picture of a serpent on a pole with him, he liked hearing the Bible stories. The fact that Marcy shared it made it more interesting. Today her comment held a deeper meaning to him. The Bible's pages ran over with images and pictures. He felt excitement at another puzzle piece discovery.

"Okay, tell me," he said with a smile.

"It's one that got me through the long days at the psychiatric ward."

Zay looked up at her and pursed his lips. Her suffering touched his heart.

"'Let their table become a snare before them,'" she quoted, "'and that which should have been for their welfare, let it become a trap. Let their eyes be darkened that they see not; and make their loins continually to shake. Pour out thine indignation upon them, and let thy wrathful anger take hold of them. Let their habitation be desolate; and let none dwell in their tents.'"

"Sounds loving," Zay pondered.

"If you read above those verses, he mentions there are more people that hate him, than the hairs on his head." she said.

Zay smirked. "I understand that."

Marcy laughed. "The sixty-third Psalm speaks to everyone. It's my lifeline when life is unfair."

A loud noise came from the hall. They both ran to investigate, but when Zay reached the door and touched the doorknob, he felt intense heat.

"Marcy, I think there's a fire. Quick! Let's see if we can get out the window."

Petite Marcy escaped through the small window easily. She offered Zay her hand.

He stared at the window. "There's no way I can get through there. I'll get stuck."

"What about the feeding bin?" She asked.

"Won't work; it's four stories down and made with smooth metal."

She starts coughing. On the outside of the lab, Marcy stands and sees flames lick around the building with black pillars of smoke wrapping themselves around the building as they burst from the windows. The flames inch closer to the lab where Zay is trapped.

Zay yells at Marcy over the roar of the fire, "I'll go to the cage. Maybe the fire won't reach it."

Marcy backed away from the heat. Zay started working on his escape or rather his survival plan. Four stories underground sat a metal cage where he may be able to avoid the flames, but not the heat. He grabbed all of the five-gallon water bottles and pushed them down the stairs. They collected on the landing of the first floor. He closed the steel door of the lab behind him and ran down the stairs to push his water bottles on down another flight of stairs. He opened the supply closet on the landing and found a full bag filled with emergency equipment. It contained goggles, flashlights, radio, and thermal blankets. At the next landing he opened that closet and pulled out another blanket and a handheld battery operated fan. When he got to the basement, he checked the supply closet there. The contents were the same, still he pulled out a big box on rollers. He rolled his water into the cage. He stopped and looked around. The fire was far above him. He threw all his loot into the cage. When he walked in he started to pull the door shut. He laughed at himself. He didn't need to lock himself in. Then a large whoosh of flame swept down only inches above his head.

Marcy ran toward the arriving fire trucks, pointing to the location of the lab. The fireman quickly assembled a rescue operation for Zay. Marcy held her hands over her mouth and watched them with tears streaming down her face. She didn't know what to do and stood there in disbelief.

"Oh, please God, get him out."

Behind her stood a large reddish-purple creature, breathing flames on the building. No one could see the creature, but the flames sparked everything in their path. The creature turned his head and started other fires.

I'll keep them busy and maybe wipe out one of the cursed Troye family members.

Marcy heard the dragon's curse on Zay. She could see the reflection of red on the side of the science building. She bowed her head and said, "Lord, I need some courage and some prayer warriors."

A few minutes after Marcy started praying, one of the firemen walked up to her and asked her to move back away from the fire. Again, she told them of Zay's dilemma. He nodded but did nothing.

Marcy heard the voice of the red dragon behind her. "He can't hear you."

Marcy knew he spoke truth. She had to do something. She ran toward the building and attempted to get in.

One of the firemen saw her and came after her.

She started screaming, "My boss is in there!"

Finally, he heard her and asked where. She told him. The fireman smiled and said, "If it doesn't roast him, he may be safer there that if I go after him."

She couldn't believe her ears.

The dragon laughed.

She looked around and saw groups of people gathering to watch the fire. *Where did they all come from?*

"People always come to see my work, I fascinate them," the invisible dragon hissed.

"You're right; evil is fascinating."

The dragon raked a clawed leg over Marcy's head.

Marcy shuddered and moved. She felt a hand touch her and jerked away from it as quickly as possible.

The hand grabbed her with more force. "Hey Marcy, it's me."

She turned and saw her friend, Christine.

"How'd you get here?"

"Tell you the truth, I'm not too sure. I was released from the hospital this morning, and I've been waiting in front of this building for hours."

Marcy scowled at her. "What do you want?"

"I didn't come looking for you. I came to see Dr. Troye."

Marcy groaned and turned up her lip. She watched the action all around her, praying the firemen would bring Zay out of the flames.

Then she heard a scream. Her hands went over her mouth. A figure came running from the building. It was burning. She ran to him and pushed him on the ground. Rolled him around, but by the time the flames were out, she dropped to her knees beside the victim and stared into the charred face of the fireman.

The man groaned, pointed at the building, and then blacked out. Two other firemen surrounded them and began to treat their fallen teammate.

Her stomach churned as she realized Zay had no hope. She turned and looked again at the building completely engulfed in flames. Tears fell down her face and built up into a full wail of agony. She fell to her knees and buried her face in her hands.

"Zay," she groaned.

31

The Meeting of the Minds

> Then Jeremiah spoke to all the officials
> and to all the people, saying, "The LORD
> sent me to prophesy against this house and
> against this city all the words that you have
> heard.
>
> ---Jeremiah 26:12

"IT'S TIME FOR the harvest!" the raspy voice of Belial spoke.

"I'm not ready," Ronnie said.

"You better make a decision, or you will watch him roast." Belial waved his tail in the air, allowing Ronnie to glimpse inside the cage where Zay cowered.

"No! leave him alone!" Ronnie yelled and hit Belial with a fist.

Belial reached out to Ronnie's chest with his claw.

Ronnie howled in agony. Pain shot through his body like lighting. He could hear the sizzle of his own organs cooking.

Michael grabbed Ronnie before he fell out of the bed. "Whoa." He pulled his hand back. "That boy's hot," he said, shaking his hand.

Ronnie struggled to speak. "Kill Zay," he muttered.

Michael wrinkled his face and said, "What?" Then Michael heard the dragon laugh and felt intense heat. He grabbed his head.

"Michael!" Sharon shouted. "The dragon is controlling everything, it's—"

"The prince of the power of the air," Michael said, describing the evil dragon working in Ronnie. "The spirit works in those who rebel."

Sharon cupped her hands over her nose and mouth. She breathed in deeply. "I think something bad is happening."

The nurse rushed into the room, short-winded and with a red face. "Have you heard about the big fire?"

"No, what fire?" Sharon asked in a raised voice.

"At the university. They said the science building is in flames. Most of the staff will be in the emergency room."

"We need to get over there," Sharon said in a high pitch voice of panic.

"You can't," the nurse said. "It's all blocked off. You will do more good here with him." she pointed at Ronnie.

Ronnie's body temperature kept rising while his spirit wrestled with a dragon in a heavenly court. He heard Davis speaking, even though he couldn't see him. "Right now, you are separated from Christ and without hope."

"But you have *me*." Belial roared and expanded his girth, making sure Ronnie wouldn't see Davis or his parents. They watched and prayed for their son.

"The monster's goal is to keep us away from Christ." Davis added.

"His plan—" Ronnie choked.

"His plan to hide Christ from us? What does that mean?" Ronnie started crying and blubbering, "Dad, dad—don't leave me."

Michael tried to understand the garbled words coming from Ronnie's parched and dry mouth.

Zay poured the water over the packing quilt wrapped around him and put on the oxygen mask from the closet. The small tank was designed for short term use. He kept a wet handkerchief around his mouth and nose. The heat surrounded him as he climbed toward the one little speck of sky.

"I don't think I'll live long enough for this to burn out," he muttered. Then he saw the sparkle of the red scales again.

"It can stop." The deep, raspy voice of the red dragon spoke.

"Your responsible for this?" Zay asked, looking toward the spot where he had seen the glistening of scales.

"I am!" came a reply.

Zay trembled at the audible voice.

"Why don't you just kill me instead of—"

"I don't want to kill you," the voice stopped him. "I want to congratulate you."

"For what?"

"Your discovery."

"I didn't discover anything," Zay argued while looking around the stairwell for a physical presence.

"The gene, the one that gives the tendency for homosexuals."

"I didn't find that," he argued.

"Once you are roasted in this meat cooker, that's how you will be remembered—the brilliant scientist that discovered the gene that your God put into certain people to make them. . .you know. . . that way. Your God that toys with people and ruins their lives with his ridiculous rules."

"I don't know what you're talking about." Zay poured more water on his quilt. The water-soaked quilt helped keep his body in balance from the heat which must be reaching roasting temperatures. The water level in the last bottle hugged the bottom.

"It doesn't matter because you'll be my greatest help in enlarging my kingdom."

"What kingdom is that?" Zay asked while trying to wrap himself in the quilt and take a breath of oxygen.

"But, for the kingdom of Satan, I am most valuable." He sneered and lowered his huge serpent-like spiked head to park in front of Zay's face. He allowed Zay to see him.

Zay let out a blood-curdling scream when he saw the face. He covered his eyes with the quilt. He knew his bowels loosened. He could smell it. Right now, death would be welcome. His breath came in short gasps. He put the oxygen mask to his face and discovered it to be empty. Still, he breathed through it for as long as he could draw breath. Then he blacked out.

When he came to, nothing had changed, except he was breathing easier. Again, he poured some water over his head and onto the quilt. The light weight of the bottle told him it was empty.

"Nice nap?" the voice of Belial said.

Zay shivered. The battle still raged. Then he heard a wicked, gravely laugh.

"This is not the battle we will fight; this is your preview of the hell you will occupy."

Zay dropped his head on his knees.

"Praying now won't help. You've already made your decision."

"You're right, I have," Zay said with confidence, remembering the conversation with his sister. He knew the image he wanted to focus upon was Christ—the bronze serpent on the cross, the One who came to remove the sting of death. He realized he no longer feared death. He dropped the quilt from his head and let it hang loosely from his shoulders.

He looked Belial straight in his horrendous face and proclaimed, "I believe and trust in the God of Abraham, Isaac, and Jacob, Jesus Christ who took my sins to give me life, the bite of a fiery serpent will not kill me."

Belial roared and thrashed his head. "You read His book!"

"Yes, and in it I found the one true image of love so deep it will not let me perish by your deceptive image."

Belial thrashed around the room and his girth shrank to the normal size of a man . . . the size of Ronnie, the dragon took on the image of Zay's lab assistant.

Zay stood firm, staring at his lab assistant. He could see the beauty in the boy. His hand reached out to touch his face. He wanted to be with him forever. He no longer felt the heat of the fire but rather the heat of desire.

He reached out and stroked the face of Ronnie. He smiled his bright smile back at Zay. He responded to his touch by grasping his hand. Then with a foul smell coming from him, he returned to the image of the menacing red dragon.

Zay stepped back, his body soaked in sweat.

"See, anyone can succumb to my lust," Belial roared.

"Where's Ronnie?"

Belial laughed, lowered his head, and opened his mouth.

There, Zay saw Ronnie in flames, thrashing around in pain.

"Take me; leave him!"

"Oh, so noble." Belial laughed.

"No, I'm not noble. I'm weak, but I know the one who removes the sting of a fiery serpent so that it cannot hurt me," Zay said, remembering the story of the serpents in the desert.

Belial said, "I will devour him."

"You already have," Zay heard himself say. He let a slight smile line his lips. Behind Belial he saw a glimpse of a white horse with a rider dressed in glistening army fatigues.

Even though Zay could feel the flesh on his bones cooking, he stood firm without fear. He smiled. The image of Belial faded, and the image of a white horse mounted by Sgt. Davis appeared.

"Greetings, my faithful and strong warrior. The Lord is with you"

Zay blushed. "Lord, if you are with us, why is this happening? I felt the strong lust for another man; how can I rescue Ronnie when I can't even fight for myself?"

Davis answered with assurance, "Surely, I will be with you, and you will defeat this dragon as one man, but Christ is the One to deliver Ronnie from the abomination."

The fire raged around Zay yet did not burn him.

Belial pitched and groaned. He fell to the floor.

The flames rescinded.

Zay kept his eyes on the white horse and its rider. "What do I do now?" he asked Davis.

"Pull down the idols." Davis said then disappeared.

Stunned by the statement, Zay stood in the middle of a roasting oven with walls blazing red. A loud clamor sounded overhead as if someone was trying to get into the vault. Coughing and sputtering for air, Zay went to the control panel and hit the emergency release button on the first floor door. *The fire must be contained.*

A fireman burst through the door, picked up the blanket and wrapped it around Zay again. Pouring the last of the water over Zay's head and body, the fireman put an oxygen mask on Zay's face, tied a tether rope around him then said, "Follow me."

Zay held tight to the rope following him through massive flames in the lab and hall and toward an exit. He recognized nothing in the lab. Flames and ashes covered everything—the last two years of his work.

When they burst out of the building, Marcy ran toward them. "I've got him," the fireman said.

Zay dropped to the ground. He lay there gasping and groaning, unable to gather his breath quick enough to tell them of the encounter with Belial and Davis.

Marcy brought him some bottled water. He gulped it down in long draws. He wiped his mouth with the back of his hand and took another draw before speaking.

Marcy wrapped her arms around him. She was crying and making garbled noises.

Zay cautiously returned the hug. He realized she felt good.

He looked around. "Have you seen Ronnie?"

32

Building an Army

For thus says the LORD of hosts, the
God of Israel, I have put a yoke of iron on
the neck of all these nations, that they may
serve Nebuchadnezzar king of Babylon; and
they will serve him, and I have also given him
the beasts of the field. Then Jeremiah the
prophet said to Hananiah the prophet,
"Listen now, Hananiah, the LORD has not
sent you, and you have made this people
trust in a lie. Therefore, says the LORD,
Behold, I am about to remove you from the
face of the earth This year you are going to
die. because you have counseled rebellion
against the LORD. So Hananiah the prophet
died in the same year in the seventh month.

---Jeremiah 28:14-17

RONNIE STOOD IN the middle of a celestial
courtroom with Belial pacing around him. He smiled when

his dad stepped up beside him with his hand on his shoulder. Standing next to Mr. Walton was a well-muscled white horse.

"You're my protector?"

"I petition the Master for you and your mother every day." Mr. Walton assured his son.

"Really, if that's true, then why is that monster always around and why is he making a plea for me?"

"It's what the council of the gods do. They are rebellious angels seeking their own kingdom."

Ronnie shook his head, "it's too weird for me to understand."

"That's the reason God gave us explicit directions about how to live our lives. He knew we couldn't understand the evil that surrounds us and wants to kill us."

"Like the thing is killing Dr. Troye right now."

The horse neighed and stomped the ground. The sound of a waterfall filled the room. A beam of broken light shone in the room and all eyes focused on that light.

"Zay entered the celestial courtroom."

Marcy screamed when Zay passed out. His breathing shallow. She touched him and realized his skin was burning hot. "Help him." She yelled at the fireman who was on his communications calling for an ambulance and EMT. They arrived within seconds and loaded Zay onto the gurney.

When the ambulance arrived at the hospital, Daniel and Barbara waited. They took him to the burn unit. There they examined his body and found it to be red and hot, but no significant burning.

"You got a really bad sunburn." Barbara said with a smile.

Zay nodded and passed out again. Daniel ordered tests. "Let's hope it's only on the outside."

Back in the celestial courtroom Ronnie smiled at Zay, "You're okay!"

"My body is still in distress, but whatever happens there won't change what happens here." Zay said as he put both hands over his chest. "My heart is sealed with Christ."

"What now?" Ronnie asked his dad.

His dad took him by the shoulders, "It's time for both of you to go back. You have been granted more time to make a decision before it becomes a permanent state. You have another trial to face. I will be praying at the Master's feet for both of you."

Ronnie grabbed his dad and hugged him, "I don't want to go back."

"I know, maybe we'll see each other again."

Belial covered Ronnie's ears when his dad said, "maybe."

33

Rumination

Seek the welfare of the city where I have sent you into exile, and pray to the LORD on its behalf; for in its welfare, you will have welfare. . . For I know the plans that I have for you, declared the LORD, plans for welfare and not for calamity to give you a future and a hope. Then you will call upon Me and come and pray to Me and I will listen to you. You will seek Me and find Me when you search for Me with all your heart.

---Jeremiah 29:7, 11-13

MONDAY MORNING ARRIVED at four a.m. for Zay. He couldn't sleep. The conversation between him and Belial kept rolling through his mind along with a hint of something else. That other thing he felt expressed urgency in his spirit. He rose and went to the kitchen, poured himself a cup of coffee, and prepared a breakfast of biscuits, bacon, eggs, sliced grapefruit, and milk. By the time he finished cooking, the morning sun has risen in the eastern sky. He called Marcy and asked her to join him. She accepted.

A few minutes later, Zay watched Marcy across the table as she sipped her coffee. He had never observed her as a woman. In the past, his eyes focused only on the beauty of Ronnie. He chuckled at the mental description of Ronnie as beautiful. He was anything but beautiful. With his square jaw and deep-set eyes, he presented the image of a GI Joe.

Belial's words came back to him; Ronnie was to be the poster child for the promotion of the homosexual movement.

"I wonder," he said aloud.

Marcy pushed her empty plate back, set her cup down, and crossed her arms in front of her. "Wonder what?"

"What is it the homosexuals are marching about?"

"I've wondered that too." she took a sip of her cooling coffee.

"Need a warmup?" he asked.

"Not now." She held up her hand over her cup.

"They aren't poor. In fact, they're some of the wealthiest and most educated in society."

"Republican Congressman Robert Bauman was exposed as gay."

"Harvey Milk served in government."

"And then there's Barney Frank."

"But . . ." Marcy paused.

"Go on."

"I think there's something desired."

"What would that be?" Zay asked.

"Respect, if one has the respect of society, then his actions are acceptable and maybe honorable," Marcy contemplated.

"Is that what they mean by gay rights?"

"Do you still want Ronnie?" Marcy asked with her head ducked.

Zay almost spit out his coffee. He gulped it down and said, "How did you know?"

"Everyone knew; it was obvious the way you look at him. And you're with him in and out of the lab. What other fellowship student spends that much time with his assistants."

Zay blushed. "I've never had much interest in girls. I didn't have time for them, but when my buds and I got together behind the barn—" He stopped before he exposed the things he didn't want anyone to know.

Marcy smiled. "Does it embarrass you to think about that time?"

He nodded. "I enjoyed it, but then I couldn't look them in the face."

"I think you may have just described the need for gay rights."

"What?" He looked at Marcy.

"The right to be gay and have no guilt."

"How's that supposed to happen?"

"I think the bigger question is, what causes the guilt?"

They finished breakfast, and Marcy finally asked the question she must have been holding all morning. "What did the monster say to you when you were roasting?"

"How do you know it said anything?"

"Zay, it's me, Marcy, remember? I know."

He smiled at her. "The monster said it's time to reap my harvest."

"What harvest?"

Zay shook his head and groaned. He buried his face in his hands. "I don't know, but any harvest to be reaped by that monster is too horrible to think about."

Marcy patted him on the back.

"When I was thirteen . . ." Zay raised up and looked at the ceiling instead of at Marcy. He stared blankly at an invisible screen playing a movie only he could see. Through stuttering words, he revealed the plot of his movie to Marcy. "My mother found a mask."

Marcy leaned in toward him to hear better, as his words were quiet as if mixed with grief.

"It came with a list of names." He leaned forward on the table and raised his head so that his eyes met Marcy's. "At the bottom of that list it said, 'The planting of seed is singular, but the harvest is reaped in multiples.'"

"What does that mean?" Marcy squinted her eyes.

"My family thought it referred to farming where you plant one seed to grow a plant that gives much fruit."

"That was also prophetic about Jesus by the high priests," Marcy said.

"How so?" Zay asked, wanting to know about this idea in the Bible since discovering a truth about God's image from his sister's study.

"It's in John 11. The high priest said it was good for Jesus to die to save the nation Israel, but not only for that nation but for all the children of God scattered around the world."

Zay smiled at the interpretation. The phrase may indicate the harvest Jesus would gather because of His death. Then his smile turned to a frown. "I think it may be a problem when the phrase comes from a dragon."

Neither of them had any explanation. Marcy left the room to go get her purse. She returned and pulled a small Bible out of her bag.

"You carry one around with you?"

She smiled at Zay and patted him on the hand. "It's better protection than a gun."

Zay laughed at her. "That may be debatable. Remember, you're in Texas."

Marcy opened the Bible to Jeremiah 25:15 and read, "'Take this cup of the wine of wrath from My hand and cause all the nations to whom I send you to drink it.'"

"Okay, you've lost me." Zay raised his hands in the air in surrender.

"Just remember that all Scripture has to be interpreted in context. This is God talking to Jeremiah because the people have started worshipping other gods."

"Still not getting the meaning of a cup of wine of wrath. Sounds like a horror movie."

"It is a horror, but it's not a movie. The other gods required child sacrifice and gross sexual acts."

"What kind of acts?" Zay wrinkled his brow.

"Any kind of activity that was outside of marriage between one man and one woman."

"Okay, why?"

"The other gods were fertility gods. The people worshipped them for success in their crops which meant wealth in their pockets."

"How could sex acts do that?" Zay leaned in toward Marcy and put his chin on his fist.

"Sex begets children; children are the sacrifice. More sex, more children, more sacrifice."

"Sounds endless." Zay sat up.

"It is, the sexual acts committed during a worship session of one of these gods became more unusual. Multiple partners of both sexes and at the same time, use of bodily fluids and excrement, all kinds of torturous deeds to one another."

"What does this have to do with the phrase?" Zay tapped his fingers on the table in rhythm.

"A dragon said it to you. Even Phobus left a message for you in ashes. What did it say?"

Zay sighed and put his hands behind his head. He pursed his lips together. Marcy didn't push, his fragile thoughts could be broken with too much conversation.

"Marcy, could Belial be? He stopped talking and paced around the kitchen.

Marcy sat still, waiting.

"Could it be the harvest is sexual?"

"Could be," she responded, avoiding interrupting his thinking.

Zay could think on many things at once. Anyone who knew him remained quiet while he was in one of these periods of pondering. He would lose all tenuous strings of thought. "Belial is not like the other dragons; it's a system. That's why it's so big and scary."

Marcy raised her eyebrows.

"A political system!" he shouted. "Remember, you mentioned, Harvey Milk, Stewart McKinney, and Barney Frank—all admitted homosexuals, and all served in a political position."

"What about Steward McKinney?"

"He died of Aids while in office."

"Even in Jeremiah, it was political. Read that verse again." Zay pointed to her Bible. He rubbed his hands together.

"'Cause all nations to whom I send you to drink it."

"Yeah, all nations."

"To whom I send you," Marcy corrected his idea.

"Okay where was . . . who is this we're talking about?"

"Israel."

"What?"

"God is addressing all the nations which took the Israelites as captives."

"What were those nations?" Zay no longer walked but bounced around the room.

Marcy laughed, "All of them, past and present."

Zay turned and looked at her. He stopped pacing. "Really?"

"Yes, every nation has a Jewish element."

"Why?

"Genesis 12. God's message to Abraham. 'I will make you a great nation.' That's Israel by the way. 'And I will bless those who bless you and curse those who curse you, and in you all the families of the earth will be blessed.'"

Zay sat down. "Wow!" He thought for a moment, and Marcy remained silent. "Why? Are nations blessed by Israel?" He asked her.

"Maybe, because they had the writings and the ways of the one true God, the creator of all things, including the other gods?"

"I think you're right. The dragons are gods, created by God. That's why Jesus is the only thing that frightens them or scares them away. Jesus is God in the flesh." Zay reasoned.

Zay stopped at the sink, poured himself a glass of water, and took deep gulps of it. He set the empty glass in the sink, smiled. and walked over to Marcy, holding his hands out to her.

She took them.

He pulled her up from her chair and pulled her close. "Marcy, why do you think marriage between one man and one woman is so important to Christians?"

"Read Genesis 1:27."

Zay led Marcy toward the coffee table in the living room. They sat down on the couch and Zay picked up the rarely used family Bible sat. One of the big white ones with the words *Family Bible* emblazoned across it in gold. He sat down and turned toward the verse Marcy gave him.

"God created man in His own image, in the image of God He created him, male and female He created them." He paused for a moment. "Sounds a little silly." Zay put his arm around her shoulders and pulled her close to him.

"You have to read the punctuation too. God created man."

"I got that part," Zay scoffed.

"How?"

"I don't know I wasn't there."

"Read it again."

Zay turned back to the verse and read it aloud without any expression.

"He created Him, male and female," she said.

"You saying God created transgenders?" Zay tweaked her nose and smiled.

"No, I'm saying he created both male and female characteristics in his human creation. Now read Genesis 2:18."

Zay complied. "'Then the Lord God said, it is not good for the man to be alone, I will make him a helper suitable for him.'"

"God saw the problem. He didn't create another man, but instead, He gave Adam a job."

Zay laughed at this. "That sounds right; have a problem? Go to work and forget it."

Marcy smiled. "Read verse twenty.

"The man gave names to all the cattle, and to the birds of the sky, and to every beast of the field, but for Adam there was not found a helper suitable for him."

"Now Adam knew he was alone, and he had a problem."

"This is all interesting, but it's not answering my question of why Christians are the enemies of gays."

Marcy sighed. "Go on to the next verse."

"'So, the Lord God caused a deep sleep to fall upon the man, and he slept, then He took one of his ribs and closed up the flesh at that place. The Lord God fashioned into a woman the rib which He had taken from the man and brought her to the man."

"See? He didn't make a new creature. He divided the man He created into two separate beings. They were both there all along. They were made in God's image. He didn't change His image by separating them, but He allowed them to see each other."

Zay pondered it for a moment. "So, you're saying it takes both a man and woman to see the image of God."

Marcy tapped her finger on the end of her nose. "On the nose."

"But we still haven't answered your question. Read on." Marcy tapped the big Bible in Zay's lap.

"'The man said, this is bone of my bone, and flesh of my flesh; She shall be called Woman, because she was taken out of Man.'"

"One more." Marcy tapped the pages again.

"'For this reason, a man shall leave his father and his mother; and be joined to his wife and they shall become one flesh. The man and his wife were both naked and were not ashamed.'"

"There's the answer to your question."

"You're going to have to explain to this educated idiot," Zay quipped.

"They were not ashamed. There was no guilt in their sexuality. It was good and wholesome. It completed the whole image of God."

Zay didn't speak, but his brain wheels churned.

"Let me give you some help," she said. Turn to John 17:20."

Zay read again, "I do not ask on behalf of these alone, but for those also who believe in Me through their word; that they may all be one; even as You, Father are in Me and I in You, that they also may be in Us, so that the world may believe that You sent Me.""

"Huh?" Zay continued to read the passage while Marcy spoke.

"This is Jesus's prayer just before He was crucified. He was praying that we may know Him and become one with Him, even as He and the Father were one."

"That's a hard concept."

"Not if you recognize the Biblical marriage."

"Are you saying that gay people can't be one with God?"

"No, I'm saying gay people can't see the concept or understand it. Like a puzzle, it may have all the correct pieces, but if one is missing or put into the wrong place, the image is still there but it's skewed."

"Marriage and sex are a picture of our relationship to Christ?" Zay asked with a raised voice.

"That's why we're called the bride of Christ."

"I explored gayness out of curiosity, but I never embraced it. What does that mean?"

"What did you discover?"

"Those who live in a homosexual relationship or desire sexual partners of the same sex, usually have short life spans; usually they die in their forties," Zay related as if he were lecturing Marcy.

"I didn't know that," she remarked.

"I also discovered they have a much higher incidence of alcoholism and drug abuse. They have lowered immunity and a higher frequency of illness."

"Where did you discover that?"

"Academic journals and my own studies on Phobus."

"Phobus?"

"I think studying him and working with Ronnie aroused my curiosity. I think the maker of Phobus may have been attempting to make a 'safe' partner."

"That's a strange goal," Marcy mused.

"Not if you want to practice homosexuality without guilt or exposure. Not even Harvey Milk wanted to be exposed, but when he was, he pursued the legality of it."

"Did you come to a personal conclusion about yourself?" Marcy asked with a guarded expression.

"I saw Ronnie's suffering. I also realized I loved the boy more like a big brother. I couldn't imagine being a mate to him."

"Did you ever talk to Ronnie about it?"

"I listened more than talked. I didn't have anything to say. I wish I had known this stuff we talked about."

Marcy sighed. Zay closed the Bible and set it back on the coffee table. They sat there is silence for several minutes, each deep in thought.

Suddenly, Zay stood up, and with much fanfare, he pulled Marcy up to her feet. He looked her in the eyes and smiled.

She blushed, and looked directly into his.

He bent down on one knee and said, "Marcy Odom, will you marry me?"

34

In His Image

> Husbands, love your wives just as Christ also loved the church and gave Himself up for her, so that He might sanctify her having cleansed her by the washing of water with the word.
>
> ---Ephesians 5:25-26

MARCY COVERED HER mouth with her right hand as Zay took her left in his and wrapped a piece of a paper napkin around her third finger. He stared at her, waiting for her answer.

"We haven't even had a date," she said.

"I guess I'm asking you for a date." Zay smiled. "A lifetime of dates."

Marcy nodded in understanding. "How could I say no? I think I fell in love with you the first day I entered your class."

"I saw you that day too. See" We've been dating." Zay smiled.

"Yes, I'll marry you."

Zay stood and embraced her. He sighed and buried his face in her hair. "There is one problem."

Marcy pushed back and looked at him. "And what is that?"

"I don't want to stay here; I want to move back home."

"Church Creek Falls?"

Zay nodded. "I know it sounds strange, but I want to set up an agriculture lab where the old fertilizer plant stood."

Marcy let go of his neck and walked away from him with her finger tapping her bottom lip. "How will we finance it?"

Zay let out a whoop. "You're with me?"

"I love the idea of having our own lab and family too. My mama lives close to Church Creek Falls; did you know that?"

"No."

"Only forty miles away."

The couple embraced. Zay picked her up and swung her around the room. When he put her down, she stumbled? He caught her, and they fell on the couch together, laughing in their ecstatic state.

Marcy leaned her head on his shoulder and quiet contentment overcame them. Then she sighed and said, "I have to have an answer to one question."

"Sure." Zay would answer anything in his subliminal state of bliss.

"Are you sure you're not gay?"

He pulled her close and kissed her forehead. "That's a viable question, but I'm sure without a doubt."

"How can you be so sure when you've been . . . you know . . . exploring it for so long?"

"How did you know?" Zay raised her chin to meet her gaze.

"A woman makes it her business to know the man she wants to marry." Marcy smiled at him.

"I questioned even before Ronnie came to work." Zay said and pushed her hair behind her ear.

"How come?"

"Curiosity. My dad always said it would get me in trouble." Zay smiled at his dad's admonition.

"That doesn't sound like a solid reason to think you're gay."

"I didn't pay any attention to girls. I really had no interest in them. But I did have interest in sex. That resulted in friends telling me I was gay."

Marcy blushed and ducked her head. "Your friends may have been teasing you. But I think I can understand. I didn't date much and really didn't care to. I always enjoyed being in a group."

"Me too, but sometimes that group got a little . . . "

"Informative and experimental?" Marcy finished the awkward sentence for him.

"Yes, you too?"

"Girls are curious too. We practice kissing on the mirrors."

Zay laughed at Marcy's description of the puberty years when the body awoke with ideas, longings, and curiosity. "I won't tell you the gross things boys do, but let it be said, curiosity can get you in trouble, mostly in your thinking."

"Zay, I need to know for sure that you want to be with me and that you're not using me as a cover for your real desire."

Zay took her hand, "I was confused by a dragon."

"What?"

"There was a dragon on our farm, and it would speak strange things to me at night. It would put ideas in my head."

Suddenly, a loud roar filled the room. Both Zay and Marcy put their hands over their ears.

Marcy moaned. "The red dragon isn't happy?"

35

The Wedding

> For your husband is your Maker whose name is the LORD of hosts; And your Redeemer the Holy One of Israel, Who is called the God of all the earth.
>
> ---Isaiah 54:5

THE GOWN FLOWED softly from Marcy's shoulders. It glowed with an effervescence against her dark skin and hair. The jeweled shoes added an inch to her five-foot, two-inch frame, and the simple locket Zay placed around her neck reminded her of his love for her. It was all the sparkle she needed.

Her future sister-in-law, Barbara, smiled and nodded. "I think it was made for you."

The music began, and Marcy clung to her father's arm for steadiness as he escorted her down the aisle to meet her bridegroom. Their eyes met, and she knew his gaze was only for her.

The words spoken by the preacher danced between their gaze. "Marriage reveals the image of God," he said.

They nodded and Zay winked at Marcy.

"He made man in His image, male and female. The institution of a holy marriage reveals the union of partners to proclaim the character of God through the separate but different roles of husband and wife."

Ronnie ambled into the ceremony and sat in the back. He had begged the doctor to let him out for the wedding. As he listened to the sermon he could tell his body grew stronger. He still had a way to go, but this trip to Zay and Marcy's wedding gave him encouragement. He felt of the wound in his chest. It didn't throb and felt less deep though still tender.

Buster Troye gripped the hand of his wife during the sermon. Merilee patted him on the hand and smiled. But her smile faded when she noticed his mouth open and a paleness on his face that bore the same expression from years past when Buster stood face to face in combat with a dragon.

She leaned over and whispered, "Buster?"

He didn't answer, he rose from his seat swiftly and dove into Zay, causing him to fall on the floor taking Marcy with him.

Marcy yelled out as she fell.

Merilee screamed and ran after Buster.

Mr. and Mrs. Odom rushed to their daughter and helped her up.

The small audience gasped and stood.

Daniel rushed to Buster and helped him up.

Rance helped Zay get up.

Daniel whispered something to Zay.

He looked up and nodded then whispered to Marcy, and they left by a back entrance.

The preacher stood in the same place staring at all the action. "What's going on?"

"It's not a joke, pastor, look over your head."

The pastor looked up at the red scales hovering over his head and yelped. He could see the drips of venomous drool coming from a sharp-toothed mouth.

"Get out of here!" Barbara told him.

Rance stood before the audience and tried to calm them. Then he announced, "Ladies and Gentlemen, there has been an unexpected guest at the wedding. For those of you who cannot see, a venomous serpent was about to bite the groom. This is the reason for my father's tackle. I ask that you quietly but quickly exit the church. The serpent has been contained but not captured."

The audience didn't hesitate.

In the back room, Marcy leaned into Zay. "I saw him too but why?"

Buster's head lay on Merilee's lap, unable to move from the open wound on his shoulder. A short groan escaped his lips before he passed out.

Daniel cleaned the poison off of Buster. "We've got to get him to the hospital, this stuff is like acid."

While Rance, Daniel, and Michael loaded Buster into the nearest car, Ronnie came running back, and he caught Michael by the arm.

"I saw him, it . . . it"

"I know." Michael patted his arm.

"I brought him here," Ronnie cried. Michael escorted Ronnie to his car.

"The dragon will not let go easily. One does not simply choose to leave a god of homosexuality or even the curious pursuit of existence."

Ronnie listened to Michael with rapt attention. "But people do it," he protested.

"You're right, but it is always difficult and for some, impossible."

"What do you mean?" Ronnie asked, shaking.

"It's like alcohol. For some people a casual drink is nothing, but others become alcoholics and a slave to their body's desires. The only way to overcome is by following the God who loves them," Michael explained.

Ronnie's hand shook, and tears flowed down his face. "How can I get out of it, if this is what will happen everywhere I go?"

"Remember, the dragon is afraid of Jesus," Michael stated.

36

When Time Erodes

> The prophets who were before me and
> before you from ancient times prophesied
> against many lands and against great
> kingdoms of war and of calamity and of
> pestilence.
>
> ---Jeremiah 28:8

RONNIE GAVE HIS life to the dragon. He didn't want
to admit it, but when he first saw the illusive drawing on
the ceiling, he couldn't believe it. When he asked friends to
see it, they shook their head and told him he was seeing
things. All except the boy across the hall.

The picture contained more than a fantastic method of
exposing the unseen to those willing to look. The more he
stared at the painting, the more intrigued he became with
the dragon. The white horse faded into obscurity. The boy
stood taller and bolder in his stance.

Ronnie found himself actually praying to the dragon. No matter what the desires he lay before the image, the dragon listened and fulfilled them. He smiled as he remembered some of those requests. The smile faded into a frown as the memory of the problems arose. His first prayer came to mind, both the prayer and the consequences. He let out a small moan at the painful memories.

Ronnie climbed the stair case to his room with some effort. He stood outside the door and reached for the doorknob. His hand was shaking uncontrollably. He pulled his hand back, leaned against the wall, and slumped to the floor. His head fell back against the wall and he sighed. His breathing heavy and his chest pounding told him, his body still suffered from the dragon bite. As he attempted to catch his breath and raise his courage before going into the room with the dragon image, he recalled the other things the dragon had done to him.

He could still see *her*. The beautiful girl who waltzed into the restaurant that day. Her blonde hair a bit disheveled, and her awkward gait as if she were wearing high-heeled shoes for the first time. She walked in the door and looked around. The tables were all full. Ronnie smiled as he remembered debating in his mind whether he should give her his table. Instead, she ambled up to him and sat down across from him.

"Mind if I join you," she purred.

He smiled at her, nodded and extended his hand toward the empty seat. "Not at all."

"Can you help me?"

"I don't know. What do you need?"

An involuntary shudder overtook Ronnie as the memory became a real-life movie in his mind. He watched this beautiful, confused girl with the deep green eyes change into a stern demanding . . . image of the dragon on his ceiling? The eyes turned yellow, and he saw smoke coming from her nostrils.

"Don't be afraid," she scolded.

The being's appearance changed back to the beautiful woman with a look of confusion.

"My name's Christine, and I don't know where I am or—"

"Or what?" How he wished he could go back and not ask that question.

"I need someone to help me find this address." She handed an ID card on it. The picture on the card was not the same woman with him.

"Who is this?"

"I need to get to her, now help me or I will let this whole restaurant see me as I really am."

"Phobus?" Ronnie quietly queried.

"Not Phobus. I'm the one that sleeps with you every night," the woman cooed and batted her eyelashes. "Of course, this is not my true appearance."

With that statement the blonde woman morphed into a blond young man, with smooth skin and deep blue eyes. Ronnie recognized him as the boy across the hall, his boyfriend.

"How?"

"It doesn't matter, the young man said and morphed back into the image of Christine. I am the answer to your prayer."

Ronnie straightened up and firmly said, "I didn't pray to anyone. I don't believe that God stuff."

"Okay, maybe not pray, but you ask."

"Ask who? For what?" Ronnie looked at her suspiciously.

Christine once again morphed into the image of the dragon on Ronnie's ceiling.

"I don't understand."

"I'm sending you your wish."

"Which is?" Ronnie prodded.

"The one where you asked for a pretty girl to like you."

"Oh!"

"So, here's your pretty girl. You better get to know her fast because she's just escaped from the psychiatric ward." The Red Dragon smiled and morphed back into Christine.

Then the two of them went to the music building. The experience with Christine the dragon proved to be horrific, exciting, sensual, and . . . shameful. He so wanted to forget it, and he never wanted to be with a girl again.

Ronnie groaned at the memory. He pulled his knees up under him, wrapped his arms around them and put his head down. That same cold chill came over him he'd felt that night. It was if he was there reliving it all over again.

Did he really pray to the dragon? Did the dragon have the ability to answer a prayer?" He learned a serious lesson that night. Be careful. Whatever thoughts occurred in his mind, the dragon fulfilled. Ronnie raised his head and let it rest on the wall behind him.

He sighed. "I wonder if I express my desires or if the dragon is expressing its desire to me."

Another more recent memory replaced the shameful one with Christine. It was the memory of the night before his vision or dream before a judge. The night before the big fire.

Dr. Troye ask him how many Christians had hurt him. The answer was none, but that had to be wrong. He hated Christians because they hated him. But his dad was a Christian. Since he saw his dad in the heavenly court, he knew he loved his dad. He also understood his dad loved him. Maybe if his dad had not been a Christian, he would still be alive.

When Dr. Troye asked him the question, he hated him for asking. When he arrived at his dorm room that night, he said, "I hate Dr. Troye and the work he is doing. He doesn't want to prove God made me like this. He thinks it's my choice. No! It wasn't." Ronnie had screamed at the image on the ceiling. His anger grew, and his ranting increased as he gathered his things. He spoke out loud even though he was the only one in the room. He spoke his anger at Dr. Troye. "I wish that whole place would just burn down."

The white horse fell down at the feet of the dragon and disappeared.

Ronnie heard the thud and looked up at the horse fading from the picture. The dragon loomed larger over the ceiling. He gasped, *I caused the fire!*

Ronnie rose from his safe spot in the hall and unlocked his dorm room. He wouldn't be there long. He would avoid the picture while he gathered his things and moved out.

He hadn't been back to the room since the fire. He took a deep breath and opened the door. Even with the resolve to hurry, his head turned toward the picture in a voluntary act of muscle memory. He couldn't help it, he scanned the picture for Belial. But the dragon and the horse were no longer visible. Only the young man and the banner with one word, 'danger.'

Could it be that Belial occupied only one place at a time? The absence of the image on the ceiling could indicate Belial roamed, but where? He was at Marcy and Zay's wedding. Where did he go from there? A trickle of cold sweat fell down the small of his back. It no longer needed Phobus or himself to move about. This vicious god roamed free. Ronnie's hands shook, and he plunged them into his jean pockets. He'd set the dragon free with his unreasonable rant against Dr. Troye.

The proof could be seen in the charred remains of the science building. Ronnie saw the dragon pouring flames upon the lab. Why would Belial seek to destroy the science building unless he wanted to kill Zay? Or could it be there was something of importance in the lab Belial had to destroy? Either way, Ronnie knew one thing for sure; just like Phobus, Belial didn't need him anymore.

He sighed. He could pinpoint the exact time his life started turning upside down. The day his college career exploded with drama, mystery, and intrigue. It was the day he saw the image of Belial on his ceiling.

37

A Father's Love

Build houses and live in them; plant gardens and eat their produce. Take wives and become the fathers of sons and daughters, and take wives for your sons and daughters; and multiply there and do not decrease.

---Jeremiah 29:5-6

ZAY SAT ON a park bench under an old oak tree. He stared at the remains of the science building. Not thinking, wishing, or contemplating. Just staring.

"What are you doing?" Ronnie asked as he sat down beside him.

"Absolutely nothing."

"Sounds inspiring." Ronnie chuckled.

"What are you doing?"

"On my way to my last PTSD support group meeting. Spending the night with Michael and Sharon and then heading to my mom's house tomorrow.

"Do you have enough strength to be doing that and come back for graduation?"

"Yes. My mom is excited to see me graduate."

"Moms are like that."

"Yeah, they are," Ronnie echoed. The two men fell into silence and stared at the burned remains of the science building which had been their home and office for the last two years.

"We learned a lot in that old building," Ronnie pondered.

Zay smiled and nodded. "We discovered a lot we didn't want to know."

This time Ronnie nodded and looked up in the sky. "Can you see it?"

"The dragon? Yeah, I see it," Zay answered.

"What do you think he wants?" Ronnie asked.

"You!"

"Me? How do you know?"

"It told me. It even said I better leave you alone."

"What does that mean?" Ronnie wrinkled his nose

"It means, if I tell you what the Bible says about your decision to live a gay existence, he will burn me again."

"First off, it wasn't a decision," Ronnie argued.

Zay turned toward Ronnie with his head tilted and his eyes staring over his nose at Ronnie. "You didn't?"

"No."

"Then tell me how it happened."

"I was born this way." Ronnie trembled.

"No, you weren't. We proved that's a lie in the lab."

Belial roared and blew a plum of fire in Zay's direction. "I told you to leave him alone."

Zay looked back at Belial and calmly said, "No."

Ronnie heard the conversation and wanted to run. He felt his chest wound throbbing. He knew Belial would scorch them both. "Dr. Troye, don't do that!"

"What? Protect you?"

"I don't think getting us roasted is protection."

"We are already roasted. I'm going to keep him from devouring you."

Ronnie smiled. "I like the image of your protection," he said. "Even if it is the action of a fool. How can one man stand against a dragon as large as an eight-story building and filled with that much hate?"

Belial reached to the ground and plucked Zay into his huge claw.

Ronnie screamed.

A small crowd gathered, but their eyes were on Zay as he dangled in the air without any visible support.

"How is he doing that?" one student asked.

Another professor queried, "And why?"

Ronnie held his hand over his mouth and whispered, "What do I do now?"

He heard an answer in his head. "Nothing."

Zay could see little of Belial other than the spear-like teeth coming upon him. He knew he would be impaled, and he prayed he would die before the fire came.

The dragon closed his jaws and turned his head. Zay could see one large yellow eye. The eye blinked.

Zay whispered in his mind, "Give me courage."

Belial lowered Zay and held him further away from him but closer to the ground. His firm grip on his body kept him from getting away from the monster, but his feet grazed the ground. He saw the crowd gathering and pointing. In the distance, behind the crowd a white horse galloped toward him carrying the tall figure of a military man.

Zay smiled and whispered, "Thank you."

"You have no reason to say thank you, I will destroy you."

Belial had not or could not see the white horse. Zay turned his face toward Ronnie. who was looking at the horse and pointing. He jumped up and down and screamed, "Look! It's Davis!"

Zay's heartbeat calmed.

A few people in the crowd staggered as if they were drunk, others fainted, and still others screamed.

One young girl pointed up at Belial and spoke the obvious, "Look, Mommy, a dragon."

The PTSD group gathered around the food, and shared jokes, events, and experiences as they gathered their plates and drinks and sat down around the large table.

Zay and Ronnie were conspicuously absent.

Sid came up close to Michael. "You ready to start?" he asked.

"Ronnie's not here yet," Michael answered. "But we can get started. He should be here any minute."

The crowd dispersed in every direction.

Belial watched. "You people are entertaining. I hate you, but you are useful idiots."

"They're not idiots!" Zay yelled out. "They are the image bearers of the Holy One. And you lie to them."

With a quick whoosh of flames spreading over the people, Belial released his revulsion at the mention of the Holy One and His image bearers. The people all fell to the ground and the flames went over them. As soon as the flames stopped, they rose and ran for safety.

The white horse with a military rider named Davis stood alone on the ground where once a large crowd gathered. Ronnie walked up to the horse and Davis. He recognized the horse as the physical reality of the image on the ceiling of his dorm room who had taken him to an unearthly courtroom. The huge dragon, with wings spread, stood over the white horse and Ronnie stood beside it. Belial grabbed Ronnie in his other claw. Davis raised his sword and lashed at the claw. Belial pulled it back.

"You'll pay for that!" he roared.

Davis responded with a voice of authority, "You will feel the wrath of the Holy One for the evil you have done."

Belial roared out a laugh. "Maybe, but not today."

The booming bass voice spoke, "Drink be drunk, vomit, fall and rise no more because of the sword which God sends to you."

Ignoring the words of Davis, Belial said, "Today, I take my prize." Belial turned his huge head toward Ronnie. "Not even that stupid angel will stop me!"

Michael felt it before he heard it. Sid, Matt, and the others turned toward him.

"Dragons!" they exclaimed.

"No, a dragon," Michael answered.

"Only one?" Matt went to the window.

"The worse, the most hateful."

"What does he want?"

"Death of a soul. . . Ronnie!"

"How do you know?" Sid asked Michael.

"He is the dragon of passion; he destroys his followers with lies." Michael stated with his face set firmly toward the campus where Zay hung in the air held by a dragon.

"What passion?" Sid asked.

"The passion of one man for another." Michael answered in a voice much deeper than his normal voice. Sid recognized the Holy Spirit filling Michael.

"I'll go with you as your prayer warrior."

Michael grabbed his Bible and umbrella and headed out the door.

Sid followed with his Bible and an umbrella.

"Guys, it's not raining," a young girl announced.

Zay saw Michael, and Sid approaching. He took a deep breath as much as possible. The big monstrosity holding him crushed his chest and made breathing difficult. Blood streamed down his body as the claws punctured him. He felt his lifeblood flowing from him. At one point, he passed out only to come back to the horror before him. *Oh, my Lord, this must have been what you faced on the cross.* A peace comes over him in spite of having the vision of pure evil clouding his face.

"What's your purpose?" he shouted at Belial.

"I want to make the gift of sex a chain of bondage and destruction to you simpleton's." Belial raised Ronnie up in his other claw. "Like this one," he roared.

Ronnie squirmed under the sharp pain of piercing claws in his side. When he heard Belial's words, he stopped, "How?" Ronnie looked into the face of the beast and raised his eyebrows.

"Do you not know, that when you abuse a gift, it is no longer a gift but a harness?"

"No, I don't understand, I love my boyfriend." Ronnie argues with the beast.

Belial raises his head toward the sky and laughs with a booming sound like a tornado. Then he moves Ronnie in front of his huge mouth and stares into his eyes. "Your boyfriend loves you, but God hates you." He relates to Ronnie's mind.

"That's not true, God loves me?"

Again, Belial roars and nods. He turns to Zay, "See how easy it is."

Zay ignores Belial and turns toward Ronnie being held in the other claw of the beast.

"Yes," Zay answered. "He loves you so much, He will protect you from this monster."

Ronnie laughed. "No, he won't. I've already been before the judgment seat."

Zay didn't have much strength left, but he knew he needed to keep Ronnie talking. He didn't know what was happening on the ground other than a battle. Zay knew he would stand in Ronnie's stead until death. He would not let this creature devour his friend.

He yelled back at him, "He will save you if you look at Him instead of this hunk of mess."

"I'll eat you both." Belial roared near Zay's ears causing him to shrink his head into his shoulders. His arms pinned to his side by the claw of this dragon made it impossible for him to cover his ears.

"You're not that strong!" Zay mocked the big monster.

Belial roared in anger. "Careful, you stupid bag of bones. I can swallow you in one bite."

"No, you can't." Zay smirked.

Michael, and Sid spotted Davis and nodded. "The army of prayer warriors is gathering." Sid said to Davis, who looked over the small band of men. "Small army, but adequate with our General." He smiled.

With each prayer, the white horse and its rider grew in girth and height. Once Davis could reach Ronnie, he pulled him from the grasp of the dragon and put him on the horse with him. "Don't be afraid; many are praying for you."

"What about Zay?" Ronnie hollered over the noise of Belial's roaring.

"He's in no danger."

Ronnie's jaw dropped, but he didn't have time to argue. Davis spurred the horse, and with the swiftness of a bullet train, the two of them charged toward the dragon. Ronnie held tight to Davis. The horse grew in height with each gallop.

When they reached the heart of the dragon, Davis pulled his two-edged sword and plunged it into the tough dragon skin between two scales and cried, "As for the wicked, God has given them to the sword!"

Belial bellowed in pain.

Davis stabbed again. "The Lord will roar from on high and utter His voice from His holy habitation."

Davis turned the horse toward the other side of the dragon and came up under Zay, catching him on the horse's rump. The three of them galloped toward the army of warriors on the ground, the horse grew smaller as they approached a landing.

Once on the ground Zay and Ronnie jumped off the horse.

Davis turned back toward the dragon.

"How can you defeat him?" Ronnie moaned.

"If you fight, you will see," Davis answered Ronnie.

Belial blew a pitiful spit of fire toward Ronnie.

"He's getting weak," Zay said.

With that statement, Zay grabbed Ronnie and pulled him into the nearest building. When they shut the door, a larger plum of fire followed them, but the metal door held the fire away from them. Zay looked around and saw the massive stone pillars of the student union building. He grabbed Ronnie and set him up behind the pillars.

Tears ran down Ronnie's face. "What's happening?" he moaned.

"The dragon is after you."

"Why me?"

"Because he has made a connection with you and claimed you as a servant in his kingdom."

"What kingdom?"

Zay put his arm around Ronnie and pulled him close. "Don't worry son, I won't let him get you."

Ronnie didn't get an answer to his question, but he relaxed when Zay called him son. He felt the love of his father in those words. His fear faded.

Davis and his stead continued to attack Belial with little impact. He returned to Michael. "I'm only holding the thing at bay. It could break free if we don't get some more support."

Michael made some notes on his little notepad he carried with him. He handed it to one of the other men, named Matt. "You're the fastest of us. Run to that building and call these people. Tell them what is happening."

Matt nodded.

"I'll distract the monster," Davis assured him.

Matt took a deep breath and ran as fast as his legs would carry him to the administration building. Once inside, he entered the first office and picked up the phone.

Belial stood up to his full height and roared again. He surveyed the campus. The signature of his disciple radiated through the student union building. But Belial could also see the signature of the Holy One's child guarding the boy. His anger grew so that steam escaped from his massive horned serpent head.

His yellow eyes turned crimson red, and he roared, "You will not get away!"

Zay pulled Ronnie closer and put his chin on the top of Ronnie's head. "Stay put, you're safe in my arms."

Ronnie didn't argue, but he did ask a question. "Dr. Troye, what did I do to enlarge the devil's kingdom?"

"You fell for his scheme and then encouraged others to follow it. You are a preacher for his agenda."

"How do you know this?" Ronnie asked, trembling.

"Because I fell for it too."

"How?"

"My thoughts of family didn't always include a mother, but two fathers."

Ronnie gasped. "Do you still believe that?"

"My science experiments with Phobus proved my theory wrong. There is not an inherited gene that makes one gay. The epigenes are fluid for survival and adaptation. Choice is a sacred gift given us by the Holy One. He programed us to seek Him. One is not born gay, but one is born with the choice of what god he will serve."

Zay knew Belial hunted them. He also knew there was an army of prayer warriors fighting for them. When I questioned God and wanted science to be my God, My dad taught me that I must first recognize what my 'god' required of me."

"What did science require of you?"

314

"The scientific community taught me to ignore God, but the science experiments kept showing me the image of God."

"The result was mass confusion," Ronnie muttered. He heard the roar of Belial and grasped Zay tighter. He wanted to keep talking to forget the beast outside that wanted to devour him.

"I always thought you believed in science over God."

"I guess I did, but deep down I always knew the truth; I just didn't want to admit it."

"What truth? I haven't seen any truth yet."

"The truth of God's ultimate sacrifice to protect us from the dragons out there."

"He's not doing a very good job."

Zay laughed at him. "You're alive, aren't you? And he hasn't taken you yet."

Ronnie raised his head from under Zay's chin to look at him eye to eye, but the moment he did, his eyes rolled back in his head and his robotic words sent chills down Zay's spine.

"Master, Belial."

Barbara hung up the phone.

Marcy noticed her pale skin. "You okay?"

"It's a dragon . . . he has Zay," Barbara answered.

"Oh no!" Marcy exclaimed while grabbing her Bible. In a loud voice she read, "'Am I a God who is near, declared the Lord, And not a God far off? Can a man hide himself in hiding places, so I do not see him?" declared the

Lord. "Do I not fill the heavens and the earth?" declared the Lord.'"

"It's time to pray," Barbara said.

Sharon came in the back door as the two women knelt. "Michael sent a message. Zay's in trouble. The dragon captured him."

Barbara responded, "We're at war again, aren't we?"

"Yes, and I think this is a fiercer battle than it was for your soul."

Mrs. Walton continued in prayer even though her phone kept ringing. She kept asking the Lord to reveal the source of the burden of her heart. After the third set of rings, she rose and answered the phone. When she hung up, she laughed and said, "My Lord, you do have a sense of humor. Thank you."

She returned to her prayer bench, and this time she knew exactly how to pray. "My Lord, my son is lost and confused. He's been captured by a system loose in the world with an evil plan to destroy Your image of a holy marriage. The devil wants the world to see the homosexual image of his own pride. Please allow my son to see the consequences of his choices."

The sting of prayer prickled Belial's skin. He shook his long tail across the campus grounds, overturning cars, and felling trees. The little repulsive humans ran for shelter. The dragon stopped and enjoyed the little circus. Before it returned his attention to Ronnie, a large thump hit against one of his scales, and the scale fell off. It revealed the skin over his chest, his vulnerable spot.

Ronnie asked Zay, "What was that?"

"It's the dragon luring you to him."

"Did I just call him master?"

"Yes, you did."

Ronnie shuddered. "Why?"

"Because you have fallen for his scheme."

"What scheme is that?"

"You don't see your own defiance, instead you seek to make everyone else defiant."

"That sounds stupid."

"Yes, but if you convince others that homosexuality has no consequences and that it should be made respectable, then you are pulling others into your own defiance against the laws of God. Most of the dragon's plans are stupid, but they are cleverly devised and masterfully carried through. Never forget that."

Zay felt Ronnie's body tense up and he could hear his teeth grinding. "I'm not defiant, God made me different."

"No, he didn't," Zay spoke calmly. "We are all born sinners, we just choose different sins to rebel. Anyone can be gay; we all have a fondness for the things we shouldn't."

"What do you mean?" Ronnie asked with trembling voice. He shuddered. "I'm cold." His teeth chattered. Zay felt sweat falling down his lip. Why would Ronnie be cold? Ronnie's eyes glazed over as they stared into a distant corner. He shivered again.

Zay spoke to Ronnie to bring him back from the image of Belial calling to him. "Being gay is determined by the god you follow."

"I follow dragon?" Ronnie said with difficulty, his words fading.

"That's the meaning of abomination—following a false god."

"How I follow?"

"You practice the things opposed to moral laws given by the moral lawgiver, God. In your heart you know, and this is why you feel guilt."

"But people say it's okay." Ronnie struggled with the words and the turn of his head.

"Just because civil law says something is okay, doesn't mean the moral law changes."

Ronnie teeth chattered fiercely. He wrapped his arms around himself as his whole body shuddered.

Zay could feel the coolness of his body, even in the warm building.

"Ronnie!" Zay wrapped his suit coat around Ronnie's shoulders and rubbed his hands between his own.

"Oh God, help me! Belial is winning."

Belial stood outside the building where Zay held Ronnie. It didn't matter, the huge dragon drew the life of Ronnie into his own. Only minutes left before Ronnie Walton would exist no more, and only evil thoughts would fill his human heart.

Michael stood before Belial and repeated the words from Jeremiah 23:32. "'The prophet who has a dream may relate his dream but let him who has My word speak My word in truth.'"

Belial roared and turned his attention to Michael. "You wimpy, little man. I'll show you." He roared again and spewed out a plume of fire. Davis raised his sword, and a lightning bolt of immense size stopped the fire of Belial before it touched Michael.

The prayer warriors took turns reading the Word of God and praying.

"'For you will no longer remember the oracle of the Lord,'" Matt read, "because you have perverted the words of the living God, the Lord of hosts our God.'"

Belial growled and grabbed at the warriors. "You foolish idiots. You read stupid words. Don't listen to them. I am the one with power. All He has is words."

Ronnie heard Belial's words. He couldn't hear the words being read by a small army fighting for his life. He turned to Zay and said, "He's right, you know."

"Who?" Zay responds.

"Belial has the power. Even in the heavenly courts, he did all the talking, and the angels or whoever there were, just sat there. Even my parents just watched me."

Ronnie wept at the memory of his parents letting Belial challenge him, and they didn't try to protect him.

Belial roared again. "You fools. I am bigger than this. You may win this battle, but I am too big for you little Christians to defeat. I will overpower you."

"Size is not the question here," Zay told Ronnie. "It's the Spirit of the Lord that will be the victor."

"Then why isn't that Spirit helping me now? Look at me."

Zay rubbed the pale-skinned hand that felt like a chuck of ice. "I don't have all the answers, and even though I'm new to this trusting game, I know God will be the victor."

As the men stand firm reading, Davis sat atop the white horse beside them. A voice came from heaven and said, "I will have regard for these men. I will give them a heart to know Me, for I am the Lord their God. They are My people."

"Ronnie, did you hear that voice? God's spirit is present in the prayers of the people out there."

"What am I supposed to do? Just lay down here and wait?"

Zay shook his head. "No, you have to make a decision."

"I made that decision a long time ago. I'm gay and I can't change."

"Not that decision, but the decision about which God you will believe."

"I need to be loved, and the dragon loves me, even if it isn't—"

"It's not love. There is no war between love and obedience to God's law."

Ronnie stopped shivering for a moment. Then he said, "Explain."

Zay wasn't prepared to give any spiritual advice to anyone. He took a deep breath and said, "Listen."

"I don't hear anything," Ronnie responded while dropping Zay's coat to the ground. His skin color returning.

"Nothing?"

"I hear people singing and talking."

"Listen to what is missing."

"No roaring." Ronnie looked around the building, "No fire, no lighting."

"Why?" Zay asked him.

"I don't know."

Zay stood up and pulled Ronnie to his feet. "Come on," he said as he waved Ronnie to follow him. When they reached the windows, they saw a small band of men, the PTSD group, Zay's sister and her husband, and a few others Ronnie didn't know.

He gasped when he saw the white horse standing in front of them with its head bowed.

The little army fell to their knees and bowed their heads.

"That's why." Zay smiled. "Prayer and God's Word. Where's the dragon?"

Ronnie saw blue sky and fluffy clouds. People milled around the prayer group as if they were inspecting the damage. He opened the door and walked outside toward the group. They called his name.

He turned to Zay, walking closely behind him. "It's not there."

"By God's Spirit, it's gone."

"How?" Ronnie asked as he felt of his chest wound.

Zay pointed to the kneeling crowd. "That's the spirit of the Lord, His Words and petitions to His throne."

"Does this mean I'm safe from the dragon now?"

"I don't know. All I can say is the dragon has no power over you while people are praying and fighting for you."

Michael and the PTSD group gave Ronnie and Zay hugs.

"That was a close call," Sid said as he slapped Ronnie on the back.

"We're going back to the house. Are you two coming to join us?"

Ronnie nodded.

"See you over there in a few, and we can have a decompression meeting," Michael said. He waved at them as he and Sharon walked back to their car.

As Ronnie and Zay walked toward their car, Ronnie said with a shaky voice, "Look Dr. Troye, I haven't had a magical experience that changed my mind. I'm still a gay man."

"I know."

"Then what is this all about?"

"We've all broken the rules, but God still has mercy on us."

"You haven't broken them."

"But I do—pride is my enemy. I'm scientifically smart and I know it."

Ronnie chuckled and nodded. "That's the truth."

"Pride fills the heart and hides in itself."

"Sounds like your saying, I'm gay because I think I am, but I think I am because I am."

Zay patted him on the back. "I knew you were a good philosopher." He chuckled.

"Come on, we need to get to the PTSD meeting before it's over."

38

Missing

> Let not a wise man boast of his wisdom, and let not the mighty man boast of his might, let not a rich man boast of his riches; but let him who boasts boast of this, that he understands and knows Me, that I am the Lord who exercises lovingkindness, justice and righteousness on earth; for I delight in these things, declares the LORD.
>
> ---Jeremiah 9:23

THE PTSD GROUP started without Zay and Ronnie. When it was over, Michael and Sid decided they needed help. They drove the route from Michael's house to the campus. About half way, they saw Zay's car parked on the side of the road with its lights on.

"No one's here," Sid said to Michael, who parked the car and joined Sid to look for the two men. They found no signs of car trouble. The keys were still in the ignition, and when Michael tried them, the car started. The tires were all up. And in spite of moist ground from a shower, they couldn't find any footprints around the car.

Michael and Sid drove to the nearest gas station and called the police, then drove back to the car and continued looking around for the two men.

"I'm worried," Michael said as he crawled over a fence into the nearby field.

"Do you think the dragon came back for them?"

"I sure hope not."

When the police arrived, they searched the place thoroughly. The crime scene investigators took pictures and measurements. Police and their dogs searched the nearby fields for scents or bodies. Neither were found.

Sharon had picked up Barbara and Marcy when Michael called her and headed to the scene. The three women held hands and moaned at each failure to find the two. Marcy would bawl for a few minutes in fear and worry, and then she would drop into total silence. Barbara stayed close to her.

"Where are they?" Marcy moaned, not expecting an answer but praying one would come.

"Ma'am we're impounding the car." a policeman said to her.

She nodded.

"We need to call Mrs. Walton," Daniel said.

The phone rang for hours, but no answer. Daniel kept trying. After four attempts to reach Mrs. Walton, he called the local police in the small town of Mineola where she lived and explained the situation.

After a couple more hours, Daniel received a response from the police stating the home at the address was vacant. They searched the place and found nothing out of place, except that Mrs. Walton's purse and keys were sitting on the kitchen counter, and her car sat in the garage.

"The only thing we found was an open Bible and a notebook filled with notations," The officer said and then hesitated.

"What is it?" Daniel prodded.

"The notes are written in a heavy hand and . . ." He paused and swallowed. "And they are written in a script we can't understand except for four words."

"What are those words?" Daniel asked.

The policeman cleared his throat and said, "The words made a simple sentence. 'The harvest has begun.'"

39

A Court Hearing

Woe to the shepherds who are destroying and scattering the sheep of My pasture!' declares the Lord.

---Jeremiah 23:1

THE HORSE REARED up on its hind legs and whinnied. It struck the dragon, drawing blood. Still, the dragon didn't remove the clawed foot firmly planted on Ronnie's chest. With his last breath Ronnie yelled out, "Help!" while holding his hand over the chest wound.

Does this mean I am doomed . . .that there is no rescue from the beast? Ronnie wondered as the dragon took a swipe at Davis, knocking him off the horse. Again, the horse reared, distracting the dragon while Davis landed a painful blow to the dragon's chest. Enough that for a moment he lost his grip on Ronnie's wound. In that instant Ronnie called to Davis, "Don't stop! It's the red dragon!"

With a heavy thud, Ronnie felt the dragon clinging to his back with its sharp claws wrapped around him and digging into his heart. Zay called to him, but he couldn't answer. Suddenly, Ronnie felt himself being swept into a whirlwind looking at his body sitting in the car. He could see and hear everything in both the spiritual realm and in the physical realm.

"Oh, please, don't stop fighting for me," he called, but only the dragon and the soldier on the white horse could hear.

The soldier came next to Ronnie and Zay and pulled them onto the horse. In the blink of an eye, the horse took off. They were no longer in Zay's car but standing in a courtroom.

Ronnie stood in front of a judge's bench. He couldn't see anyone behind it due to the enormous height, but he did see a beautiful rainbow over a glistening light. He smiled at the sight of the rainbow, the symbol for homosexual rights. But this rainbow was different; it throbbed with life and beauty.

He stood mesmerized by the sight and the comforting sounds. It didn't startle him when he heard his mother's voice, but he turned when he heard a male voice beside him.

"Where am I?" Ronnie asked.

His Father put his arm around Ronnie, "We are at the judgment seat of the Ancient One."

Ronnie smiled when his mother kissed his father on the cheek. "I'm so glad to see you again."

He pulled her close to him.

"Dad?" Ronnie asked.

With a bright smile and eyes plastered on him, she answered, "Hello son, it's good to see you again."

Ronnie looked at his mother, "What's happening, Mom?"

"I don't know, I was praying for you, and the next thing I know I'm here," she said then squeezed the arm of his father and gazed into his face.

He returned the look of love to her.

Ronnie smiled at them.

A sound like a great waterfall called their attention to a new party entering the courtroom. A glistening creature of untold beauty stepped out from behind the desk and stood in front of it. He spoke, and his words sounded like the harmony of chords carried by a philharmonic orchestra.

"Welcome into the family, Zay Troye." The voice sang.

Ronnie's jaw fell, and his eyes widened at the sight of Dr. Troye. "What are you doing here?"

"We were together, remember? And where is *here*?" Zay asked, swiveling his head from side to side and drinking in the sights and sounds. Before Zay could receive any answers, he heard the beautiful voice make an announcement.

"Mr. Ronnie Walton, Sgt. Davis will be your advocate," He said.

"Mom, is this a dream?"

"I wish it were." She ducked her head

At that moment, the four of them shuddered at the sounds of war around them. They witnessed a door open in the mist, and a huge figure in shadow walked into the courtroom.

He approached the group and sat several feet from them in shadow. Davis moved toward the shadow, allowing his light to fall upon the features of the figure.

Ronnie gasped. It was Belial.

"I'm to be judged by the red dragon who bit me?" Ronnie asked as he reached for his mom's hand.

"This is a hearing not a judgment, Ronnie Walton. Belial will make arguments for your soul before the Holy One. Your parents will make their arguments to you. Your destiny is to be determined." The voice speaking the words filled the surrounding air with vibrations. The Walton's stood on each side of their son and put their arms around him.

"We cannot speak in your behalf, son," his dad said. "But we will stand with you through any trail you must endure."

"Dad, did someone stand with you in Vietnam?" Ronnie asked.

He nodded. "You've met them."

"Who?" Ronnie gasped at the idea he met someone who knew his father.

"The group you attend."

"They said they didn't know you."

"They didn't know my name, but they were there with me when I died. Michael helped load me onto the Huey."

Ronnie smiled at the connection. While he mulled it over, a series of trumpets sounded. The Walton family turned toward the multi-directional sound of the trumpets.

The mist rolled around their feet and cleared from around their face. A scene of multiple figures, including Davis, appeared in front of them.

Belial stood next to Ronnie and his parents.

Ronnie focused on the central figure who appeared so bright he looked as if he were burning. He sat on a deep blue seat, highlighted by his white hair and beard. The beautiful rainbow arched over His throne.

"God!" he whispered.

Belial laughed.

How can he be here? Ronnie wondered.

"The figures sitting around God all rose to their feet. At that moment, Ronnie saw a large number of people behind those sitting—thousands of figures, and many of them were dragons.

"Where are we?"

Mr. Walton answered his son, "We are in the council of the gods."

"I don't understand."

Mrs. Walton stepped up beside her husband and said, "It's from Psalm 82, God stands in the council of gods. It's also where Satan argued with God over Job."

"But why are we here?" Ronnie asked.

Belial stepped up and faced God. "May I answer the young man?"

God nodded at the dragon.

"I requested this gathering." Belial turned to the three humans and growled the answer.

"But why?" Ronnie asked.

"Today, I make my argument for you. I'm here to prove you belong to me. . .forever."

Ronnie looked at the figure he recognized as God. He could see the great compassion on his face. He opened his mouth and wrinkled his brow. "Why?"

"I will hear his case, and I will hear your cause," God said, but the blue eyes burned into Ronnie's heart so deeply he felt as though a fist gripped his chest like a vise, but the wound didn't throb with pain.

Belial stepped up in front of the group. "Please have a seat." He put a clawed foot on Ronnie and looked him in the eye. "I will prove you belong to me."

Ronnie shuddered and grabbed his parents' hands. "Help me."

40

A Dragon's Revenge

> Why has the way of the wicked
> prospered? Why are all those who deal in
> treachery at ease? You are near to their lips
> but far from their mind, You know me and
> examine my heart's attitude toward you.
> How long is the land to mourn?
>
> ---Jeremiah 12:2,4ff

BELIAL GATHERED HIS army of demons, dragons, and spirits and made demands of them. "We must not lose the boy. We're going to have to fight harder to keep him. He's heard too much of the words of the Holy One, and he heard that blasted sermon about the Holy One's purpose in marriage."

"What's the plan now?" growled a little minion.

"Revenge!" Belial roared. Then he spread his wings and flew to the courtroom of the council of the gods.

Ronnie sat opposite his parents in a seat in front of the bench but raised two steps higher than his parents. Belial paced between him and his parents in a manner that made it difficult for them to see each other.

"If you follow only after me, you will be free from the condemnation of your fellow humans. You will no longer be plunged into the pits of guilt from the commands of the Holy One. You will have the freedom to love whom your heart desires, and even the Holy One says love endures all things. If there is love between two people, then what difference does their gender make?"

Ronnie cocked his head to one side.

"If you follow me," Belial continued his argument. "You will not be rejecting the God of your father. By examining His own book, we see that Jesus, who claimed He was God, never addressed the topic of homosexuality."

Ronnie nodded. He made a glimpse at his parents and noticed his mother's wide eyes and her hand over her mouth. His father held her close but ducked his head.

Belial stepped between them and Ronnie and spoke again. "Historically, older men would use young boys for their sexual appetites while they still had wives and children, but they were basically criminals. You haven't done that." Belial ended with a sing song lilt in his voice.

Ronnie smiled, he would never do that. He respected other people's rights.

On the cusp of his thinking, Belial made his final argument. "In fact, homosexuality is just a minor thing that it is only mentioned six times in the God's Holy Book. If He didn't give it any more attention than that, it must not be that important to Him. Thus, you may choose to love whom you desire."

Ronnie nodded at the logic of Belial's argument. He may hate the dragon, but he did make sense. Even Ronnie knew there was a chapter about love in the Bible. It was read at almost every wedding and quoted by those of faith and non-faith alike. He smiled at Belial.

Davis stood to take his turn. He paced a few times in front of Ronnie, and then he stood to the side of the seat so Ronnie could see his parents and his mentor, Zay.

"He says if you love someone, then it's okay, because God's Word says so." Davis tapped his chin and moved his head from side to side.

"I must first ask you, how can you love someone who is abusing you or whom you are abusing?"

Ronnie wrinkled his brow. Davis turned to face Ronnie and continued. "When the disciples asked Jesus what the greatest commandment is, Do you know what he answered?"

Ronnie shook his head.

"Jesus said, the first and greatest commandment is to love the Lord with all your heart, and the second is like it, to love your neighbor as yourself."

Ronnie stared at Davis with a blank expression.

"Now I ask you again, how can you love someone you are abusing?"

Ronnie tightened his lips. "How can I abuse someone I love?"

"When you use another for your own gain or pleasure, are you abusing them?"

Ronnie nodded, "I guess so."

Belial raised his head and puffed loudly, "You're out of order."

"How so?" Davis asked Belial.

"You're talking about obeying the law, not love."

Davis' eyes met Ronnie's. He turned his gaze to the Walton's. "Is love inconsistent with the law?"

"Yes!" Belial roared.

"If the law is summarized in the statements made by Christ, then the law states to love others as oneself. If one loves another as themselves then they will not abuse them in any way that is harmful, degrading, humiliating, or divisive, for they would not want to suffer such things."

Ronnie nodded at the statement.

Belial once again stepped between Ronnie and his parents and his friend. "I will give you the desires of your heart without guilt. That's love. Life will be pleasant and fulfilling," Belial cooed.

Ronnie couldn't see his parents or the Holy One. He thought both arguments were sound. They offered no guilt or need for repentance. Ronnie was about to declare his allegiance to Belial when he caught a glimpse of a horse's hoof. It brought to mind the word across the banner in his dorm room—shame.

"I'm tired of being ashamed, guilty, and scared!" Ronnie shouted out in the courtroom. The light from the bench came closer to him. He felt a warmth and security he had never known before.

At stake in this court hearing was Ronnie's life and soul.

With Belial between him and his parents, Ronnie lashed out. "Why would a loving God take my dad away from me when I needed him most? Then He makes me gay?"

"Good question," Davis replied.

His simple answer took Ronnie by surprise; he was expecting more of a fight. "So, what's the answer?" he shouted. "It was my choice!"

"Why does that seem repugnant to you?" Davis asked him.

"If I had a choice, I wouldn't be like this."

"I understand that you are saying that if you had a choice, you would not be gay, correct?"

Ronnie shrugged and ducked his head. He didn't answer the question.

Davis walked back and forth in front of Ronnie, pushing Belial out of the way. Ronnie saw the great audience watching. *Who are they?* Their presence seemed to calm his spirit, and he felt himself melt into the chair ready to listen to Davis. His mother smiled at him, and his father nodded at him with a smile.

"Choice is a sacred thing." Davis looked Ronnie in the eye when he made the statement. He paused and put his index finger over his lips. He continued to stare into Ronnie's eyes, waiting for his attention.

"What does that mean?" Ronnie sneered.

"If you don't mind, I would like to quote from God's Holy Book."

"Okay." Ronnie conceded. All the fight flowed from him, and curiosity replaced his defiance.

"In God's Holy book, the word *choice*, meaning to select one thing over another, is most often used in connection with God's choice of a place to put His name. In other words, a place God designates for His people to come and worship Him."

Ronnie watched Davis walk back and forth as he laid out his argument. Davis would stop occasionally and make contact with Ronnie, looking him directly in the eyes. Once Davis knew Ronnie listened, he would continue.

"Except!" Davis raised an index finger in the air and lifted the tone of his voice. "In the occasion when God gives a choice to man." Again, he raised his hand in the air and lifted his voice. "And, that choice is almost always the same. Do you know what it is?" Davis stopped in front of Ronnie with only a couple of inches between their noses.

"No," Ronnie answered with a quiet tone.

"The choice—to follow Him and have life or to reject him and follow evil which ends in death. Did you know that choice is sacred?"

At that question, Ronnie felt himself fading from the courtroom. He and Zay stood in front of Michael's door.

"How did we get here?" Ronnie muttered.

"I think it's where we are supposed to be."

The door swung open and Michael called their names, "We've been looking for you for the last three days. Where have you been?"

Zay and Ronnie looked at each other, "Three days!" they said in unison.

41

Images

> My heart is broken within me, All my bones tremble; I have become like a drunken man, Even like a man overcome with wine, Because of the LORD and because of His holy words.
>
> ---Jeremiah 23:9

PATTI DUMPED THE dustpan into the trash can and hung the broom up on a hook in the closet. When she shut the door, she looked around the clean lab. The house shined from the top floor to the basement.

The real estate agent would be arriving soon. Patti slapped her hands together. *At last I will be rid of the evil woman.*

It felt empty with Cook, Michelle, and the other children gone. Cook went to a small town called Church Creek Falls three hundred miles away. She and Michelle planned to open a restaurant. Patti knew she would succeed, especially with Michelle joining in their new venture.

The kids had been reunited with their parents or guardians. As soon as the place sold, Patti would be out. *Maybe I'll go there too.*

She walked around the lab. The paint job in the basement changed the image completely. It was no longer a chamber of horrors, but a nice family recreation area. The hall contained several small rooms which could be used for storage or closets. She walked down the hall to make one last inspection.

Patti hated going into these cells, even if all the images the kids painted on the walls were gone. The images of stick figures and oversized hands and hash marks marking off the days and years. She kept some of the murals of artistic talent. They both fascinated and horrified her with their graphic images of other boys and girls with sad faces. The one drawing of Lapetos as the mad scientist with Einstein hair and Frankenstein sparks of electricity made her chuckle.

There was but one picture of Madame Lilith, or Grandmamma as she would have them call her. Strangely, the painting revealed a grossly beautiful woman. The artist had captured her seductive spirit exactly. She loathed the children but treated them with the temptation of giving them love. Which she never did. She destroyed everything she touched.

Patti didn't want to hide this historical record of the events of the previous decade. She studied the paintings with a critical eye. Would a potential buyer be repulsed or delighted with the art?

She looked up at the wall she was about to paint and noticed a painting she hadn't seen before—a depiction of a large man pointing to a small boy with his hands behind him and his head bowed in a submissive pose. The man looked to be reddish purplish and covered in spikes of differing sizes.

Patti moaned. The head of the drawing depicted a plum of flames coming from the man's mouth, which drew an eerie resemblance to the head of a dragon. She had seen that dragon before. She knew him as Belial, the chief of all the dragons. The one who inflicted the most pain on young boys by using the evil of men. His name meant worthless. Patti moved back from the drawing. It felt alive.

"You are worthless, you beast!" She shouted at the painting, knowing the pain and anguish the artist had put into it. But it was only a painting, not a dragon.

"Are you sure?" The painting suddenly animated and opened its eyes to look at Patti.

She screamed and dropped the paintbrush. She backed up against the opposite wall.

"Don't be afraid, I'm your friend," the painting cooed.

"You're a demon. I want nothing to do with you."

"This is your home, your life, and this is your wealth."

Patti buried her head in her hands and wept. "I don't want this life any more. I want Paps."

"But Paps left you, remember?"

"He didn't leave me. He died."

"He left you here as a baby."

"But—"

"You belong here, my sweet."

With the last statement by the dragon, he stepped out of the painting on the wall and stood before her in a full horrific tangible image.

"Leave me alone!" she screamed again and turned her back to him.

She heard the clacking of his claws on the floor. Sweat poured down her back and the sides of her face. If she turned, she would die from the horror, and if she didn't, she would die from the thought of the horror. She let out a gut-wrenching, spine-chilling scream. She kept screaming until she felt a hand on her shoulder. She stopped and dared to turn and look into the face of a soldier. His smile relaxed her tense body.

"Who are you?"

"Paps sent me. My name is Davis." His words gave her hope.

Patti fell to the floor as the soldier sat beside her wrapping his arms around her. She could feel a sensation of caring and safety. *This must be what love feels like.*

She cautiously looked around for Belial. He wasn't there, and neither was the disgusting painting. She sighed and pulled her knees up to her chest and she held them and cried, releasing the adrenaline collected from facing Belial. Then she did something she had never done in her life, she prayed.

"God, if you're real, please help me."

42

Home

> I will set My eyes on them for good, and
> I will bring them again to this land; and I will
> build them up and not overthrow them, and
> I will plant them and not pluck them up. I
> will give them a heart to know Me, for I am
> the LORD; and they will be My people, and
> I will be their God, for they will return to Me
> with their whole heart.
>
> ---Jeremiah 24:6-7

WHEN RONNIE AND ZAY entered Michael's home, they saw Ronnie's mother. "Mom?" He turned toward her.

"What are you doing here, Mom?"

"This is where I was dropped off, apparently like you."

She stroked his face. "I love you, son, and so does your father."

Michael and Sharon watched the scene for a few minutes before Michael asked for clarity about the strange disappearance and reappearance of the three people in his living room.

"Are we fighting a dragon?" Michael asked Mrs. Walton as he handed her a glass of water.

"Yep," she responded. "Mr. Walton is pleading our case now before the Holy One."

"Sit down, Ronnie. We need to talk," Michael said.

Ronnie complied.

"Your mom told me about the experience you had in the heavenly courts."

Ronnie turned toward his mom. "You mean that was real?" he asked incredulously.

She nodded.

"You mean that really was my dad?"

"Yes, he stands at the throne room and brings you before Jesus every day."

Ronnie's mouth opened, and he shook his head. "My dad prays for me?"

"Uh-Huh."

"Ronnie, it's not easy being the son of a soldier killed in action, but it doesn't mean he left you."

"He said you were there when he died!" Ronnie exclaimed.

Michael looked at Mrs. Walton. "Where did he die?"

"He was in the 101st Airborne division to carry out a covert operation. It was called Firebase Ripcord."

Michael smiled. "Yes, I was there. I helped load a wounded man on the UH-1 dustoff, a nickname for the Iroquois huey medevac."

"That was my dad."

Michael nodded at the thin connection between himself and Ronnie. "Your dad's prayers have stopped the evil plans of that dragon to kill you."

"Oh!" Ronnie buried his head in his hands.

"Listen to me, son. You make your decision. But before you do, learn as much as you can about God from His book. Then learn to know the schemes of Belial and all the other dragons."

"How can I know God?"

"He makes Himself knowable. In Psalm 100:3, He says we are made by God. If we are made by God, we must know Him."

Michael reached over and touched Ronnie. "Remember at the wedding, the preacher said marriage is a picture of God."

Ronnie nodded.

"That's why God warns against homosexuality; it blinds one to the image of God, and one cannot know Him and won't choose Him if they don't know Him."

"Zay said it depended on the god we follow."

"He's right, your god is whatever you worship, and you will worship what you love."

"So, if I choose homosexuality, I am choosing Belial as my god?"

"I think you have it backward. Homosexuality is a deed you do, not a god. But like all sin, it takes you away from finding the truth about God."

"So, I'm hopeless."

"No, you're not. But you are in a bad place. If you follow Belial and his agenda of destroying Christianity and preventing people from hearing about it, then you have chosen to reject God."

"Can I choose later in life to change?"

"That's a tricky question," his mom said. "Once you give your heart and soul to a dragon or to the one true God, you become like the one you choose. Whatever sin draws you to a dragon will chain you to it."

Sharon, Marcy joined Michael, Zay, Ronnie, and Mrs. Walton.

"I'm so sorry," Ronnie moaned when they walked in and sat down.

"What for?" Marcy asked as she walked over to Zay and hugged his neck.

"Ruining your wedding."

Zay and Marcy both gave a little snicker. "You didn't ruin it," Zay said. "We're still married, and we'll have quite the story to tell our grandchildren."

Michael caught them up on the discussion.

"Ronnie, the only difference between being a victim and a victor is knowing God with your whole heart," Marcy said.

"He knows you, and He'll give you every opportunity to know Him and see Him and follow Him," Zay explained. "Our wedding was a picture of the image of

God. It's the reason the dragon wants to distort God's image with the unholy union of same-sex or with adulterous affairs or multiple pre-marital partners. All sin makes it difficult to see God with our whole heart, but sexual sins hide Him most because in marriage and the sexual union He revealed Himself."

"Why is same-sex the target for Christians?"

"It isn't," Zay answered. "Christians are the target of the homosexual movement. That's why Belial is attacking us. That horrible dragon is the movement. In Moses's time, the dragon killed the babies to prevent the Redeemer from being born. He did it again when Jesus was born. But Jesus still came. Then the dragons thought they won when Jesus died on the cross."

Ronnie listened to Zay's explanation.

His mother took his hand and held it between hers. She continued the scene. "Then He rose from the grave, to defeat the power of the dragons, which is death. That's why He's the only one they fear."

"Christians are the only ones who tell the truth about the dragons," Zay added.

"Christians are compassionate, by telling sinners how He redeems them," Marcy said.

"You mean make them stop their love for one of the same sex?" Ronnie snorted.

"No, to tell them to choose to follow Him," Sharon jumped in. "All of us are sinners and sin is sin. His salvation is a free gift, not because we deserve it, but because we need it in the middle of our problems. He knows we have no hope without Him."

Ronnie looked at his chest. The hole wasn't as deep and the wound not as painful, but it was still present.

"Why is my wound better?" Ronnie asked Zay.

"Because you are hearing the Words of Christ. They are a healing salve to a wounded heart."

"That sounds preachy," Ronnie scoffed.

"Truth often does because only Christ is truth."

Ronnie shook his head. "Do you think we can heal this blasted hole in my chest if we keep talking about Christ?"

"No, we can't. The words are comforting, but it won't be until you choose to be a follower of Christ that the wound will be healed," Sharon answered. "Remember who made the hole and search for the one who can fill it with healing.

The others all nodded in agreement.

"What does that mean?" Ronnie growled.

"Zay and I are looking forward to being together and learning from each other," Marcy said. "I'll learn strength from him, and he will learn tenderness from me."

"What does that have to do with anything?"

"The purpose of marriage is to see the complete picture of God's heart toward us," she answered. "That's how we follow Him, by learning more about Him and responding to situations as He would."

"You're saying I can't see God with my boyfriend?"

The group nodded.

"Ask yourself, what is the purpose of a same-sex relationship." Michael suggested. "What does it reveal? What can it produce? What's its purpose? Other than rebellion against the Creator and the law-giver."

Ronnie pondered an answer. Then he grabbed his chest. "It hurts!" he exclaimed.

In the unseen realm, Belial snarled. The Angel of the Lord beheld Ronnie with misty eyes and a loving smile. Mr. Walton stood before the throne of God, pleading for mercy.

Ronnie found himself standing in the celestial courts again. This time he saw his dad before the throne on his knees.

He heard the full tender voice of the Supreme One say, "Choose your words wisely, for I set before you life and death, I want you to choose life and choose it more abundantly. Choose you this day whom you will serve."

Belial and his minions surrounded Ronnie, hoping to block the prayers and interference of the Holy One.

Mrs. Walton spoke softly, "He has no defense against our prayers." Then she bowed her head and prayed. The others joined her.

Ronnie saw the bowed heads of the group and his mother around him. Tears ran down his face as he heard their pleas for his salvation. He knew the pain, and he wanted peace, but how could he give it up?

"He's not asking you to give it up," Marcy said. "He's asking you to acknowledge Him as you are."

Ronnie sat us a little straighter in his chair, spread his arms, and proclaimed, "I need you Jesus." Then he dropped his arms and head and whispered a prayer no one else heard but the advocate standing in front of the judge's bench.

He raised his head and clasped his hands over his chest. "It's gone! The hole in my chest is gone!" He danced around the room with a freedom he had never known before.

Immediately, Davis and a band of warrior angels descended on Belial and the lesser dragons. It only took a few minutes for the dragons to be beaten and limping.

"Go!" Davis commanded, and they were sent back to the wilderness without mercy.

"Listen!" Marcy raised her head.

"I don't hear anything," Ronnie said.

"Exactly. The dragons are gone."

Ronnie looked at the group now staring at him and smiling. "He did it? He healed my heart. I chose Jesus."

A chorus of angels sang as they watched Ronnie Walton's name written in the Book of Life.

Major Walton stood next to Sgt. Davis, with a beaming smile.

"He's going to need your prayers more than ever now," Davis said to Mr. Walton.

Mr. Walton smiled. "At least the harvest is delayed."

Epilogue

Christine slumbered in her bed. Her night stretched into the noonday sun. When she arose, she stumbled through the apartment wondering . . . not about anything in particular . . . just wondering. She ambled into the living room in her pajamas with a pillow-styled Mohawk hairdo stumbling into the kitchen to grab some food.

Belial laid the roots of his plan for Christine in her mind. Her compliance to his wishes exceeded his own expectations. She served him as the most loyal servant he possessed . . . and he possessed billions; more than the Holy One could ever bring together.

Christine crawled back into bed.

Belial took a hooked claw and grabbed her by the back of the neck.

"Ow!" she hollered. Looking around the room, she saw nothing to inflict the sting on her back.

The pain subsided.

She aimed for her pillow, and her head landed with a dynamite blast of a headache. She sat up and held her head in her hands. *What's going on?*

"Your master is calling you," Belial said.

Even though Christine couldn't actually hear him, his words in the air would conduct her thinking. "You need to buy a house."

Christine didn't argue. She rose and got dressed, called a taxi, and waited outside for it.

While waiting, she asked Belial, "How do I pay for all this?"

The monster cooed instructions in her ear. Christine smiled and nodded.

Ronnie continued his relationship with his boyfriend for the next few months but slowly pulled away from him as he made new friends in his Bible study group. As time passed, the same sex attraction grew less, and his desire waned.

Barbara, Daniel, Michael and Sharon, and Zay and Marcy all moved back to Church Creek Falls.

Barbara and Daniel opened a local medical clinic and raised money for a hospital.

Zay opened a lab to assist the hospital and farmers. He gave lectures about soil treatments and seeds. Marcy served as his assistant.

Sharon served the hospital as Director of Nurses while Michael joined Rance in helping to rebuild the community with legal and financial services.

Rance came face to face with a most profane dragon when he opened the pages of a girlie magazine.

Author's Notes:

In 1970 Nixon started pulling troops out of Vietnam. However, there was one last ground mission. The purpose of the mission was to re-establish a Fire Base to destroy supply bases of the People's Army of North Vietnam.

The media was requested not to cover the covert operation in order to prevent a publicity nightmare such as the one that accompanied Hamburger Hill. There were no additional troops sent into help the beleaguered and outnumbered troops fighting on the hill against 30,000 of the enemy.

The Vietnamese had watched the operations on the firebase and on the first day of July the PAVN released mortar shells on the workers at the base, killing seventy-five Americans. It was soon clear the base was indefensible, and after twenty-three days, the troops were removed, leaving a southern trail for the Vietnamese.

The last combat battle of the war received little attention at the time. Additional materials that relate more of the details can be found in a National Geographic special in the third hour, "Inside the Vietnam War."

Books written about the battle are:

Ripcord: Screaming Eagles Under Siege, Vietnam 1970, by Keith Nolan, Presidio Press, Ballantine Books, Copyright © 2007

Hell On A Hill Top: America's Last Major Battle In Vietnam, by Benjamin L. Harrison, Published by iUniverse, Inc., New York, NY. Copyright © 2004 by Benjamin Harrison

Note: This book relates the view of the battle from the two leader's viewpoint.

Remembering Fire Base Ripcord by Christopher J. Brady, Outskirts Press, Inc. Copyright © 2015 Christopher J. Brady

Ghost of Ripcord, directed by John Ryan Daily, Written by John Ryan Daily, Starring: Ralph Young, Adam Segal, and John Ryan Daily, (2015 documentary, available on Netflix)

Recommendations for information about homosexuality:

First Stone Ministries, https://www.firststone.org
Stephen Bennett Ministries,
https://www.sbmworldwide.com/tools/lp/sbm

Money! Money! Money! - Destruction, ruined lives by a profane dragon.

Rance Troye uses his financial investment skills to rebuild his broken community.   His heart grows hard with the loss of his fiance. Rance can't see the dragon conducting the orchestra of his life out of tune. Will finding his beloved return the melody to his heart?

Dragon Series

Buster Troye comes face to face with a horrid Dragon. Will he overcome the dreadful beast?

Barbara Troye is lured by her selfish needs into revolt? Can she be rescued from the Dragon's demon?

Dr. Zay Troye sees a Dragon carrying the secret of hell. Can science find the truth?

Rance Troye's wedding is cut short when the Dragon steals the bride. Will Rance's search save her or destroy him?

The pain of Buster Troye's Dragon bite grows from a family division. His final battle is fought by the Dragon warrior.

During World War II, military "Operation High Jump" explores Antarctica and finds the Dragon's lair.

Available wherever books are sold.

Stones in Clay PUBLISHING